PRAISE

FOR MICHAEL BOTUR

"Michael Botur's writing is a breath of fresh air in a country gone stale on its own literary midgets' bad breath. Just read him. You'll see what I mean. This dude can write."
—Alan Duff, MBE, author of *Once Were Warriors*

"Michael Botur's work grabs you by the throat and won't let you go. His stories throb with what feel like real people, real conversations, real moments of pain and hope, misunderstanding and reconciliation, remorse and surprise. And that's the magic of this collection."
—Maggie Trapp, *New Zealand Listener*

"Michael Botur's talent shows a skill broad, diverse and still very focused. He has mastered the art of the short story. The authenticity is so scary, you wonder where this man has been and what demons followed him home."
—Paul Brooks, *Wanganui Midweek*

"Written in unvarnished street language about the rougher side of life—drugs, jail and death, the book shows rare bravery and honesty. The thing about Michael Botur is his voice is very much a street voice. His language is street language: it's raw, it's coarse, it's obscene. It's tough and it's confronting. There are gems—some of them are absolutely great."
—Ian Telfer, *Radio New Zealand*

"It's as if Mr. Botur hung out at CBD fast-food outlets after midnight—swilling bad coffee on a hard-plastic seat, listening to conversations, and jotting observational notes under the garish yellow lighting. There is a ring of authenticity about these stories—both in the language used by the characters and in the physical descriptions of their environments. Botur is not so much a moralist, as an informer—without ever becoming a show-off."

—Jeremy Roberts, *Takahē*

"Botur wields demotic vocabulary, and agitated rhythms, combined in collages of invective and obscenity, with much skill. It's a neat trick that's easy to stuff up, but he consistently gets it right."

— Paul Little, *North & South*

"As a former journalist he has perfected the skill of telling a story and evoking emotion. Botur is a clever writer. He has mastered the art of leaving things unsaid."

—Rebekah Fraser, *New Zealand Book Lovers*

"These stories are energetic, often breathless, containing concrete detail, close observation, originality and power. Most of them use street language in a playful, or serious manner. The collection is peppered with expletives, topics about sex, drugs, viciousness and breaking the law."

—Patricia Prime, *Takahē*

ALSO
BY MICHAEL BOTUR

Crimechurch

Loudmouth (poetry)

True?

Moneyland

LowLife

Spitshine

Mean

Hot Bible!

HELL OF A THING

SIXTEEN STORIES

MICHAEL BOTUR

Hell of a Thing: Sixteen Stories

Copyright ©2020 Michael Botur

Cover Designed by Siori Kitajima, SF AppWorks LLC
Interior design by Siori Kitajima, SF AppWorks LLC
Formatting by Ovidiu Vlad

Cataloging-in-Publication data for this book
is available from the Library of Congress.
ISBN-13s:
Paperback: 978-1-950154-13-5
eBook: 978-1-950154-14-2

Published by The Sager Group LLC
www.TheSagerGroup.net
info@MikeSager.com

HELL OF A THING

SIXTEEN STORIES

MICHAEL BOTUR

GLOSSARY

Kiwi Slang and Māori Expressions in *Hell of a Thing*

Hiding: a violent beating

Skux: sexually attractive

Lino: linoleum

Pash: tongue kissing, making out

Bach: beach house or holiday home

Dux: top of school class

Marae: Māori meeting house, similar to a temple

Tupuna: Māori. A grandparent or any ancestor more remote than parent

Kūpapa: Collaborator—Māori who sided with Pākehā or the Government during 19th century wars in New Zealand

Whakatauki: Māori wisdom or proverb.

Haka: Māori ceremonial dance or challenge

Whanau: Māori for extended family

Tokutoku: Māori pattern designs

Tēna koe: Māori for "hello"

Waiata: Māori lament song

Kapa haka: Māori performing arts

CONTENTS

HIDING

1.

You're at the intersection where the road points north, thinking about how the Dutch have zero traffic lights and it's entirely roundabouts and no crashes ever occur when your steering wheel headbutts you. Your dashboard rears back for another assault and you're rolling forward into the tulips in the centre of the doughnut and you're ripping the handbrake up and running to the back of the car to check if Livvy's okay in her black plastic shell and you can see a big cocky white Jeep backing away and the driver, a man with tattoos on his neck and a gold chain with a dollar sign, a man who looks about 24, 25, same age as you, actually, he could be a companion in another dimension, he's about to drive away until you tell Livvy you'll be right back and step in front of the Jeep waving your arms like you're putting out a fire and bellow STOOOOOP.

'You hit us! What the hell? I have a kid in the back.'

'Shouldn'ta stopped all sudden, lady.'

He's chewing gum and staring ahead. Your car is half in the roundabout flowers, half on the road. You are blocking his way.

'I was—I don't know my directions very– we've only just moved here, and look I'm sorry if I did, I mean I just... *Hang on.* It's a Give Way sign. You're supposed to *stop.*'

Jeep Man is a jaw and fingers high in the driver's seat of a big white metal cube. His black-tinted windows are wound mostly up and he has thick black sunglasses on too. He doesn't want to look at you.

'You're sposda just slow down at Give Ways, else peeps'll rear-end ya,' he says.

'But I have a baby in the back.'

'Yeah yeah. Heard you the first time.'

'DON'T YOU HAVE KIDS?'

'Listen, I gotta jet. Got clients to see. Back in ya car, already.' He sounds his horn twice.

'I'm pretty sure we need to swap, um, swap details, I mean—'

'So you lost a coupla chips off your bumper. Get yaself a can of spraypaint from Mitre 10, problem solved.'

'But—but I mean, don't you need to hop out and, um, like, check for dents?'

'Did I stutter? You gonna move or what?'

You ask Livvy for her patience, give your little girl a quick thousand kisses, promise you'll make this horrible incident up to her, get back in your car and reverse with the hazard lights on. There must be ten, twelve cars waiting patiently at each mouth of the roundabout. You're holding everybody up. A few hours into the day and already you've fucked up. Typical.

You drive thirty metres north, find a spot to pull over, race to the back seat to inspect Livvy.

Jeep Man follows, slowing as he passes you. He winds down the black passenger window. You duck as he aims a dark gun-barrel. It's the man's pursed lips. He's blowing you a kiss as he tosses a business card out the window. Stiff charcoal card. Gold letters.

CuzzyCutz. 12 John St. Get 5 haircutz 6 is free.

On the back are empty squares you can have stamped or clipped before claiming your bonus haircut.

Livvy's face is the pale yellow of wet bone and she's saying she needs a ambliance, squeezing SuckyDucky's neck. You pay for an hour in the underground car park beneath the bank, drive into the farthest, darkest corner. Your face stretches. Livvy begs Mummy to stop crying, be smiley, mum-mum. You sniff yourself dry, reverse carefully and cruise over to the Emergency Department.

*

Anton is giving you and Livvy his updates through the MacBook positioned at the head of the table. A finger of steam curls into the air from Daddy's cooling cannelloni. It took 40 minutes to stuff the tubes of pasta with the mince and herbs and cottage cheese. Hopefully he can smell the coriander. You went out of your way to buy the actual leafy herb for him instead of the powdered stuff, not that he'll even eat it, all the way over in Sydney. Putting his portion on a plate is just a gesture to keep him appreciating you and Liv while he's away across the Tasman makin' money. You would've poured cheese sauce directly into the cannelloni tubes except you couldn't get the sauce jar open, even by running it under hot water, even by using the rubber glove. Just one of the many things that need doing around here. The u-pipe under the sink is leaking, leaf gutters on the roof need scraping out, plus there's some critter caught in the humane mouse trap you're afraid to shake into the yard.

From his little goldfish bowl of a screen, Anton is giving you and Livvy a lecture about how his team are drilling a four inch cable-tunnel through a mountain of solid granite. They've got their soil samples approved, they have the permits, now Anton's looking at a five figure bonus for every week the proj-ect is completed ahead of—

Anton has frozen. Colored squares are eating his beard.

Livvy makes noise and looks at you from her high chair, choking SuckyDucky, her eyes big and terrified. She's still pale from the crash.

'Daddy's fine, honey. He's not hurt. See?'

Anton wriggles out of his mosaic prison, asks what you and bubs got up to today.

Church play group, you tell him, then Wriggle & Rhyme, then the swimming pool.

All lies.

You waggle your bottle of unopenable sauce. 'I spent half the day wrestling with this freaking thing, ha ha, wish you were here for that!'

'The relevance of which is... ?'

'You know. Cause you've got strong hands.'

'Anyway, pools, yeah, wicked, that reminds me,' Anton says, doing a drum beat with his fingers, 'We've been tryina get some fibre through these swamps and we made eeeeepic progress with the Parramatta council, right, they're as invested in digital highway partnerships as we are, really putting some serious finance into this thing which means some tasty kays but what's really eating me is getting the copper relayers in place by January else my arse is grass, so that's us for the next few months, eh, if we're going to land that 18 mil we promised the shareholders. We're really forging ahead in terms of systematic lines revisioning. Exciting times, you oughta be here.'

'So are you coming home for Christmas?'

'What?'

'I don't know anyone in this town. We need you here.'

Anton's face freezes in disgust. The signal isn't lagging. He's just unimpressed your life doesn't move as fast as his.

'I have to drop something important cause you can't open some sauce jar on your own? Literally? Look: January I can pop over. Will that suffice?'

Anton's fingers get large as they reach to switch the camera off.

'I got hit by a car today.'

Anton frowns at the webcam. For a moment, you're sure Skype has frozen again.

'I don't think I heard you right.'

'Well, not me. The car. *Our* car.'

'*My* car, if we're being technical, since you don't earn anything—but no, what in God's name happened? Insurance haven't phoned me. It's my name on the papers.'

You tell him about the crushed flowers, the chipped bumper. Holding up traffic, speared with embarrassment. Burning cheeks. Jeep Man's gunbarrel lips blowing the deadly kiss. Jeep Man in his white metal armour. *Don't cry, Mum-mum. You get your kneepants wet.*

'And you got his details?'

'I Googled... he does haircuts from home, he's like a famous barber and everyone in town knows him and—'

'How much is this gonna cost me?'

'It's.... not? I dunno, the man said it wasn't that big a deal and he just sorta drove off... .'

'But you're not hurt?'

'I'm shaken. And you should've seen Livvy's color, she was ashen, she was shaking on the drive home, she was—'

'JESUS. Please don't frighten me like that again. We have insurance for a reason. I'm really busy, seriously, you're lucky I scheduled you guys in. I got a report that won't write itself. Liv: g'night, baby girl. Love you.'

Livvy waggles her cup of juice at the webcam but the screen's already black.

So is the inside of Livvy's mouth as she screams four hours later when she wakes from the nightmare.

So is the inside of the car she swears she'll never get back into because your baby has been traumatized.

2.

You watch Livvy stack blocks in the barred pen in the corner of the waiting room beside a plastic Christmas tree. Usually she stuffs the toy cars with tiny dolls and rams them together. Today, she's not interested in crashing cars.

Ahead of you in line to see the doctor will be Mrs. Lowndes, who sits with a Marian Keyes novel perched on top of her knees, glowering down at it. You can tell Mrs. Lowndes wants to ask about the jar of pasta sauce in your handbag. You know Mrs. Lowndes from church play group. She's okay, and she's the closest thing you've got to a friend in this ocean of strangers, though she asks about your husband's job way too much. The only other person in the waiting room is an ex-con-looking man in his 50s. His skull is shaved shiny with silver speckles on it. His skin is dark with curls and twists of blue ink, skulls, slogans. His knuckles have spiderwebs on them. There's a faded bulldog printed on his neck. While he waits, he crushes a pamphlet. Squinty eyes behind little glasses. One flip flop tapping the floor.

At the ED Livvy was found not to have a concussion, but having your family doctor give a second opinion is essential. You've read that the symptoms of whiplash might not show up for a week. Livvy is the most beautiful wee schnookum in the entire world and she deserves attention and praise and concern. It's annoying, actually, when the nurse comes out and tells you for the second time that the doctor's late by another 15 minutes on top of the existing 15 minutes of lateness. Jesus Christ. Livvy's brain could be bleeding right now. You could enroll with a better doctor if you wanted—the money's not a problem. The only reason you keep coming to a clinic in the muddy, broken-fenced part of town where the streets sparkle with broken glass is because Dr. Tana is a good listener. Once you cried into her tissues while she stroked your knuckles and printed you a very generous scrip for Paxil and Lorazepam.

Livvy reaches out and says your name. She needs help separating the pages of a cardboard book glued shut with something sticky.

'She yours?' the shiny dark man asks.

Strange question. Why would a person not have their own child? You suppose whatever culture this man came from, the children are raised by their village, or something.

You tell him yes, Livvy is yours, two years old going on 16, ha ha, a little stroppy when her dad's not around but she has a heart of gold, ha ha.

Gold teeth. Black windows. Gunbarrel.

The shiny dark man nods once as he processes what you've told him. He's stocky and bulging with flesh and has jowls with white stubble. He wears a rugby league shirt and shorts even though he looks too old and squat to play any sport. He jiggles the single foot relentlessly. It's freezing in here. The man must have thick skin.

'Me, I had a couple nieces come stay after m'daughter died,' the dark man says.

'Oh, I'm so sorry. That sounds.... painful.'

'Yep. Gout's bad enough as it is.'

You play with your cellphone.

'I SAYS GOUT'S WORSE.'

Mrs. Lowndes looks at you, tilts her book away from the angry ranting man and checks the time on her watch.

'It was her time to go, anywho. Had some bronchial shit. What's that expression—Make plans; God laughs?'

God laughs? LAUGHS at your pain, your humiliation? End of conversation, surely. You smile, pull your scarf tight and tuck your head down. You read an email on your phone from Anton, stroking through his words.

'Whatchu in for?'

Anton begins his email with an apology for telling you what to do, reminds you that he honors the sovereignty of women everywhere who should never be mansplained to, especially after thousands of years of oppression, but having said that, he's emailed you a list of services which you can use to find friends and hobbies. There's the Women in Business club, the tennis club, the Women's LARP League, macramé, Boxfit, SPS, which is the Solo Parents' Suppor-

'I SAYS WHATCHU IN FOR, MISS?'

Mrs. Lowndes gets up and shifts into the hall, clutching her novel against her chest and tutting.

'Sorry, I didn't... I had a car crash—no, I crashed into another car and—actually, no, no, another man, he crashed into us, sorry.'

'Quit sayin sorry. Sign of weakness.'

'I'm just worried cause Livvy hasn't been herself.'

'Is her head all fucked up?'

'Iiiii'm hoping to get an expert opinion on that.' You move a seat closer to your daughter, then another, kicking your handbag deep under your chair. There is a thunk as the glass jar hits the wall.

'D'you give 'im a slap?'

'Give who a slap?'

'That cunt what ploughed into you.'

Even the receptionist has disappeared. There is no one around to help you get out of this conversation. Livvy is trying to cram a plastic T-rex inside a Sylvanian Families cot.

'Oh, ohhhhh—no it wasn't that bad at all, no. Just a ding.'

'Was it ya enemies?'

'Oh no, no no no. A complete stranger. Just some local barber guy. Cuts hair and dings people's cars, I spose, ha h— '

'Cuzzy Cutz, oi? That guy's a snitch. No one likes that arsehole.'

'Um, yes, actually, as a matter of fac- '

'What's with the jar?'

Dark Man walks across the waiting room, squats, reaches between your legs, finds the jar of cheesy pasta sauce and hefts it like a brick.

'I can't open it. Sorry.'

'Shoulda got your man to open it, miss.'

'Oh, he's at work.'

'After work, then.'

If you run from this conversation, this insane person is likely to choke you. You look at your babygirl, but Livvy has no idea you're drowning.

'He works overseas, mostly.... He's not around.'

'Fuck kinda man leaves his woman all alone? Anyway: ding my ride, you fuckin die. Specially if my kids is in it. I'd'a given him the hiding of a lifetime. Put the fear of God in the cunt. Want me to fuck im up?'

'No, no it's perfectly okay. It was my fault.'

'OI: it was not your fuckin fault. Y'understand?'

You spread a Woman's Weekly magazine in front of your face and block the scary man out.

BLOOSH.

From outside a thud and the crack of broken glass.

You're out of your seat and rushing to the window. It's just an old man across the road dumping his recycling bin on the sidewalk but when you turn back, Livvy's looking at you from the arms of the bald beast. She has a question in her eyes and she has started to bawl.

Dark Man waltzes your baby girl as he shushes her, roaming the room, not looking to see if his knees will bump the chairs.

'Unkie Graeme's gonna smash the bad man isn't he, yes he is, yes he is,' the scary man is saying to your daughter. "Graeme" he's called, apparently.

A nurse appears and begins to announce your name. Then her eyes bulge.

From beneath Livvy's legs, four spiderwebbed fingers and a thumb emerge. In Graeme's fingers is a cellphone.

'Chuck your number in, I'll text you,' he's saying to you, though his face is smiling down on your daughter, 'We'll go see Mr. Cuzzy Cutz, yes we will, yes we will.'

3.

You're in your car five houses down from the house of the villain, Jeep Man, Cuzzy Cutz, waiting for him to return home.

Slumped low in your seat, you watch the white-Jeep-metal-tank pull into the driveway eight minutes after four. Out hops Mr. Cuzzy Cutz in a pure white hoodie with his black cap with a gold sticker on it and a stack of colorful boxes that look like pizzas with pink stripes. He approaches his front doorstep.

Graeme has told you you need to be close enough to "come in for a peep" as justice is served but far enough away that you won't get spotted.

You hear something like 'Yoooooo, what up?' as Graeme waddles up behind him. Graeme is sticking one hand out OH MY GOD THEY KNOW EACH OTHER, THEY'RE FRIENDS, OF COURSE THEY ARE, YOU'VE BEEN SET UP, CRANK THE KEYS AND GET OUT OF HERE then Cuzzy has his fingers out like a blind person trying to grasp air because he's sinking, he's dropped the boxes, which appear to have ribbons on them, and he's searching for something to hold his weight as he faints and Graeme's arm swings back behind his head and there is a hammer in his fist and he's putting his fingers inside Jeep Man's pants—all this publicly visible! Anyone could drive past!—and Graeme's pulling Jeep Man's keys off him and unlocking the house and dragging the floppy, rubbery, sleepy body of Jeep Man by his hood up the steps. *Ohmygodohmygodohmygod.* Graeme puts fingers in his lips and spits a powerful whistle down the street at you—oh my God, he can see you, you're totally busted—then he hefts Cuzzy inside the house and disappears.

You open your car's back door, flop Livvy into your arms and run with her as if you've stolen a paper bag of groceries, stepping over Cuzzy's dropped pizzas wrapped with little tiny trains, teddy bears, unicorns.

Not pizzas. *Presents*. Presents for his *children*.

This is not your place. You cannot be seen here.

You get inside his house quickly, breathlessly. Graeme has told you ten times over the past week that this whole thing is in-out, quick as a flash. Hundred seconds and it's done.

'*DOOR.*'

'Sorry!'

You seal the room and stand with your back against the exit, pulling a Christmas tree half-over your chest, trying not to knock over a mirror and table stacked with clippers and razors and combs in pots of blue disinfectant.

Cuzzy is on his knees, burrowing between the legs of his dining table like a loose rat. Graeme is stalking the victim, hammer in hand, pulling the chairs out one by one then putting each chair immediately back, tidy and respectful.

Musical Chairs concludes after a few seconds when Graeme whacks the hammer directly into the centre of Cuzzy's cap, stunning him. Graeme grabs the man's gold chain, which snaps. He tosses it at you. 'Catch. Souvenir.'

Graeme gives three efficient smacks of the hammer on Cuzzy's throat, nose and chin.

The victim has pulled his limbs into his body now like a dying spider. He's small when he's being bashed. Deflated. Scurrying in retreat. He bumps the wall and a photo of three kids slumps off its hook.

Graeme pulls Cuzzy's pure white hood over his head then gives a further three smacks into the skull. A purple stain blooms in the white fabric.

Graeme sets to work on the spider's legs and arms, bashing ankles, toes, shins, kneecaps, elbows and fingers, any piece of bone sticking out of the bleeding bundle. The wet *thplack* of snapping celery.

Finally Graeme catches up to you, panting. He bends backwards and his spine makes a *crick*. 'Whoo whee. Haven't had a workout like that in a while! Here: want a whack?'

You press yourself into the corner of the room and test the door handle. Livvy's face is sickly pale again. You cram your fingertips behind her ears and press her face into your shoulder and joggle her. You pull a bauble off the Christmas tree, offer it to Livvy, who offers the bauble to SuckyDucky.

Graeme pulls an inhaler from his pocket and gives it a mighty suck. He puts his hands on his knees, and catches his breath. 'We've gotta boost. Any last words?'

It stinks like a longdrop in here, raw and salty, like farts and rot and cold dripping public toilets with shit splattered on the walls. There is a dark beetroot stain creeping through the fibres of the carpet. The crushed bug in a hoodie polka dotted with blood is jiggling as if something is electrocuting him. His fingers twitch. His head has withdrawn deep inside his hood like a turtle.

You try to come up with a threat.

'Anton,' you begin, 'I mean, not... .'

Easier to shut up.

'Get ya photos in now. HURRY.'

You unlock your cellphone, aim and extend it like a slingshot.

'NOW, miss. *NOW.*'

*

Anton speaks through the computer screen over a steaming plate of ravioli and cheesy pasta sauce. He's leading his cable into the fibre splicing station now that the shareholders have permitted a loan of two mil to lease a borer imported from Germany to get the tunnel dug ahead of schedule and Anton's company's next step will be to report to a committee of stakeholders who—

'Stop. Just stop.'

'I beg your—

'Stop. TALKING. Your boring. Work. SHIT.' Livvy pulls the pasta bowtie out of her mouth and watches. 'We need you here. So get back home already.'

Anton checks the time on his FitBit and frowns. 'I sacrificed a very important call with San Fran for this and if you think—'

'SHUT UP. SHUT. *UP.*' You point your cellphone directly into the webcam like a knife. Your finger hovers over the Play triangle. With a single click you could show him. Show him what you are. Show him the power you've got in you.

'You wanna be man of the house, be a man, and be in the FUCKING *HOUSE.*'

You pick up the laptop, walk to the dark cold end of the table. Put Anton down. Shut the lid.

Livvy grins, cheese sauce on her teeth.

D_ OUCH _E

1.

Andi finds Lotus on the steps of Auckland Art Gallery. There are black paw-prints under Lotus's shoes. She's been playing in the fountain while she waits for Andi, who is late. God damn electric buses only run once an hour.

Lotus could've gone inside the gallery already but it's too awkward, dealing with the guard-dicks on the door, plus she's finishing her chamomile tea and you're not allowed to take drinks in, so sayeth the authorities. Their title is *minder*, officially, these door-dicks. That's one of the many things the girls hate—why does a painting need a chaperone? This is supposed to be a public gallery where courageous ideas can stand. Let it be free to view 24/7. Let it be an open air gallery. Let the art be unguarded and free.

Door-dick Marcus sees the girls entering and pulls a bollard close. He strokes the velvet rope. Secure. Now the girls have to stand in the lobby's concentration camp of retractable seatbelt tape and chrome bollards. Marcus is a student too but he does this door-guard shit to try get a better chance of having his art on the walls here.

'Tickets, please.'

'Gimme a break,' Andi says, 'This is a public place.'

Marcus flops his weary head. His chins crease. 'You gonna shoplift from us today, Andrea?'

'True artists don't repeat themselves, sellout. I'm here to check out wall space. I'll have a piece in here real soon, trust me.'

'Kay, well, you'd be the first. Students've never had their stuff on display in here, it's a meritocracy 'n shit so.... Yay for ambition, lady.'

'Don't call me lady, fatass. It's an ARIStocracy. This place invalidates women of color, that's the problem. It's all white artists.'

Marcus coughs into his fist.

'Dude, before you try to say I'm white, okay, I don't identify as white, so fuck what you're thinking. Will you let us past?'

'I still need to check in your bag; stuff's insured for millions in there. Sup, Lotus.'

Lotus blushes.

'Why would I want to steal phallocentric white-o-cratic bullshit anyway?' Andi pushes her backpack into Marcus's shirt and tie and his fat jiggles. She's nearly six feet tall, Andi, with shoulders like soccer balls and a thick neck. 'Here's my stupid bag.'

Marcus attempts to rummage through the backpack. Andi snatches it out of his grasp and the girls sprint onto the golden parquet and begin catching up on the new artworks. Andi and Lotus have just 20 minutes until the gallery closes.

The girls love this place and hate it. They have to visit at least once a week to remain part of the conversation, though most of the artworks on the walls are conservative and deserve to be destroyed. The indigenous stuff needs to be repatriated to its homeland.

From the ground floor up to the mezzanine, the girls give Auckland Art Gallery a lightning tour, looking for new pieces to *hmm* over. Mostly it's the same old stale pale males on the walls. They tally up what the value would be if it were all torn down. There is millions of dollars in insurance behind this art. Irreplaceable, sure, but overvalued, not to mention over*rated*.

It's hard to agree on which piece is the number one most offensive, actually. The ten square metre Jackson Pollock in the South Atrium is pretty undeserving—just another Caucasian abrasion. Then there are the Colin McCahons taking up far too many metres of wall. That wannabe Christ appropriated Māori culture and there's never been redress.

The girls reach the Contemporary Art rooms which host works by some graduates of Elam School of Fine Arts. Pretty much every Elam-ite has spent a few years in Prague and Berlin then returned to the art school on Symonds Street to tutor, though Andi and Lotus have been told that's not an option for them. Sellout suckups anyway, those tutors. Total Quislings. One Elam grad has a whole room to himself. His so-called masterpiece: an open bucket of paint on a pedestal. It still has the Bunnings Warehouse 'SOLD' sticker on the side. The bucket contains dried white paint solids frozen into a frisbee. The label claims the piece makes an introspective postmodernist statement about Syria. Really, the white disc of dried paint represents a contraceptive pill, the girls agree. A very subtle misogyny, though impossible to ignore.

Andi leads the tour, waving her dismissive fingers at each disappointing artwork. Lotus follows up with her tablet, live-Tweeting her outrage.

Just as bad as the Eurocentric art colonizing every level of the gallery is the *Do Not Touch Please* barrier frame on the floor around the Haisla totem pole in the Indigenous Suite, a totem built to honor forest god Tsoda who saved the Haisla people from smallpox. Lotus appreciates the font, a variation on Highway Gothic, very autumn 2010, perfect for the cover of the next edition of her zine, though the message spelled out by the gorgeously ironic font is impossible to stomach. *Do Not Touch Please*, it says. Like, literally? The frame around the totem pole is a square of gold poles lain in four sections a couple inches above the ground. The girls look at each other and wordlessly agree what needs to be done. They lift the four bars of the *Do Not Touch* frame, grunting, dismantle it and shunt it aside. In a corner of the ceiling, the security camera twitches. Andi feels it burn her neck. She points her middle finger at it. Fuck rules. Fuck *Do Not Touch*. First Nations peoples can decide for themselves whether they want to be touched or not.

Andi grabs Lotus's wrist and checks the time on Lotus's FitBit. Nine minutes till the place closes.

The Hubbard Room is the next travesty. Its centre is cordoned off with four road cones with caution tape around them, a wet floor sign, a coffee cup with an inch of blonde coffee with a milk-skin floating on the surface parked on the third step of a stepladder positioned under a displaced ceiling panel. Some wires are dangling down. The actual room itself becomes the artwork as people orbit the stepladder. The piece makes a statement about the purpose of art galleries in post-New World Order western cultures. It won this year's Walters Prize.

Andi swallows, saves her outrage for the Mackelvie Collection of imperialist racist shit upstairs. Seven minutes 'til closing time. Better get to work. Lotus takes care of the Grade D offensive, following the plan they've agreed for today. Lotus lowers her glasses, ensures she's not being followed then backs into the women's bathroom. She visits every stall, pulls ten zines from her underwear and uses double-sided tape to stick a copy of *Routon* to the toilet walls. *Routon* is revolution without the evil. The plan is the zines will be spotted by patrons, assuming they actually bother to sit on the toilet.

The Grade D operation complete, Andi and Lotus get to work on Grade C.

Lotus trots diligently to the lobby and stands in front of Marcus, who has been pulling the tall blinds closed with a long rod. She doesn't think of him as a door-dick. He's a cog in a discriminatory machine, that's all. Without saying a word—and Lotus hasn't spoken in days, apart from Tweeting—Lotus twirls, showing off a skirt made of woven plastic fibre upcycled from plastic bags found on the beach at Mission Bay. Marcus asks to touch the dress, his canines creeping over his lips. Letting him touch the dress will buy her comrade a few more minutes. Lotus stands still and silent while he fondles her.

In the Indigenous Room, Andi checks over her right shoulder then reaches under her right legging and pulls out knitting needles. From her left, she produces a mostly-completed woollen web. She moves outside the Indigenous Room, closes the doors, wraps yarn around the handles and with sixty seconds of twisting wrists and fingers links the door handles with knitted woollen yarn, woven tightly enough to hold the doors closed. Andi then reaches deep inside her skort, produces a one page A4 paper manifesto from the front of her underwear and holds it against the wood of the door. She dips back into her skort, under her knickers this time, puts two scooping fingers inside her labia, pulls a glob out and pastes the corners of the poster on the doors with four smears of blackberry blood.

Andi is confronted immediately, palms on her shoulders, fingers digging into her collar bone. As she is guided outside onto the street, she warns door-dick Marcus that if he puts a finger on her she'll begin civil proceedings of sexual assault and will also lodge a compensation claim with the gallery. Marcus looks at little Lotus to see if she, too, feels harassed. Lotus shrugs.

Fuck this place anyway. No point in patronizing it if it won't support student artists. Andi bans herself. Lotus stays away in solidarity.

2.

They return within days, this time in black pants and white shirts and black bow ties.

Wednesday night's fundraiser begins with the Manukau String Quartet playing Schubert while the tuxedo'd and ball-gown'd sponsors stand against the six metre curtains waiting to applaud. Poised in the dark half of the room, with trolleys and trays, are Andi and Lotus and the other dozen catering staff. They were warned they'd be busy tonight. Lotus keeps the barrier arm open out in the alley while vanloads of food are delivered. The code to open the garage door is 5465. Amber Anderson repeats the code three times in Lotus's face because Amber Anderson is too God damn busy to stand by and type in four simple digits, mmkay, and there's a rule against writing it down. 5465. Got it? Yay. Hurrah. The code is good for a month; some of tonight's staff will have to get up bright and early and come back here to pick up Amber's platters and breadboards and keg and folding tables as the vans can't take them tonight. Come down the ramp to the loading bay, enter the PIN, through the service roller door. The PIN opens the gate and deactivates the alarm.

Lotus nods and nods. She stoops lower than her five feet one inch of height. Amber Anderson runs off to yell at some moron who's forgotten to dust powdered lime flakes on the oysters before carrying them out.

Reductions and nibbles and tasting platters are wheeled in, unpackaged, heated or iced, seasoned, lain on porcelain and silver and served to the hundred-odd people splashed across the floors, fora and stairs of the gallery.

The reason for tonight's fundraiser is the unveiling of a half-paid-for Banksy discovered in an alleyway in Clendon, transported brick by brick and given the south wall position on the first floor. The gallery borrowed $2.2 million to buy the bricks, which has cut into next year's budget, hence tonight's whip-round. There is a Diamond guest list, a Gold guest list and Silver and Bronze integuments so the names and profile photos of likely donors are easily identifiable to members of the board who carve paths through the room, hit their philanthropic target, squeeze his or her shoulder, pump his or her hand and sell sponsorship and brand platforming rights. The Herald has sent its *Spy* photographer Ricardo. He's paid to photograph each handshake. It helps turn a suggested donation into an embarrassing-if-it's-not-confirmed donation.

Looking through the throng at her BFF, Lotus can tell Andi is pissed. Andi—half a head taller than most of the plebs here—is moving like a Terminator, nudging people aside with her big arms. Andi wants the night over. Andi wants the routon to kick off.

Secreted in a corner, cupping her mouth over a platter, Andi hoiks up a batch of her private reserve spit, the snotgreen phlegm at the back of her nostrils she has to pull down with an emphatic hoik and use throat muscles to force onto her tongue so she can perfectly spit the goo into the reduction of spinach and feta she's about to serve to these creeps. She also spits toward the floor, waddles up to the Banksy and toes the spit onto the bottom of Banksy's bricks so nobody notices and she doesn't get told off.

Lotus sees Andi's snot games but her attention is elsewhere. She's staring past these fancy zombies, tallying the value of the paintings in the Mackelvie room. This whole desperate art student-resorting-to-catering-thing? It's a front for the girls' real purpose: getting deep inside the enemy's base.

Not surprising, of course, is that the gallery tonight is staffed with Lotus's biggest fan, the fatass door-dick with the tie and shoulderpads. He's sidling through the throng and saying Wassup and—ope -no no no, no no no, please don't do that—Marcus is leaning in for a kiss on the cheek.

Lotus grins 110 percent, forcing her cheeks outward so the ceiling lights burn Marcus' saliva off and it doesn't soak past the second layer of epidermis. After a couple seconds' awkward silence, Lotus realizes no one is watching. She doesn't have to pretend to hate him without Andi around. He can't hear her tiny voice so he squeezes her arm and leans in. He's talking about the artwork on the new *Call of Duty* game but she's in sensory overload. She can smell his Listerine and count the number of chest hairs with zits forming where the follicles are blocked with grease. Kind of sexy, in a dorkish way, but Lotus has to get back to work. She can't be distracted by fantasies of sleeping with the enemy. After serving lab-grown hamburger patties to Heart of the City board members Max Gimblett and Barbara Kirshenblatt-Gimblett as they deconstruct Ralph Hotere's *Godwit/Kuaka*, Lotus is pulled aside by her boss, who's so stressed that she is shaking. Lotus HAS to return in the morning to pick up two beer kegs and a stack of tablecloths with driver Willy. Lotus needs to open up and disarm because Willy isn't trustworthy.

Lotus nods to indicate she'll be there. She wants to speak, but she's saving her words for intellectual übermensches. She holds up the numbers using her fingers. 5465. Grin? Grin. Attagirl.

On the dais at the end of the room, Andi is shoving a prawn kebab into the hands of Auckland City Councillor Cathy Casey and shunting her to the right so she's not blocking *Te Whenua, Te Whenua, Engari Kaore He Turangawaewae* by Robyn Kahukiwa. It's one of the few pieces in the place worthy of respect and Andi wants to look at it without a fucking bureaucrat in the way.

At the end of the night, Lotus passes Andi in the stainless steel kitchen and they exchange a few whispered words that mean everything.

Coming in at 7.30. Picking up the shit at 8.

3.

Andi enters Auckland Art Gallery, strides through the lobby and into the bowels of the building. Nobody stops her. She is in disguise as an ordinary aristocrat, after all. Andi wears a navy blue suit, bow tie and five colorful barrettes to draw attention away from her face. Lotus follows eight minutes later disguised in a thick raincoat with a pull-over hood. The girls waited three hours today for rain and in the end it was only a speckle, but the rain justified the disguise. The girls have something serious planned.

They're hesitant to enter the Mackelvie collection at first. Just being in the room feels like a vote of support for Western supremacy. It's all Edwardian and Victorian oils on the walls in here with three marble sculptures and four bronze. The oldest of the paintings dates to 1603. The most valuable is insured for 10 million Euro. All of the paintings are deeply problematic. There's the Lawrence Alma-Tadema portrait of Cleopatra which appropriates Afro-Arabian cultures. Then there are the more subtle inflections—a bongo drum in the background of Bundy's *The Day of Sedgemoor*; the body language of the male authority in *Pope Makes Love To Lady Mary Wortley Montagu* by William Frith.

The girls crouch, creeping around the room, ready to sprint, keening their ears for the twitch of the ceiling cameras. If security knew what they had planned, they'd be arrested already.

'D'you think Marcus is on shift?' Lotus rasps.

Andi is momentarily speechless. Lotus breaks her silence only to waste words on some door-dick?

'Who? That guard-boy? Yes, no? Who cares?'

'It'd be good to know,' Lotus mutters.

'The hell's that supposed to—will you do your thing already?'

Lotus takes her slingshot from her handbag and aims at the security camera. She unpackages the tampon Andi has wrapped in silver foil, puts the soggy crimson cartridge in the barrel of the slingshot, aims at the camera and launches the bloody bullet. It hits and leaves a smear of dark red juice on the camera lens.

Andi reaches into her underwear, extracts a 110ml tube of spray adhesive from her vagina, peels off the $4.99 *Gordon's Art Supplies* sticker then takes a scroll of A3 protest art messages from her left breast pocket. Each of the twelve A3s is lain on the public bench, quickly sprayed with adhesive then plastered over the chief white male imperialist in each of the Victorian artworks. First to have his face covered up with poster paper is the distasteful 1915 *Simpson and his Donkey* by Horace Moore-Jones, a truly sickening slapstick designed to manipulate the public into support for the modern-day Crusader conquest of Turkey. Other paintings are plastered with protest too. Posters over moustaches. Posters over tricorner hats. Excited, nervous, hearts hammering, the girls barely breathe.

The chiffon-wearing waif beside the swan pond in the Frederick Goodall painting from 1788 is now standing beside a square of white paper with some scandalous words. The diaphanously draped sister in John Godward's *Memories* finds herself staring at a man with a staunch white poster for a head. Andi and Lotus plaster posters over every repressive male until the room is woke, then stand against the wall as the cops arrive.

Door-dick Marcus is glimpsed, pacing, pissed-off, conflicted, piles of blubber under his hunched elbows as he thinks about what to do. Two electric blue police constables ask the girls to come out to the street. There'll be no force, no cuffs, no roughness. The girls put down their spare posters and adhesive and descend the stairs, sniffing. On the way out, before her arm is bent and she drops the pen, Andi produces a silver Sharpie from her cleavage and with three strokes draws a penis on the mouth of the portrait of Governor Grey.

4.

Andi and Lotus fall into their flat at 4 am. They've managed to find an Uber with a Driver of Color. His headlights carved through the black and then he was gone. An IMMIGRANT has done the hard labour to drive them to KING'S land. So much significance in those words, significance doubled, no, TRIPLED by the wines they glugged in the pub after the pigs let them go. MAAAAAAhahahahaha. Jesus fucking Christ. The driver was a business student at AUT University, originally from Waziristan. His life story was utterly fascinating and the girls wish they could have more time to honor him. The girls don't deserve this flat. Too spacious. You could fit fifty families in here. They stare out different windows, studying the towers of Kingsland lit like Christmas lights.

Lotus wraps her duvet around her, yawns as if to say goodnight, but Andi slaps the island tabletop in the kitchen and announces a meeting. Don't you dare go to bed, Lotus Chua. Revolution begins, bitch. This is no time to back away.

It's been an insane night—day as well, actually. It was 3.04 pm when they were arrested. Lotus filmed the whole thing. The car ride to Auckland Central Station was eight minutes. They were each dumped in holding cells while police tried to get confirmation from Auckland Art Gallery's chief executive whether she wanted charges lain. Fingerprinting and photographing the girls took 90 minutes. They were then returned to a holding cell, which Andi didn't want to be released from as she was engrossed in conversation with an indigenous cellmate whose rights had been violated. The two were released after being given a formal warning, typed on a sheet of paper with an NZ Police letterhead.

The mission to achieve the Grade B offensive was successful, no doubt about it. The challenge for the girls now is to achieve a Grade A. Up the ante. Push the structure over.

Lotus, wobbling on her feet with tiredness, nods to agree she's keen, she's down, she's committed, absolutely. The state has shown it will retreat when confronted. Lotus will join the daylight strike against the target, she's just battling the yawns right now, YERRRRRRR, she's seriously sleepy and has to say goodnight.

Andi tells her comrade that's absolutely fine, go for it, girl, you enjoy your beauty sleep. Andi is loading the coffee machine with two bullets of Nespresso as she puts out the threatening platitudes. While the coffee is pouring, Andi is pushing tiny tablets of No-Doz out of their package. Pushing the No-Doz into the espresso Lotus Chua better seriously fucking drink unless she wants to be outed as a Little Eichmann.

Andi isn't sleeping tonight and nor is Lotus. Back off now and there'll never be a student presence in the city's public art gallery. Back off now and the establishment will win.

Andi is placing her laptop computer on the kitchen island and switching it on, jabbing the password in, tapping her foot, chewing No-Doz, laying down a rectangle of poster paper to draw on. What the girls are having right now is a summit, and apogee, a peak, a pass. Lotus shivers inside her blanket, holds the fabric against her ears, trying to quell the yawns.

'Oi! Wakey-wakey!' Andi is clicking under her friend's chin. 'Stop dreaming about your boyfriend. Draw a comic about your imaginary marriage if you're that desperate. I need your attention here.'

Andi takes a sharpie and begins sketching the plan on the back of the poster. She forces Lotus to finish the drawing. Make it look good. Buy in. Get complicit. Spread the struggle.

5.

It is 4.59 am when Andi types 5465 into the keypad and the roller door opens. Birds scream in the trees. The black sky is stained blue. Amber Anderson Caterer will shortly receive a dawn phone call from IMS Security to ask why she's using a supplier's security access code even though no catering has been planned tonight. Amber Anderson Caterer will tell those inbred rejects to fuck off and call back when their computer ain't spazzing.

The sky is indigo now with pink diluting it. They can't afford to have anything other than moonlight in here. The girls struggle to find the light switches so it takes four minutes and 48 seconds to cut the wires holding each Mackelvie monstrosity to its wall. The girls bump into each other once, twice,—FUCK!- as they scamper around the room, tearing each painting down and chucking the artworks in the middle of the floor. None of the paintings can be simply yanked—Andi knows this, having tried to tug a couple of them off as she was plastering them with her manifesto. There's a certain twist, then a jiggle, then a hard oomph to yank the screws out of the walls.

Thirteen pieces of European art are unclipped from the wall within three minutes. An alarm sounds after the Waterhouse is pulled down. Motes of plaster dust dance in the light. The darkness thins and the girls' eyes adjust. Blue floor, grey walls, black city with a coat of orange. The alarm remains a consistently shrill 99 decibels no matter how many misogynist artworks are pulled onto the pile. Sledgehammers and drills in the ear.

The girls are pleased to see chips of dried paint ₆and gold splinters as they stack the pile. The art's damaged, chipped: Fantastic. Andi scampers to the Indigenous Room, seizes two lengths of the bronze barrier arms and drags them through to the Mackelvie Room. The girls erect a barrier around the pile of paintings. DO NOT TOUCH PLEASE is redacted with a Sharpie so it reads D____OUCH____E.

They've failed to plan for the absence of lighting. This isn't enough daylight to film with. They're working in watery blackness. Lotus finds the Torch app on her phone and lights the pile of paintings. The thickness of the gilded frames has given each painting several inches of height. Combined, the stack of paintings is four feet deep.

Andi kicks the glass cabinet housing the fire extinguisher and axe. She has her weapon. Yusss.

Lotus takes photos while Andi hacks at the paintings with the fire axe, using her feet to stomp them into position for choice chops. She injures her foot trying to stomp through the Bramley, which weighs 150 kilograms. Chips fly into the air as Andi hacks at the Bundy, the Burne-Jones and that so-called lovemaking one by he-who-shall-not-be-named which is deeply rape-y. Andi's thick shoulders endure the lactic acid, the burn, the exhaustion, but she's glad when the destruction is done. After three blows, the axe is stuck in a thick wooden backing. She has to kick it loose. Andi picks up a shard of oily board and snaps it over her knee. Lotus continues to document the Grade A offensive with the camera on her iPhone. It's a three step technique, over the next two minutes, systematically damaging the paintings. Andi penetrates half of the canvases. The other half at least have wedges cut out of their frames. Three works have glass on their faces; Andi ensures these are all smashed.

Before they've fled the scene, Lotus sends the video reel and a couple of the best photographs from her phone to the *NZ Herald* newsroom. It's 5-ish, now, possibly 5.30. Print time, the girls hope. Yo, bourgeoisie? Eat yourself for breakfast.

The girls exit through the service entrance into an orangey world that smells of coffee and exhaust pipes and damp shadows steaming. The sun is coming up. The seagulls are stirring.

From Albert Park the girls dash hand in hand down Vulcan Lane, across Queen Street, up past the beggars, the bungy rocket, Sky City and over to Victoria Street West and towards the NZME building where Andi hunts for the *NZ Herald* logo as she produces a small reservoir of vaginal mucous. She moistens the corners of her last manifesto then plasters it on the glass walls of the entrance of the building. The Herald must take notice. The manifesto demands to spread through media. What the girls did was Grade A. What they did deserves discussion.

The girls are picked up moments later and invited to get inside the cop car. Not even manhandled, just politely asked in, then informed they're under arrest. Sick with post-adrenaline nausea, they're glad of a warm ride to the station, a blanket and a cup of sugary tea.

6.

Andi begins reading *Long Walk To Freedom* on the bench in her cell. The bench is a rude rectangle of stainless steel riveted to the wall. It's not even ironic architecture. It's unintentional bad taste design. She feels like writing an essay on it.

As if the design-crime weren't bad enough, they've taken her shoelaces and piercings. The conditions really are barbaric. No fresh water, no mattress. Andi is mentally composing her letter of complaint to the United Nations when her cell is unlocked and she's told "Time to go."

'Seriously? You'll dismiss People of Color that easily? Pfft.'

Andi is escorted through a series of yellow-painted concrete corridors which veer off one another at 90 degrees. She's sure the corridors are lain out in a swastika shape and is attempting to prove it when she's released into a visiting room. Mum is on the phone on the far side of the plexiglass; Dad is pacing the room, chewing the end of his necktie nervously, his Italian shoes clacking on the hard cold concrete. Mum's hair has been razored painfully short and angular; Dad's has spilled into a silver topknot some barber has convinced him is trendy. Mum and Dad explain they'll kill the next two hours at a café across the road. The police charges have been negotiated by Uncle Baz, who is a barrister with Kensington Swan. There will be zero court time so long as the girls agree to sell their piece to the gallery. Thanks to the video on the Herald website, the Mackelvie Room revolution has gone viral. It's all the art world can talk about.

In the backseat of the car they toss her a *Weekend Herald*. The headline is a brand, a burn.

Protestors' $20m Gallery Bomb.

*

Andi doesn't see Lotus for ages. The two lay low at their parents' houses until the contract is settled and there's definitely going to be money and the charges are definitely not going to happen.

Heart of the City has talked to the girls' lawyers. The girls' lawyers have talked to the girls' parents. The girls' parents and lawyers have talked to Elam and Whitecliffe and Creative New Zealand. Nobody has talked to the *Herald* until the whole thing's been finalized.

Known to have cost $20 million to create, the installation titled D__OUCH__E tops every art discussion worldwide. *Douche* is preposterously postmodern, powerfully provocative, creatively confrontational. The way two of the paintings face one another in the perfectly-positioned pile obviously represents the artists' demand that the art establishment face itself, concludes Peter Schjeldahl of the New Yorker.

Andrew Paul Wood describes *Douche* as "A work of gynocentric genius and a timely rejoinder to Georgia O'Keeffe's triptychs and Judy Chicago's *The Dinner Party*."

The Guardian suggests a Turner Prize may be likely for Andi, considering her mother still holds a baronet title for a family castle near Penzance. She's English, if she chooses to be.

There are endorsements from Banksy, from Damien Hirst, and the Demarco European Art Foundation.

Douche is sold for an undisclosed sum to a buyer who allows it to remain in Auckland Art Gallery. The piles of chopped paintings are fixed forever in the Mackelvie Room with epoxy resin and invisible screws and piano wire. The walls of the Mackelvie Room remain exquisitely damaged, sporting tiny white craters in the plaster where the wire fixtures have torn chunks of wall out as they crashed, details which are thought to represent a desire for the fall of Cecil Rhodes and other pillars of the old establishment.

Andi visits her installation regularly, asks the door-dick to screen off the room, as her deed requires, and sits on a padded bench and stares at her artwork, usually clad in an expensive shawl from Donatella. She thinks about Frith and Goodall and Godward fighting for a position in the Royal Academy of Arts. She thinks about her younger self fighting for a bowl of fried cabbage in the queue outside the Hare Krishna yurt on campus.

Lotus catches up with her occasionally, during Douche board meetings, though she's busy supporting Keas and Brownies at the Howick Scout Hall. Her daughters have just hit five years old and while Marcus is a good father and drives her to art gallery fundraisers every month, Lotus doesn't have much time for the revolution any more.

BAADER-MEINHOF BOY

The fat little razorback tries to shake his minder off so he can beat up your son. The kid is a tornado of ugly meat—a black mullet, thick eyebrows, a face puffy and bloated. He's enraged, bellowing, spitting, swinging wild overarms. The minder follows, sidestepping stray fists from the boy he has lost control of. The minder is a big 30-something giant dressed in a childish backwards cap and basketball shorts, chasing the stroppy pig-boy across the netball courts. You're half-stunned, trailing belatedly in the wake while your boy cops a beating. You've seen dogs fight like this.

Ainsley is on his back in the sandpit by the time you catch up with him. Your delicate little ten year old is traumatized, looking up at his attacker to see when it's going to end, his cheeks hot, his mouth black with fear. Neither your boy nor the bully should be in this junior section of Ribboncreek Primary School. From the jungle gym where it started, the fight has spilled eighty metres across the school.

Your son's no fighter, nor are you. You stand behind the razorback-boy, unsure of the law around restraining the bully, looking for an opportunity to intervene while he batters your shrieking son. As he bombards Ainsley with fistfuls of sand

and knuckle, the bully's shirt lifts and you get glimpses of pink scars on a mottled belly. Burns and blotches.

Finally the minder knots his hands around the crazed kid's head and under his elbows, lifts the crazed hog out of the sandpit and marches him away.

The minder notes your aghast expression as he leaves.

'Sall good, he does this,' the minder calls, hitching up his silken shorts with a spare hand, 'We cool.'

*

You are anything but cool. Bursting into your house and locking the door behind, you give Ainsley a bath to wash off the shame. Stalactites of snotty sand hang out of your son's nose. On his back are purple and pink splotches where he's been pummelled. It's mere minutes before the boy's mother, Philippa, is due home from work. You have sixty seconds to extrude for your wife an explanation as to why your boy was singled out by the brute. She'll scold you, Philippa will, plus you're already in trouble with your team leader for taking the afternoon off to clean up this godforsaken mess.

The bully—Legion is the little shit's name—had been lunging like a leashed dog at the seniors from the high school who take their daily shortcut through Ribboncreek, Ainsley explains, sitting in his tub of sandy water, sniffling. This Legion child was transferred from some other school just last week, dumped like a brick into a serene pond. Angry after a day of being sent to the principal's office and back by Ms. Marshall, the boy had been nipping like a stray dog, confident no teenager would fight him. Legion had picked fights with at least four teens before your angel suggested he stop, confident his Big Safe Daddy was coming to dignify the playground in just a moment or two. You really fumbled that one. Shouldn't have pulled over to respond to that email from your team leader. It cost fifty valuable seconds, and at the rate of one punch per second... Christmas crackers.

You dry your boy with a fluffy yellow towel with a hood stylized to look like a gosling, make a mug of hot chocolate with marshmallows and lay your boy on the couch under a blanket. He drops into sleep watching *Toy Story*, sucking his thumb.

Philippa comes in the front door, drops her groceries on the mat in the hall, calling out questions about the trail of sandy footprints and the dot of blood on Ainsley's gumboot. Within a minute, she's shrieking and shaking Ainsley awake, rattling his story out. Ainsley cost $30,000 of invitro fertilisation therapy to produce. He's precious, one-of-a-kind. No one has a right to touch him but God Above. She aims her angry eyes and demands to know what you're going to do.

2.

Of course the bully's mother doesn't show up to the meeting at which Legion is supposed to apologize to Ainsley. No father shows up, and no child, either. Everyone in the office is scrambling to locate him. The minder stands outside the office vaping, not bothering to pursue his charge, occasionally calling out 'Leeee-jaaaaarn?' in his monotonous oaf-voice. It's pointless—out the window you can all see the child off scrounging in the garbage tip on the edge of the woods where the school ends. Hundreds of metres away. As far from this so-called Restorative Mediation and Healing Conference as one could get.

Mediator Ms. Meadows peers at her written notes about the so-called fight. Her lips slip like kelp in an ocean of jowls as she formulates some words about honesty and openness and forgiveness. It's all ludicrous, of course. The perpetrator's a free man. There's no justice here.

Ms. Meadows says she'd like to proceed to the final page of notes: the compromise. Compromise? COMpromise?! You shake your head at the sickening obsequiousness of it all. Philippa will be unimpressed, to say the least; Elizabeth at work will demand a stronger result as to why you have taken time off. Ainsley, sinking in a bean bag in the corner, isn't even invited to participate. Sullen, he plays Python Code Quest on his tablet.

What stands out from Ms. Meadows' compromise document is the Legion child will be returned to class because there is some school values policy about "not stigmatizing" children, apparently, and by law he cannot be expelled without the Board of Trustees voting for the child to be removed, which would ultimately cost the school funding, which, Sir, we are not here to do.

'We are here to heal, as we agreed at the start,' Ms. Meadows says, smiling down at Ainsley.

You can hear the minder outside on the deck bellowing *LeeeJAAAARN* towards the woods.

Utterly dysfunctional, all of it. Sickening complacency. Borderline corrupt, actually.

You haul your creaking body off your chair and prepare to return to the office to work through your lunch break to make up missed time while Ms. Meadows protests about waiting for Legion "So everyone's on the same spiritual page." You close your ears, pause Ainsley at the door as you leave, putting your fingers on Ainsley's throat, fastening that top button he's always neglecting.

On the deck outside, you fume and frown. The minder shuffles over and attempts to stand beside you supportively. He points his vaporizer at a distant blob on the corner of the sports field where the school ends.

'Can't wait to clock off,' the oaf laments, shaking his head, his childish shorts swaying. 'Least the lil' clown goes to Residential in six hours, let them handle it, know what I'm sayin? Lucky it's payday on Thursday.'

You think of Ainsley trembling. You think of your team leader's frown. This society is falling apart. It's time transgressors had some sense slapped into them.

Past the playground, through the final goal posts and into the weeds you stomp. Fear rises from your toes into your groin. It's unsafe out here. Civilisation has receded. The school dissolves into wild woods, rusty washing machines, a small mountain of junk mail, a little stream, gravel, mosquitoes.

The trees close behind you. The sun hides. You're alone in the boondocks, now, two hundred yards from safety. The child appears, snapping something, building, constructing. Making a nest.

The boy pauses, gives you a quick assessment with black raisin eyes in his potato-face. He's peering around your body, checking to see if you have backup.

He's building—it's hard to tell at first—no, not building anything, *digging* a pit, a pit with a commotion in it, a muddy pit with—with a duck's head sticking out?

The boy has buried a—for Christ's sake, surely not—a *duck?!* Several ducklings are nipping around it in a panic.

'LEAVE MY BOY ALONE.' Your words are missiles which approach the boy but fall to earth. He's barely listening.

'YOU HEARD ME. MY SON: NO MORE BULLYING. He's delicate. Y'hear me?'

Legion tips his head sideways.

'What one's your boy, mista?'

The feral boy shunts more mud around his repulsive buried duck.

Your hands are in your pocket so he can't see them quivering.

'YOU WILL LEAVE THIS SCHOOL AT ONCE.'

'School says I hafta go. They make me. Sure you don't wanna play wiv me?'

He plops a dollop of mud on the mother duck's head and it disappears. He picks the ducklings up easily, rearranges some matches in his pocket and tucks the ducklings in instead.

Play with you? PLAY WITH YOU?

You pin vicious words with your teeth, count to 13 as the counsellor at Marriage Matters encouraged last month. You pull the poor duck out of the earth, turn and walk away, armpits black with worried sweat.

3.

Though you try to go through the usual shower, shave, coffee and yoghurt routine and do your buttons and tie responsibly, you can't get into the right headspace for a normal day. Your nemesis invades your headspace. It begins in the *Ribboncreek Report* newsletter which welcomes the school's newest brat, a certain Year 5 named Legion Jones. The school is attempting to exorcize the child's demons with lashings of kindness. Straightaway you're seeing the little prick's name everywhere. They have a name for it, you recall from that Dr. Robert Sapolsky tome you read last Christmas: it's called the Baader-Meinhof Effect. Encounter a significant name once and you'll begin to see it everywhere.

The obese little fucker returns to your consciousness later in the week with another newsletter update: he's been given a so-called 'Wonderful Wednesday' certificate. It's a desperate piece of appeasement, like when Hitler was granted the Sudetenland in the hope his violence would subside. In the newsletter is the Baader-Meinhof boy's ridiculous mugshot, certificate in hand against a trophy cabinet, as if the kid is normal.

You crumple the newsletter and biff it at the bin, missing of course. You were always useless at sports. More of a reader. Forbidden by Mother to so much as snap flowers off stems or buy yourself a hot pastry on a foggy day.

Ainsley walks into the kitchen hunting for his Minecraft cap and sees the crumpled newsletter. His face crumples accordingly.

You ask him if the Baader-Meinhof Bastard is still a bother. Ainsley asks what *bastard* means, and what *Baader-Meinhof* means. *It means something you'll never be, Softy,* you think with a snort. *If you would just stand up for yourself once in a while, you'd save me a tonne of trouble.*

Dropping Ainsley at the gates with an extra-special lunch in his backpack, you spy none other than Legion and his so-called minder marching the school grounds in the company of Silvia Meadows. They're picking up rubbish or lecturing the boy or somesuch. The child lags behind the minder, head swinging side to side in search of mischief. He's a big'un, you note, tall as the grownups' elbows. The child's eyes penetrate through the school fence and through your windscreen and nearly lock on you and your son. You take the long way round to the far gate, ignoring Ainsley's questions in that weak squeaky voice of his. You guide him to class, give him instructions on how to keep safe during the day and leave him with a special kiss on his fluffy eyelashes.

Thirty thousand bucks to brew this kid. What was that phrase from the Dan Ariely economics book? Opportunity cost, yes, that's it. He cost you opportunities.

Five hours later in the office, you're preparing to endure a one-on-one in the Fern Room with your team leader Elizabeth when a Seesaw alert interrupts your phone. Something about people marking themselves safe. Ribboncreek had been placed into lockdown while the firefighters put out a blaze. Traffic is backed up right into the centre of town. Elizabeth fumes as you ask permission to postpone today's meeting. You'll have the report in her inbox tomorrow, you swear.

You park 600 metres from Ribboncreek. You're nearly hit by that bloody real estate woman coming out of her driveway. A bus honks as you sprint in front of it. Finally your toes touch Ribboncreek's asphalt and you're amongst emergency services, their flashing reds and blues, the hi-vis vests, and a firehose which snakes for fifty metres.

Ainsleyyyy! Ainsley? AINZ?

Hundreds of children are gathered on the grass, a sea of yellow and blue uniforms, obedient little faces. You can hear Ms. Meadows and the teachers fussing. Something about hats.

The firefighters look unhappy. They are gathering up a firehose. Just as you're beginning to think the alert has misled you, your nose catches the sharp tang of petrol. A firefighter is holding a yellow Ribboncreek shirt far away from his chest, wincing. The school shirt, evidently, has been doused with petrol. Another firefighter follows, this time holding a saturated Teen Titans backpack.

You spot your freckled ten-year-old in the ocean of colorful children lined up obediently on the grass. You wade into the kids, pick Ainsley up and paint him with kisses and hugs. His pockets crunch—they're filled with chess pieces and he has a little game going on the grass. He's safe—deliriously happy to have a spare few minutes to enjoy his passion, actually.

A teacher gently asks you to fetch Ainsley's bag. The kids will be free to go home soon.

You go in search of Ainsley's backpack in the central corridor, several blocks of coat hooks and benches and lockers. In the hall are two police crouched in front of a fat, hunched, shirtless blob of trouble. He's trying to push through their legs; they're nudging the black-eyed boy back and ordering him to stay put.

Matches are sprinkled through the hall. To your right, a red plastic gas can is on its side, still hiccoughing a dribble of fuel.

Between the knees of the grownups, Legion's eyes catch yours.

Light it up, mista, says a rubbery little voice in your head. Play wiv me.

4.

Philippa insists on doing school drop offs for the next month, though she can't get away from court for pickups so she supposes you're competent to handle the 3 o'clock shift. It's about his safety, Poopsie, she tells you. Really it's Philippa reminding you you need to stay powerless. You'll need to communicate better with his teacher if you want to give him a good future, she tells you as an aside, and that starts with effective communication. You understand, Silly-billy?

It's not your fault, Philippa adds, not really. She squeezes your shoulder. God didn't mix bravery evenly when he was baking each of us, did he now.

At work Elizabeth confronts you before you've even taken your seat. There's no way your numbers are going to stack up for her report. Also, missing that meeting two days ago really fucked her week, Elizabeth tells you. Salary review? Forget it. She got Timothy from Communications to take care of your report for you. He can handle legions of responsibility.

Legions?

You heard me, she snaps.

You begin to ask her if she's ever heard of that Baader-Meinhof thing by which a person can't tell a coincidence from an omen then cut yourself off with a silent snigger. Elizabeth hasn't read half the books you have. Stooping to her level is pointless.

Hello? HellOOOOooo? She's snapping her fingers in front of your eyelids. If you're not going to engage professionally, you may as well just go home. She stares you down and you accept the defeat, blinking, though maybe not next time.

Nothing to do but hover outside Ribboncreek Primary so there's zero chance of being late. You crash down the emergency stairs, get into your car, honk at aggravating drivers, pull over near the school.

He's—he out?!

Legion steps in front of your car, tilting his head sideways like an owl. Amused.

'YOU!' you tell him, getting out, ready to throttle a neck as thick as your thigh, 'This is all your fault. QUIT BULLYING MY SON.'

'I already done that, mista.'

'You're a menace.'

'How come you're not in school, mista?'

Legion rests the object he's holding, some sort of club—a table leg—a TABLE LEG?! With a bolt protruding from it?—and waddles around some cars, disappearing momentarily.

Then he opens your passenger door and hops in.

'What in God's name are you doing?'

'Let's do fun stuff.'

'I have to do some work from home.'

'You like your work, mista?'

'I do not.'

'Don't go, then.'

You glare at the boy, order him not to touch anything, take the handbrake off, reverse out and creep slowly up the street.

Legion points west, far away from school. Fine. You can dump him on the outskirts of town like a sackful of kittens. Until then, you suppose you'd better comply with the law. You pull a seatbelt over the boy's breasts and plug it in.

You take Streamscape Drive. The street just keeps on giving. Generous lights pointing north, then you veer towards the river where a dozen small, identical buildings with gleaming windows are lined up amongst the oaks. The Shelter Independent Living Village, it's called. There is a parking lot outside the perfect houses with their red roofs and brown bricks. Legion spots a corner of the parking lot where the security cameras are blind. Okay: deposit the child there. You ease the car slowly into a space under a low branch, set the handbrake. Legion is out of the car and scuttling into the village. Legion's a lot more energetic than his blubber would indicate. You help the boy haul a garage door open. There's a loading dock where trucks deliver to the village's kitchen. Bag after bag of flour, onions, instant pudding. Racks of soft white bread.

Taking his time, calmly brushing his fingers across the bulk bags of food, Legion selects a sack of potatoes and drags it out. You ease the roller door back down, covering for the boy. What on earth is this? What's his plan? Surely school is missing him. Surely the police are following. In the thirty seconds you waste pondering what to do, Legion makes swift, efficient progress.

He plants a single potato on the asphalt behind each of the shiny hatchback cars. The boy budgets exactly 32 potatoes then once they're each lain out and prepped, he goes back to the first potato and crams one after another up the exhaust pipes moving right to left.

You don't want to enable a child to do such a thing, of course, so you shove the last dozen potatoes up exhaust pipes yourself, squatting so you can't be seen behind the cars. Your work pants strain and you make a mental note to wear something less restrictive. You dash back to your car and rev the engine impatiently, urging the boy to retreat to safety.

Soon as Legion has plugged the exhaust pipes with potatoes and jumped back in the passenger seat, the car screams out from its leafy den and you take several detours before resting on a grassy hill overlooking the village. Heart knocking, you watch through a pair of binoculars taken from Ainsley's Scout kit. Nothing happens for a few minutes, then the first family leaves the Reception building, waving goodbye to nana, strapping their seatbelts, driving to the Give Way, preparing to roll onto the road... and BANG!

You and your little accomplice can't hold the binoculars up, you're laughing too much, an apish, caveman chortle which you pass back and forth, exciting one another.

God, you haven't laughed like this since you were a kid. Your blood warms. Your eyes sparkle. You wipe a tear from your cheek. You drive a curve back towards the city through a boulevard in a wealthy part of town with wide berms and cherry blossoms and high walls.

Legion says he needs to go toilet. Right now? Right now, mista. You're on a street of mansions, four storey fortresses set back from their walls. Palms and fig trees on the lawns, sculptures, fountains. At 1005 Pallisades Parkway you keep the engine running while Legion hops out, pulls down his shorts and blasts shit onto the perfectly shorn Bermuda grass. His faeces resembles brown scrambled eggs. The boy's diet must be all grease and candy. He needs someone to feed him properly. Working together, you scoop the shit onto a fig leaf and guide the shit inside the mouth of the mailbox of mansion number 1007, trying to breathe around your laughter. You're sure to get busted any moment now! Never have you had such a thrill!

You're creeping away, desperate to flee, when Legion says Oi, check this out, and adds the cherry on top: he moves the red flag on the mailbox from down to up.

'You got mail!' he bellows over and over, and you're clutching your guts in exquisite amusement. Of course the boy deserves a chocolate shake from Burger King for his effort. Of course Legion takes the shake as it's handed to him by the girl in the red cap and bowtie, takes the lid off, enjoys a quick slurp and then tosses brown goo all over the girl. Of course he takes the wheel while you try to dry your laughing eyes. You can barely see the road.

It's almost 3 o'clock by the time you've splashed and smashed and sprayed and shat your way through the city. Your jaw aches with permagrin; you think you might need Deep Heat to cool the pain in your ribs from laughing all day. You've stopped at the supermarket, picked up a packet of marshmallows and crackers and a barbecue lighter and melted delicious Smores in a car park looking out over the river. The taste brought back memories of sitting round a camp fire with your Scout troupe, tossing fistfuls of pine needles into the orange and feeling thrilled, back when you used to get chased by caretakers, caned by nuns who rammed your face into the newspaper. You want to end up like this Carlos the Jackal brute? Eh? EH? Detention. Firecrackers, pipe bombs. Rocks and windows. Freedom. Adrenaline. Pure glee. Squashed by the academy, business school, the grey internship. Sensations you've buried and dragged a rock over.

You leave the boy at the gates, spitting on your handerchief, wiping chocolate from Legion's sticky cheeks.

The bell rings. A tsunami of grinning children yeeee across the plaza.

You extend your hand to shake Legion's.

It's not the end, mista, Legion tells you. No need to shake on nothin.

5.

Philippa swirls her Gewürztraminer in a huge glass and remarks on its notes of mandarin and sandalwood. She slides her glass along the breakfast bar. You can smell that, surely? What's wrong with you? You need your nose checked, that's what. She's been taking a night class in wine appreciation and wishes you'd join her. Our Lord and Saviour wants us to appreciate the gifts he's bestowed upon us. How can you not be appreciative?

From your barstool, you nod so much it's hard to bring your head back up.

Listen, Poopsie, she says, rubbing your back, gargling her wine, I know. About the little secret rendezvous.

Your blood cools. There is a wine knife on the counter. You smuggle it inside your fingers, store it on your lap. Might need it if a fight breaks out.

There's nothing to be ashamed of, she continues. You're doing a wonderful thing for that child. A Christian thing. We both know his guardian's useless. Just do it by the books, eh? You have to let the school know if you're giving one of their children a lift home. Get it on paper. Authorized. Besides, Ainsley's jealous.

You aim your fist towards her. The wine knife is poking your palm, eager to escape. Tell me who the hell narked.

Narked?!

Who squealed on me?

She recoils, says she doesn't like that street language. It's vulgar. Your son's just concerned about his father, that's all. Plus, you can't be taking any more hours off work.

Motherfuckin Ainsley. You fume all night and catch him next morning.

Ever heard of blinders, boy? Blinders are the things you strap on a horse's head when you want to keep its vision focused. Keep your eyes where they oughta be or you're gonna get hurt.

You clench his shoulder until he promises to keep his God damn eyes to himself.

*

You're 40 minutes late to work and Elizabeth's flapping her arms, waving you into a meeting room where she's got Australia on speakerphone and a couple secretaries behind her, recording minutes.

She tells you, with her molars glued together and her lips barely moving, that you need to *SRRT. YOUR BRRRT. DWWWN.*

You give her a hard shove in the chest and brace yourself. How a person reacts in the first second after a shove determines how a fight finishes, Legion taught you.

C'mon lady. Gimme one reason.

She backs down, of course, and flees to another room. A secretary follows her, rubbing her back.

You get stood down for a week, with pay. Perfect: the pressure cooker's been boiling over anyway. Time to work on mindfulness. Reconnect with your inner child.

6.

You spend the morning in the woods on the edge of the school, showing the boy how to mix epoxy resin, which until now Legion has only been pouring into a sock and sniffing. Epoxy resin, when mixed correctly, is strong enough to glue razor blades discretely behind every door handle of every class. Ms. Meadows puts her fingers on her door handle, slicey-slicey nicey-nicey, so long as you mix the correct proportions of epoxy. The boy is way behind on his units of measurement and you know he's not understanding how milli means one thousandth, as in it takes three thousandths of a litre of epoxy resin to glue each blade to each door handle. Still, he demonstrates some tactile learning and you get the blades glued to all of the handles around 5 as the sun is setting. Ainsley has been waiting patiently and he wants a lift home but you tell him to harden up and walk. You could've walked home already, son! The hell's wrong with you? He's interrupting your lesson. The little sniveller pleads, cries, moans about the rottweiler's snout sticking out the gate at house number 88. Finally he walks away and you resume working with your boy.

*

As you read Thursday's *Ribboncreek Report* at the breakfast bar, laughter squeezes your ribs. Oh, mercy: the first line of Principal Mohammed's editorial literally says "Looking over the list of terrorism conducted against my school, its buildings and its people over the past month brought a tear to my eye."

The big baby's been crying! You can't wait to tell Legion. Like these idiots can't fight back! Pathetic. These babies need to harden the fuck up.

The principal apparently can't handle a few dead rats planted in pencil cases, concrete poured into a toilet, plus that hole covered with cardboard you dug into the sandpit. Kids walk over the hole, they fall in, sand falls on 'em: comedy gold.

What Principal Mohammed has his knickers in a twist about is paramedics had to be called to gently lift some little Korean girl out cause her leg got all twisted and her dad's a diplomat and the family are thinking of suing. The school may have to ask for extra donations to cover this unanticipated cost, the editorial tells you. As for the Case of the Deadly Doorknobs, several teachers have had to have tetanus vaccinations after their nasty cuts. All children must urgently update their immunisation records with the school. It'll cost hundreds of hours of admin.

Your abdominal muscles pulsate with laughter. Your cheeks ache. As Philippa heads for the door, dolled up in heels and a short skirt, looking more fuckable than she has in years, she asks you to load the dishwasher, please. You throw a ripe juicy tomato at her which spatters on her $1800 Dalbergia wood door and trickles down onto her stupid fuckin imported Etruscan tiles. While she's stunned, you put your arms on either side of her and tell her who's boss. Her thighs quiver. You tug her into the bedroom. She works for you then spreads herself, holding you inside her with her fingers, stroking you afterward, gushing gratitude.

Later, you pull on flip flops and a singlet and trudge down to school. It's a good day to walk. You even pick up a pack of cigarettes from the dairy. The first smoke brings a dizzy rush to your head and sparks a suppressed memory of sneaking smokes in an orchard. Pressing chests with a girl at a disco. Running from a taxi driver.

You tell the piece of skirt at the school reception that you're Legion's lawyer and the child needs to be called out of class for an urgent meeting. The receptionist obeys and summons the child. His suspicious black squint spreads into a smile when he walks into the office and realizes it's you, here to spend a day together in your war corner.

You trudge over to the boondocks, carrying two milk bottles filled with gas and show the boy how you can dissolve polystyrene into the petroleum, each chunk turning into a blob until the bottle is full of a sticky cream colored sludge. That's napalm, son. You position yourself around Legion's back, wrap your arms over his as you prepare a second batch, tearing off chunks of polystyrene, guiding his fingers as he pushes the white tufts inside the snout of the milk bottle. There. The two of you stand back and admire what you've created together.

Later, Ainsley limps over and finds the two of you as you're scraping a battleplan into the mud. Legion has stolen the keys to a steamroller parked round the corner on that site where they're putting up the new special ed prefab classes. You're going to flatten the school's fence, maybe the whole damn school. It's just a matter of timing. You'll chain the Minder to the fence and flatten him as well. Ms. Meadows and the principal, too. You'll flatten anyone who's ever questioned you. The firemen. Philippa. That nark at work. Your boy –

'Dad?'

He says your name with a lilt at the end. A question.

As in, Dad, is that you? Are you still in there?

Legion walks straight at Ainsley, ready to smash him.

'Legion: halt.'

He stops, looks over his shoulder, awaiting instructions.

7.

It's black tonight. There's steam in the air. The orange letters glowing on the digital noticeboard spell BOARD MTNG 730.

The Board of Trustees has had Legion Jones enrolled for the legal minimum of 60 days and they're now permitted to expel the boy provided everyone votes Aye. The Board has gathered in the middle of the school hall, dragging together four trestle tables to form a wagon-circle. In the middle the secretary sits on a revolving office chair, giving instructions. All families "victimized" by the boy are invited. You can't not attend. He's jumped out the window of Residential especially to be with you tonight. The boy's fate is sealed, Board-wise. If one fails to show up, one gets moved to Juvenile Detention Facility.

You're not surrendering the boy. No, he's safe in your car.

Legion, half-leaned back in his seat, tells you what you must do tonight.

You keep the engine running until you spot the Minder in the parking lot, resting his bulk against the boot of the car, pulling back the cuff of the sleeve of his billowing FUBU sweatshirt, looking at the watch on his wrist in frustration.

Now, Legion tells you as your car eases into the school, Hit 'im.

The Minder cranes his head forward, trying to peer through the dark and see who's that thumping over the speed bumps, coming right towards him.

The Minder steps forward.

'FASTER,' Legion instructs, and there's a crunch as your windscreen shatters and you're slamming on the brakes and the body on the bonnet rolls onto the ground where it splats like a watermelon.

You get out of the car. The hall is right ahead, the Board, the wagon circle, so many targets. There's a groan from the sack of meat on the asphalt. He's not dead, just down.

Fuck. Change of plan. You leave the car in the middle of the school and walk briskly away. The napalm will still be in the boot when you get back, don't worry. It's bright, the car is—the moon catches the corners of every cube of glass. The broken windscreen glows.

Glowing, too, is the illustrious McDonald's sign just up the road. You feel a hard fat warm little bun placed in your palm. It's Legion's hand, his chubby callouses clutching yours.

You park the upsetting thought and try to enjoy the safe, warm reliable family restaurant. McDonald's has a playground with a yellow plastic slide and a climbing wall and—look, son—somebody's even left you a balloon. Here.

The boy's favorite food turns out to be hot, sweet, sticky apple pie. The pies are just a dollar ninety nine; you buy him five. The way he carries his tray delicately, held up beneath his fat little chin, warms your core.

You find a booth in the play area where you can keep your backs to the wall. One of your favorite hacks when you were a kid, the one that earned you that two day Time Out, was to eat 9/10 of the pie then pick a dead wasp from the glass walls, stick the wasp in the remnant pie and take it to the counter to get compensation—free milkshakes, burgers, toys.

He's scared of wasps, your boy. Legion studies you with wide appreciative eyes as you inject the delicate corpse of a windowsill wasp into half a pie then send him over to the counter to hustle, patting his cute wee bottom. It's okay, son. There's a lot to be scared of in this world. The red and blue lights licking the walls, the whoop of a siren, the crackle of a police radio outside. Approaching the counter he looks over his shoulder at you, his eyebrows bending in appeal. Poor little fella's frightened he might get told off.

He hesitates in front of the counter, nervous.

You ease out of the booth, put your hand on his back and walk with him.

DINER'S CLUB

1.

Wayne returns to the table from the bathroom wiping his fingers in a careful motion, slip-slurp, slip-slurp, trying to get people in the restaurant to notice how skux he is. His shirt collar's up, covering his neck tats, and he keeps stroking his own chest as he comes back to our table. He yanks out his seat real elegant and plops his bum onto the wood, pulling himself up against the table in a perfect little tug.

'Madame,' he says, as teeth leak out of the cheeky slit in his face, 'Let us begin.'

I'm trying to see if I can sneak something from the children's menu, we really should've come here between 11.30-1.30 on Thursdays when everything's massively discounted, instead of tonight, but Wayne yanks the cardboard out of my hands and tells me to stop panicking about money. He adjusts the single candle yellowing our table till it's positioned just right. He forces the wine list into my fingers and tells me to order anything.

'*Anything*,' he goes, then leans back, tapping his fingertips together like a fatcat. Wayne must've scored some money somehow but he's being all espionage about it. I wanna escape the upper class meanies and crack a box of Cody's on the couch and watch *X-Factor* and snuggle but Wayne told me on the bus here that me and him need to show the world that we're moving up, starting tonight.

The waiter—one of the good ones, without tattoos on his neck—arrives and holds his pad ready for our order. He doesn't even look down my tits. Ducasse is a swanky joint.

'Scuse me, um, what's a… a… can of apies?' I ask him, 'Can apes?'

'It's can-a-paize,' he explains. 'Sort of like a vol-au-vent. A teaser. We're talking pastry-bread with a morsel of savoury filling.' He kisses his fingertip. 'Tonight's are pumpkin and sunflower with salmon.'

A woman in pearls at the table opposite us turns her head to listen. I blush beetroot red. Everyone else's table's got an electric light on it. Wayne demanded we get a real legit candle of actual wax.

The waiter begins talking us through the specials but Wayne interrupts him with an 'Ub-ub-ub-ub-UB!' and five fingers jammed against the waiter's mouth and it's Wayne, the king of culture, the man-who-got-a-massive-promotion-today, who's in charge.

Wayne adjusts the cuffs and shirtsleeves of his brand new Hallenstein Brothers suit and snaps his fingers.

'You'd better get cooking…. .' Wayne looks at the waiter's nametag, squinting, '…Better get cooking, *Marcel*. Here we go: Beef tart thingy for our canapé. Then first course we'll have that hardout cauliflower one.'

'The velouté dubarry, sir?'

'Obviously. The artichoke sourdough next, then the… how do I say this? Folie a deux?'

'*Foie de volaille paté por deux*. It means paté for two. It's chicken liver. I'm not sure you're going to like— '

'Garkon, shut up and write this down: we'll take the degustation.' Wayne yanks my menu out of my hands and snaps it closed, discarding it over his shoulder so the waiter is forced to bend for it. The hotness is creeping down my neck now.

Wayne reaches inside his breast and produces a Diner's Club card. Its silver shines in the candle light. 'Don't forget the amuse bouche.'

'They gave you this at work?' I go.

'So to speak.'

He's supposed to be committed to a job selling water purification filters with Love Springs Eternal, letting customers know the council's poisonously high levels of calcite won't come into their glass of water so long as they invest in the right purifying-y system, with a basic setup starting at $4999. I thought Wayne was doing alright at his job, going around the retirement villages knocking on doors, asking for a glass of water, spitting it into the bushes, saying it's poison, he was getting decent commission for his sales but it seems like Wayne's got a new business venture he's brought me here to announce.

'Did you have to pay for the card thing or...?'

'Total opposite, babe. They pay ME.'

Wayne slides a pamphlet across the table and drums his fingers on the tabletop to indicate I oughta hurry up and read it. The pamphlet says Diner's Club gives us free access to over 800 airport lounges worldwide, plus advance notifications of concert tickets, exclusive discounts on spas and makeovers, plus we can withdraw cash advances at any Westpac money machine.

The club card makes me feel like I can tip back into a nice safe cloud. They don't just give out credit cards to anyone. For once in my life I can chill about the bills while I chew the first thing on the degustation that arrives, which turns out to be Saint Jacque scallops with garlic from Java that makes me totally mouthgasm. Wayne updates me on Love Springs in a past-tense sorta way, as if he's moved onto something else, which I don't quite get, since that's where he's been going every morning, or at least he's been telling me he's been going. What Wayne reveals, twirling a forkful of lamb saddle with handmade ratatouille, is he's about to undergo the R&D phase of a vapourless vaporizer he's been building out in the garage. Wayne says he expects to get some angel investors hopefully this year to put in some serious seed money, not necessarily

Sean Parker or Richard Branson, but those types of dudes, and I nod and chew and nod and swallow and nod and sip and I'm in heaven, honestly, but heaven stained with some serious worry about the bill, cause I'd rather not have a fancy dinner date if there's like a fifteen dollar limit on the card.

He waves his Diner's Club around though and promises me everything's sweet, babygirl, and we eat til we're in agony. When Wayne can't fit any more inside him, he fills my handbag with sachets of Sweet'n Low and breath mints. My heart stops when Marcel brings the credit card swiper machine round and Wayne slices his Diner's Club card and it's dot dot dot, thinking about calling the cops on our broke asses, but then the receipt spurts out and my heart starts beating as the purchase goes through. I fall asleep on the bus home with my head on Wayney's lap. He strokes my hair and makes up little raps about the rubbish he finds tucked into the seats.

2.

It's two months later when Wayne brings me back to Ducasse and he's pointing his fingertips at the maître d' and saying some nickname for her, even though I'm pretty sure he's never met the maître d' before.

I'm nervous and I don't want to take my jacket off, at first, but Wayne says the secret to getting ahead in life is looking the part. I shrug out of it and a waiter wrestles me for it, hanging it on a coat tree.

Wayne pays the waiter two bucks to pull out our chairs. People turn their heads, forks hovering.

'Would you like a couple of cushions to sit on, sir?'

'Fuggoff, I ain't that short,' Wayne grumbles.

When Marcel the waiter asks what kind of wine we want, I'm about to cringe and slide under the table and admit I don't know any kinds of wine, but Wayne's thought of literally EVERYthing.

'We'll take the Burger Chanson Pinot Noir first,' he goes. 'I'll signal when we're ready for a ...Jabba... Syria. And, oi.' Wayne produces a rolled-up note which looks purple—purple! A fifty!—and tucks it deep into Marcel the waiter's pocket. 'I want some SERIOUS service. I'm talkin the BEST.'

I spot Marcel the waiter pausing on the lip of the kitchen and unfurling the note to check if it's real. If it is, it can only mean....

'MASSIVE progress,' Wayne goes, swirling his sparkling water, adjusting his Diner's Club card so it's perfectly positioned on the table. 'That's why I wanted to celebrate.' His ankle caresses my calf.

'Wayyyney,' I whisper, glancing from side to side, 'Are you sure there's room on the... you know.'

'Diner's Club isn't a credit card, babycakes. Does it SOUND like a credit card? It's a CLUB. That's why they call it a club.

We're MEMBERS, babe. And it's for entrepreneurs, so just chill, would ya?' Wayne makes himself laugh and looks at the people on either side of us to make sure they know what a good time he's having. 'Worrying takes ten years off your life. I read that in Forbes.'

'I just don't know how we're gonna pay for —

'Babe, look: did Steve Jobs listen to some jellyfish when Microsoft told Apple they were never gonna survive? I think not. And you know where Steve Jobs is now? Exactly: livin it up.'

Wayne's not supposed to be an entrepreneur. The bank rung us up and said unless he took that job with Kirby, he'd have to consolidate all his credit card debt and it would get deducted out of our bank every week. With every slurp and every story tonight, though, it becomes more and more obvious Wayne's outgrown the things holding him back. He doesn't have to get refugees to sign direct debit forms for vacuum cleaners any more. My man is unstoppable.

Marcel the Waiter plops down some creamy saucy stuff with ham and a chunk of cheese on it, that real good cheese you get with the Big Angus burger at Maccas.

'Anyway, the reason I called you here tonight,' Wayne goes, sees no one around us is eavesdropping, and starts again, louder. 'SO THE REASON I CALLED US HERE IS TO CELEBRATE. Ever heard of a little company called HRV? Yeah? And ever heard of a little job position called *SALES REP*?'

I'm so excited for my Wayney I sob into my napkin for a moment then flutter my fingertips til I'm chill again and he can continue his big news, leaning through the yellowy blackness of our candle, his fangs peeking out of his lips. 'Tell me, bae.'

Wayne is destined to flourish in his new role selling the home ventilation system that's proven to save lives purifying the air in the households of our most vulnerable citizens. All he has to do is hit daily sales targets for a couple months, and Wayne's sales experience at Love Spring and Kirby practically puts him on the pathway to management, he says. His words start to melt and swirl as I get drunk on cold wine and hot excitement. I can feel the anxiety drain down my legs and out my toes and I make a note to myself that Wayne's definitely getting head tonight. As I'm eating prosciutto and swishing sweet syrah on my tongue, I decide that we actually do fit in here. I've been stressed out cause I'm studying early childhood education and cause laying out a career seems so predictable. I wish I had Wayney's courage. He makes badass business decisions every day.

Things are gonna change for the better, I decide, tapping the last drops out of the wine bottle. No more debt collectors. No more changing the expiry date on Pizza Hut coupons and holding my breath every time I place an order.

As he leans towards the candle, the light glints on his eyebrow ring. He's moved it from the left eyebrow to the right since it got ripped out when those hoodrats jumped him and the eyebrow got all infected and puffy.

'HERE'S what's the next big thing with the economy, babe: the human body. What if I told you there was a miracle product that could literally melt the fat off you. Well, not *literally*… '

'Fat… ?'

'Not, FAT-fat, I didn't say that… not, like… look, you've got the *good* fat on you. Unsaturated or whatever. Baby fat. You're making me lose my point. What if I told you there are dietetic milkshakes designed by actual NASA scientists, expertly calibrated to synthesize with the body's nutritional rhythms, and I could be the exCLUSive representative in this city. I'm talkin 50 percent commission. Every time one of my shareholders makes a sale, I go up a level.'

'Level?'

'Can't spell Multi Level Marketing without Level, bae.'

'Milkshakes?'

Wayne tears his paper napkin in half and tosses the scraps towards this black man eating with this Asian girl so they'll look over at us. 'Legally, technically they resemble.... Y'know what? No. NOT milkshakes. That's obtuse thinking right there. Herbalife nutritional supplements are a complete meal in drinkable form, okay? It's an insult to call 'em milkshakes. Herbalife is listed on the NASDAQ. Is Mr. Whippy on the NAS-DAQ? I don't think so. And I've got 400 Herbalife shares with our name on 'em, like, I mean, well technically it's your name cause of bankruptcy rules and all that, y'know, I'm not allowed to trade for seven— GARKON! Yo! That escargot ready, huh? Got enough parsley butter on it? Plonk it down, attaboy.'

The world has been swaying like kelp in the ocean. Now it stops.

'The power bill's... it's bad. We owe, like, fourteen hundred, Wayne.' I flap my fingers and dab my face with my giant white serviette. I sniff wet boogers. 'I need to do my assignments—'

'What you need to DO is STOP before you EMBARRASS yourself.' Wayne has leapt around the table and he's on his knee, squeezing my wrist.

'Now, as I was saying, we have CREDIT becauuuuse, drum-roll please, you ready, this is why I brought you here: our bacon's been saved. Tell me: who has two thumbs and just got start-up capital from a certain angel investor by the name of Save My Bacon Little Loans?'

I sniff my face dry and wait for the smartest man I know to correct my dumb ignorance.

He points his thumbs back towards himself. 'THIS GUYYYYYY.'

I feel Wayne's ankle sliding up my calf like an alley cat. I'm on a plateau of ecstasy.

Forget the bus. We take a taxi home like rich people.

3.

I.... just... GRADUATEDDDDD!!!

It's seriously like I'm tripping. Of course we head to Ducasse to celebrate.

We have to walk tonight to get here, with a quick detour to Warehouse Stationery to pick up some printing. Wayne reckons walking is part of our new carbon neutral stance as a family but secretly we both know it's cause our car got repo'd.

But, like, anyway, hooray for me!!! Early childhood care's always been my dream. It took me three years to complete my diploma cause we moved around, then I couldn't get my student loan for a while cause Wayne'd got us to both change our names so we could open fresh bank accounts with new overdrafts (he took the Y out of his name but he said mostly it was a branding decision because his investors never have to ask why, which is pretty genius if you think about it).

Tonight, even though the maître d' gives Wayne a reeeeal concerned look as we come in, we finally we get to celebrate my achievement with our favorite waitstaff making our night special. This new waiter, a girl whose nametag says Emma, takes Wayne's Diner's Club card away *before* we've had our meal, which is weird, though I guess she's keeping it safe cause it caus-es a lot of envy and people might jack us. In the corner I see the maître d' getting out these big shiny scissors and snipping it in half and suddenly it's baking in here and my face glows red.

This new waitress Emma comes back over to us, like all cringe, explaining she'll be happy to take cash for our order, but only in advance. Wayne gets out his wad and gives her what looks like a hundy and Emma-the-waitress puts the money in her bumbag and works out the change before they process our order. He tries to give her a two dollar tip but she tells him to keep it. Rude, sure, but soon enough we're nibbling breadsticks and sipping drinks and concentrating on having a good time, keeping our relationship strong, gazing at each other through the candle.

That is until Wayne changes the subject.

'So I've done the math and you can't start work,' Wayne says. 'Early childhood teaching, you only start on 17 an hour. Factor in commuting costs, new car, depreciation, lunch, makeup and whatnot, I don't think you'll be bringing in enough.'

'But... but the Herbalife thing? You had the exclusive franchise for our region?'

Wayne waves my words away, looks around at the other tables, chewing grumpy-styles.

'Listen, I'm going to need you to re-enroll for a couple more years so you can keep borrowing on your student loan living costs thingy. We can't afford not to have Studylink coming in every week. It's free money. You'll have to go do another course. Grab yourself a Bachelor degree. Master's after.'

The waitstaff begin a commotion and Emma holds up her fingers which I can see are green and inky as if she's been playing with finger paint.

Wayne reaches across the table, grabs my hand, squeezes, pulls my attention back towards him. My little magic man. My GI Joe. My big boy propped up on cushions like a king.

'Babe: most of sales is thinking on your feet, yeah, and if we want a good financial outcome, we're both going to have to think on our feet right now. Like RIGHT now.'

I don't get what the fuck he's on about but I nod anyway.

'That baby you always wanted? *Start having it right now.*'

'Whuh?'

'*Pretend you're pregnant. Go. GO.*'

I push my seat back from the table as Wayne comes around, lifts up my dress, puts his ear against my tummy and starts making a big commotion.

'For the love of God, we need an ambulance,' Wayne is yelling, 'THIS WOMAN IS HAVING A BABY. WHAT'S THE MATTER WITH YOU PEOPLE?! DIAL 111 ALREADY.'

Pretty soon an ambo is pulling into the parking lot, its lights turning the restaurant rose-red, my favorite color, and all in all tonight is—what was that thing Wayney used to spend all our money on at the trots?—a *trifecta*. Yeah, tonight's a trifecta of three wins, cause the first win is they forget to bill us as we scream and wince and stumble to the door, me clutching the top of my butt, and we've had another divine dinner, so that's the second win, and thirdly, best of all, thanks to the ambulance we don't have to take the bus home.

THE COOLEST

The moment we agreed Matt Lamb Junior was the coolest kid was when he turned the tables on Jake, who was like a mean-as bully. Jakeyboy had this thing he loved doing—sticking his finger up his butt then jamming it in people's noses, progressing from the back of the class up to the front while the teacher was off running errands and class was unattended.

See, this one Tuesday, Jakeyboy was flitting around the class all demented, his eyes blue with insanity, hair shocked white as a lightbulb, when he arrived at Matt Lamb Junior's desk and jammed the finger right up in Matt's nostril. Matt didn't flinch. He looked in the eye of the pale-skinned, googly-eyed bully and calmly said, 'Smells like your mum.'

A torrent of laughter flooded our eardrums. Kids were getting out of their chairs and falling to the ground in hysterics. Jakeyboy began twitching, looking over his shoulder at the howling seven year olds, not sure which way to react.

'*You're dead.*'

Matt coolly folded one knee over the other, laced his fingers behind his head and eased back in his chair.

'If I'm dead, why you talkin to a zombie?'

It was the sassiest comeback any of us had ever heard. Already popular because his mum drove a cool car and he was allowed to watch R-rated movies and because he always had snacks in his lunch that hadn't even been on commercials yet, Matt now had a non-stick coating of cool. The rest of us would have to eat shit from bullies occasionally, but not MLJ.

At eight, he ran the cross-country race backwards, glancing over his shoulder every ten seconds to stay on track. We dumped an avalanche of cheers on him.

At nine, Matt Lamb Junior put a story in the school newsletter, labelling a photograph of Principal Finlayson standing beside the newly-raised war monument with the legend, 'Finlayson shows off his erection.'

At ten, Matt Lamb got Missy Chrissy Townsend, the big redhead girl in the wheelchair who'd been held back a year, to surrender her bra. Matt strapped Missy Chrissy Townsend's bra round his belly, pulled his Reebok shirt down over it and charged each of us fifty cents for a peek. We imagined we saw milk stains on it, perhaps a crimson curl of pubic hair, the imprint of her nipple, maybe. It was an artefact from an alien dimension.

By eleven and twelve, Matt was getting other kids to do stuff for him. That kid from the Outback was dared to climb to the top of the water tower and piss off it. Cedric Chang was tasked with writing his history speech in Igpay Atlinay. Matt bullshitted to Avinash Rao that Friday was a Pyjama Day fundraiser and you should show up in your jammy-jams with a sleeping bag and a hot water bottle.

Thirteen was the turning point. Our parties were suddenly hardwired into the rest of the world. There were expectations, now. You had to play Spin The Bottle and get with somebody. It began in a basement at the house of that rich prince-kid from Germany, Matt shushing the party with a conductor's finger, spinning his bottle deftly and sharing a perfect pash. The trend was set. We copied the spin of his bottle, the positioning of his fingers, the dance of his eyebrows.

Pussies wanted to know how they could stare someone like Jakeyboy in the face and say real-life Schwarzenegger shit. Nerds wanted to know how they could keep pimples repressed. Matt Lamb's hair grew as long as a rockstar, thick tight curls like a river of tater tots, sometimes in a topknot, a couple times as an undercut. Once, threaded in glowing golden braids. A gorgeous fleece no other kid could sport.

Girls wanted to date Matt, of course, though you couldn't get to him. Soon as the bell rang and Matt's mum picked him up, he was inaccessible. Every day she dropped him at school in her convertible and fetched him at 3, often early, always revving and rumbling, never leaving the driver seat before whipping him away from the parking lot, as if she didn't want a drop of dirt on him. She had a fierce ferret face, tiny lips, eyes ringed with black. People said her spine was fused. A short woman with a head of blonde that didn't seem to belong to her. A smoker, a driver of an expensive glowing car. A buyer of weekly Reeboks and NBA caps for her son, always shopping and tossing bags at her boy. Mrs. Lamb had clawed her way out of some slum, some monetary miracle that elevated her from pauper to posh overnight, it was said, though this raised questions about a husband. Trinidad claimed to have seen a father-figure in a fragment of memory from kindergarten, though the man in his story had wheels and a cape, that story went. Trinidad had an X-men pencil case, so he was probably just thinking of Professor X. We all assumed that if there ever was a dad, the man had given up competing to be man of the house when Matt was two and scarpered.

At fourteen, Matt was dressing years ahead of us. He wore a bandana to the exact day that bandanas entered the mainstream—then dropped his bandana that very afternoon. He got to Rubix Cubes before they got to us, and Chatter Rings, plus he knew yo-yo tricks. He taught us how to glue our lunch trays to the tabletops with McDonald's ketchup. He showed us how to get lifetime free refills at Burger King by buying a single 99 cent cup, folding the waxed paper cup down to the size of a postage stamp and cramming the cup between the cushions of the vinyl booth where you could extract it any time. Matt Lamb told us tales of napalm and alleyways and how to rattle a fence and make a pitbull so angry it would explode.

His boogers were flicked effortlessly into the backs-of-heads of kids in front of us. His paper planes were stealth bombers. He would flip his bag over one shoulder and head for the exit door at 2.59.59 every day, saying 'Smell you later' and high-fiving hands and the bell would herald him as he headed for the convertible growling in the parking lot. Mrs. Lamb would lurch out into traffic and hoon away, leaving us in her wake. Mother and son, Bonnie and Clyde, sitting on some mountain of mystery money.

*

Around 15 or 16 we all got obsessed with wrestling, which of course led to weights and protein powder and we convinced Mr. Mears to let us in the gym at lunch time. Matt was dating Gemma Lancaster at the time. Gemma Skankass-ter, we secretly called her, because she dressed like a slut but didn't put out for anyone who wasn't elite. She had suspicious eyes and a body that mutated constantly, purple hair and black leather one month morphing to red the next month with neon and highlighter tights. Piercings in her eyebrows, her lips, her tongue. Gemma despised everything—except Matt Lamb. She knew she should never take him for granted.

Gemma Skankasster would walk Matt to the gym door and leave him with us to lift through lunch, though she never had any place in the gym itself—she disdained sports and preferred vodka, which of course made her ten times sexier. She'd guide him in then go wait in the parking lot in her car, sipping Smirnoff poured into a plastic bottle. Most of Matt's workout session would consist of chestbumps and hugs and wassups. Actually pumping iron was too low to stoop. Matt got changed into expensive white cotton and immaculate Air Jordans but he never broke a sweat. He had just enough muscle to appear like he belonged in the gym, while also being slim enough to be accepted by the soccer kids, what with soccer shooting into popularity because of our country kicking ass in the World Cup and all the European kids suddenly becoming cool.

It was for a Thursday night soccer practice, actually, that Gemma Skankasster picked us up. We slid into her ride and clicked our belts without commentary, looking forward. Watching TV on a weeknight just couldn't cut it any more. Talking to people on the phone for an hour was pretty rad, but driving someplace was even cooler, and driving to a viewing of Matt Lamb was the coolest.

We pulled into the carpark by the soccer field and eeled up to the edge of the lights. Ahead, in the green misty heaven, the soccer boys had Matt on their shoulder. It looked like he'd just scored a goal. The players scattered for a break and began zipping hoodies over their steaming bodies.

There was a spare three minutes before practice resumed. Gemma tugged Matt towards the concrete bunker bathroom with a female sign on top of it and Matt whistled casually as he followed her in. Someone had to keep watch outside the toilets while Gemma got Matt inside her. Matt was the first to exit—jogging briskly, boots hitting the backs of his buttocks. Gemma swore and complained and was scratching inside the straps of her tank top as she emerged half a minute after.

We watched our boy immerse himself back in the team, receive the ball, make some serious metres, boot for goal.

He got some decent headers. When he was asked to play Back, he stopped a couple goals. A fistfight broke out. Matt strolled through the melee, stretching his arms theatrically, calling encouragement. The coach dashed around like he was trying to herd bees back inside a hive.

Afterwards, Matt said he was going off to play Dance Dance Revolution with the Chinese kids. Of course he was. Chinese stuff would be trending soon.

Gemma drove around the park, pissed, directionless without Matt Lamb Junior. She smoked five cigarettes in a row, smashing them out half-smoked, then drove home.

Her place was a caravan bobbing in an ocean of grass out the back of a house with an old lady snoring on an armchair, waking occasionally to suck a cigarette. Inside Gemma's caravan, yearbooks from school were Sellotaped open showing the parts with Matt. In the Year 9 photo, Matt had a *Ssh* finger over his lips. The Year 10 one, he was doing a hilariously serene Gandhi pose. By the third photo, Matt had inspired the rest of his class to pull goofy faces, while Matt alone held up his chin and with a dignified smile.

'I got more,' Gemma said, pulling a box from under her bed. In it were clippings, love notes, condom wrappers, assorted drinks—a Nestea bottle with a little juice in the bottom; a Diet Coke from the clean eating fad he'd introduced; an apple juice.

'He drank that, umm, let's see... .' Gemma pulled a diary from under her mattress, fingered the pages. 'Oh yeah, duh: that's Last-day-of-school Juice. Matt was drinking that final day, last term. 'Bout 1 pm, 1.15.'

We asked her about the empty packet of pork rinds. Matt had eaten them during assembly right behind the principal's head. Every time the principal's head had turned, Matt had held the pork rinds packet up and frowned, playing the part of an authority disappointed to have discovered the unhealthy snack.

The prank worked on so many levels.

Gemma smoked as we pored over the Matt Museum. We got to flicking through his baby photos—that cheeky twinkle in his eyes! It was so Matt Lamb!—and we eventually crawled into bed with a thick photo album and fell asleep on each other.

*

Matt Lamb's seventeenth birthday, at Bowlapalooza, was widely open to anyone. Nobody was surprised that, yet again, the party wasn't at his house. One kid had snuck onto the lawn and taken photos of Matt's supposed property, but no kid had ever seen inside.

The Bowlapalooza crowd gathered early, humming like a hive, waiting for our leader to show up. He was five minutes late, then 15, then 25. We wondered if we'd been pranked, humiliated large-scale, for which we would have given our leader a round of applause.

We flinched every time Bowlapalooza's sliding doors opened, expecting to see Matt enter. Instead, when it hit 12.30, Matt coolly spun around from the Speed Racer slide-in game he'd been playing all this time, hiding over in the games corner, and got up and stretched. All of his clothes were white—a cotton hoodie contoured perfectly to his body, tearaway trackpants and puffy white Nikes.

'You niggas got PUNKED,' he said to our stunned ensemble, hefting a bowling ball. 'Ladies? Gentlemen? Shall we get down to business?'

Many of us got spares, turkeys, with the occasional strike. We occupied four lanes. Matt's name was on each. He strolled from lane to lane, keeping up four or five conversations; he'd toss in ripostes when required. A joke here; sarcasm there. A sprinkling of philosophy; a threat against one kid who borrowed his ball; some sexy suggestions whispered in ears that made the girls titter.

Three strikes in a row earned him a bonus roll, and he came from behind to lead two, then three, then all the games. 'Oh, sorry, have we started?' he would say, tossing his bowling ball into the ten pin tonsils.

His anxious, irritable mum was the only person at Bowlapalooza unimpressed. She shuffled the handbag on her shoulder, checked her watch, fielded phone call after phone call, pacing, resting her leopard print pants against the wall, rubbing her knee-high leather boots together. Something about the pharmacy was overheard. Something about 'What do you mean my painkillers aren't ready?'

A birthday cake arrived, gifted from a bowling alley manager besotted with our haloed leader. Matt—who was leaning against the bar, sipping the same gin and tonic as his mum—took a twenty metre run-up, blew the candles out in a single breath as he walked through our claps and cheers before bowling a final strike, bowing, strutting out to his mum's car and into history.

*

School began spluttering and fizzing out. We'd all hit seventeen-and-a-half and a few of us were toeing 18 and spilling over. Booze; driver licenses. The first few pregnant girls. Yearbooks. There was the first party where a kid got stabbed; the first quiet wallflower kids who enlisted in the army, sending us instant messages, imploring the rest of us to be all we could be.

It was disappointing, to us, to be outside of the terrarium of school. To not get to glimpse Matt Lamb Junior every day. Still, it would have been wrong to stain him with our boring ordinariness. He had great things to achieve out in the real world.

We tried to keep the group coagulated where we could. We chose Gemma's checkout at the supermarket and made chit-chat with her while she beeped our groceries. No matter what her hair color that month we could spot her from the colored patch on her throat, the dark letters she'd been dared to get etched one night when we were passing around a goon bag of wine. In curling, graceful script, she'd had *Property of Matt Lamb* inked forever on her neck.

We talked about these things when we hooked up. Gemma was always available a couple times each month for sex. Inside her trailer (her parents were dead; the trailer lived on) she adjusted us behind her till our angle was perfect, exactly the angle Matt Lamb used to make love to her, and she guided us inside. She got us to nibble her spine exactly as Matt had.

Gemma told us precisely where Matt's fingers slotted between her ribs, sliding till the fingers could pinch her nipples. There was one hot night when Matt had ejaculated deep inside her with no condom when they were drunk on summer. She'd counted each of the 148 thrusts and made notes. We recreated the sex exactly and erupted warmth into Gemma's core, our eyes rolling back inside our skulls. For a moment, we were him, a titan, a god, living on a cloud.

We made it a regular thing, Gemma and us, adding a sand-colored curly wig which roughly approximated Matt Lamb's head of hair, drawing his tribal tattoos on our arms with a Sharpie. We kept his memory alive. He wasn't erased, he'd just taken a plane to Surfer's Paradise one evening during a party. It was his biggest mike drop ever, a stunt that spanned years. A pop-up advert to come work in Australia had materialized on his phone, he looked at the foam lapping the land, the salt air and skyscrapers and blue horizon. He went to his room, packed a suitcase, took a taxi and left us standing around his house holding plastic cups of beer and debating when he'd be back.

*

Gemma was the first to turn 21, or was it 25? She'd always lived a couple of months more of life than the rest of us. She'd been scarred and scared and shocked by what was out there in the future. The cold cruel grownup world had pocked her cream skin, made her voice sharp, made any optimism in her eyes dwindle and die.

Her party was in a country barn in a cornfield. People heaped pallets and broken armchairs on the bonfire. There were shitloads of new faces at the party. It wasn't a school thing anymore now we were all in our 20s. Our circle been infiltrated by new people from other schools, other codes. Churchies, musos, thugs, personal trainers. New haircuts. Adult jobs. Some kids even trained as teachers and went to work at our old school.

Out among the gravel and cornrows Gemma went from group to group, squinting into the black to check on each of us. She was getting fat around the arms and she carried heft in her hips. She'd been partying since she was 10. Tonight was just work to her. We asked her how were things at the supermarket and she snorted and sucked her ciggy. She was working full time as a massage therapist, now, well, with some sideline stuff as an escort. Her voice had sunk so deep it seemed to thud on the ground.

Matt Lamb Junior didn't make the surprise entrance into the party some of us bet money on. Every conversation slowed to namedrop him, though, as if we could summon him from the night. Charn and Trinidad recreated that time Matt had been set upon by a pack of juveniles in the city, how he'd laughed as he tossed one of the hoodrats into the fountain, pushed another through the safety glass of a bus stop, shoved the third kid into the path of a passing car. The boys' wild violent theatrical re-enactment, lit by lapping bonfire flames, attracted one or two of us at a time, till we were all standing in a circle, contributing lines, details, keeping Matt Lamb alive, *and then he did this, and can you believe he said THAT, and you'll never believe what he did next!* Gemma had a new anecdote she agreed to unwrap only when everybody was silent and the bonfire was under control and she had a fresh white cigarette and a glass of brandy. Gemma sat on a beer keg, cleared her throat, held her hands up for silence, then began. She had once needed to hand in an assignment about Hamlet, and she'd been clubbing and driving all night. 9 am was looming and she had nothing to hand in. Matt had escorted her right up to old Mrs. Rahmati's desk then looked Mrs. Rahmati right in the eyes to hypnotize her while his subtle spider fingers deftly pasted a sticker saying *Gemma Lancaster* right over the name of some poor other kid. Gemma had gotten an A-minus thanks to the other kid's work.

Mrs. Rahmati even wrote in red pen her appreciation for the neatly printed name.

When there was five seconds' silence and we realized her speech had ended we gave Gemma a standing ovation. This woman had lain with a king. That made her a queen.

New tidbits about Matt Lamb emerged first as a trickle, then a spout. B-sides, offcuts, demos. Undiscovered insight. There was one new story about the time Matt Lamb persuaded girl scouts that came to his door to give him a dozen packets of cookies, which he promised to on-sell and—at a later date—return profit to the scout troupe. Of course he ate half the cookies and threw the rest at the neighbour's labrador.

There was the story about Matt secretly recording an R&B album, though he supposedly did it under a pseudonym so you'd never know.

There was a story revealing Matt Lamb's middle name, the effortlessly cool *Ethan*, about which we nodded and said 'Ohh-hh' and raised our cans in a toast.

Rumour had it there were little Matt Lambs out there somewhere, with powerful blue eyes and incredible angles in their little faces and that HAIR, the golden fleece. Perhaps Matt wouldn't be hard to find. He was a builder, apparently, which somewhat rang true, though it wasn't exactly sailor or secret agent or rockstar. His new-built three bedroom house in Surfer's looked exactly like that of his neighbours. It was buried in a maze of suburban cul-de-sacs with freshly-poured tarmac and weed matting and baby trees, nowhere near the beach, a well-informed source had told us. He had bikes and a boat in the garage, a patio and a four burner barbecue. He rolled his truck onto the same blacktop at 7 every morning and drove to work like a normal person.

The hours spilled over til 1am, then the giddying gossip kept us in a trance which lasted til 3, and then the sun was coming up and we were throwing onto the embers every detail we remembered about our leader. How he swum, how he played basketball, how his basketball hoodies smelled of fabric softener. We recounted his patois, his proverbs, his idioms. We recited what he ate for morning tea on day 24 of term 2 of Year 12. Jane Scranth had once come to his door selling magazine subscriptions and when his mum had answered (wearing a kimono), she'd spotted a shag carpet conversation pit and some mechanical lifting device, like a hoist which presumably Matt used to cultivate his power. Paul Wrightson told us he'd once seen a black van hovering outside Matt's house, engine running as it lowered a robotic ramp. There was that one time Trinidad was walking to school and he realized that for ten minutes, Matt had been silently aping each of his footsteps, a spy with a satisfied smirk.

These days he never posted about his life on social, though you could tag his empty profile.

All of the stories combined gave us 60 percent of the man's life, maybe 70. There remained a mystery about the man somebody had to speak on.

*

At our high school reunion, we nursed our bottles of beer, standing in a circle on the pitted floorboards, just off the disco, where nobody could force us to dance.

We had the election to talk about, and that thing the council was doing, putting a roundabout in instead of traffic lights, and how the polar ice caps were shrinking. There was decent sport on over the coming month and our discussion about the FIFA World Cup led to a remembrance of that time Matt scored a goal off a header. We tried to steer the conversation back to our plans for waterskiing on the lake and how some kid broke his back, which then morphed into conjecture about the zimmer frame amongst the shoes on Matt Lamb's doorstep and the physiotherapist seen pulling up in her health board car 14 years ago.

We talked of his mailbox, his basic building qualification spotted on LinkedIn, the lichen-free sidewalks in the boring cul-de-sac where his children cycled on their BMXs. What were the children's names? We opened our wallets and lay down bets beside the punchbowl.

We talked of the regular old Toyota he drove to his ordinary job where Matt had ended up painfully normal, surely unappreciated. We talked of the rare glimpses inside his life: a lift home in the mum's car; a swim in his pool; seeing inside Matt's school bag; that time Matt was encountered at K-mart.

Finally, after everyone was full of quiche and potato chips and looking at their watches, the doors opened and a man scuttled in, dodging dancing couples, and stood in the middle of the hall. He spotted us and slowly walked over.

Matt Lamb began with an apology. He'd struggled to find a babysitter, plus his motel was miles from here. He was sorry. He hadn't lived here for a decade. He'd remembered the city all wrong.

All good Matt, we told him. We do it too.

We gave Matt a position near the middle of the circle. Everybody squeezed his hand and kissed his sunburned cheeks. His eyes were faded and squinty, now. He scratched his bald, shiny head. It was coated in fine sandpaper stubble glowing more silver than gold. He rested a glass of punch on his belly fat.

As we passed around baby photos on our cellphones, Matt became lost in the circle. Half the people were taller than him, many of us equally fat and faded. He answered questions with a hand cupped around his ear, apologizing for being slightly deaf with an occasional polite "Not to worry" or "Hmm?" Yes, he had two little boys, both with a babysitter who was costing him an arm and a leg right now. No, he'd never shagged that trainee teacher, but she had hugged him at the school disco. No, his mum wasn't a Rothschild—she had received a payout because his father was crushed in an accident at the flour factory when he was three. His mum was an alcoholic, always angry at him cause he reminded her of his dad, a man with bent limbs shivering under a shawl where he spent decades with a colostomy bag as a friend. All the money was gone by the time Matt hit 20; his mum carried on borrowing till she died of liver failure.

Matt was surprised at the information about himself coming across the circle, but he nodded as he took in each description. His wife, sitting in the car, was texting him. He would have to go shortly. She couldn't drink alcohol cause of her diabetes, plus she didn't like people. He began to issue thanks and see you laters, but we convinced him to stop as he tiptoed towards the exit door. Somebody shunted a chair under his arse. We pushed his shoulders down. Just one more story.

We told him about the time Matt Lamb had climbed the rope in gym class to the top of the building then stayed up there, living in the rafters till the Fire Service brought a ladder in. We let him know it was Matt Lamb who turned the school pool pink with industrial tins of beetroot stolen from the camp supplies. We recounted the fable of *Why you talkin to a zombie?* which caused Matt to burst out laughing, spraying us with mist.

Gemma had a live webcast on RealGirls which had to start at 8.30 on the dot and she had to get going but she stared at him as she backed out, smiling.

Several times Matt looked poised to contradict the memories, or ask a question about himself, but he couldn't get a word in. We were the last in the hall. The security guard yawned, checked his watch, tapped his foot. We told Matt Lamb Junior every legend we could come up with, laughing till our stomachs hurt and we had to put our beers on the ground as we doubled-over, faces burning with joy. We kept him as long as we could.

SEROTONIN

1.

Monica is stifling giggles as she packs up the bookstore, sniffling, shaking her head. Little snorts of disbelief at her own stupidity. She has doomed the business. She says it's absurd that she had faith in herself in the first place, really. The event at the book shop tonight—the launch of an anthology from some ageing first-time writers—was a dirty bomb. A cluster of misers in pharmacy perfume recited dreary flash fiction before an audience of fifteen. They kept the store open late, spent almost no money. Monica can't believe she trusted the small-town publishing collective, trusted God, fate, destiny. She can't believe she trusted herself. She could've been home fixing her marriage, trying to cheer Peter up. He's going to glower and criticize. She tells you you don't need to stick around to watch her humiliation. Your job is to sell books, not to rub her back. It's okay. You can go.

You tell her no way. You're here to support. Lebanese men are faithful. Leb men stick around.

Hosting the old fogeys' book launch after hours was typical Monica selflessness. Her body –thick wavy mahogany hair, skirt bright as crayons—was aged by the disappointment of tonight. She has filaments of silver in her hair now. Sad creases by her hooded eyes as the let-downs pile up. Her husband is a cold fish who sleeps in a separate bed. Her kids are both

partying at university and they never call. She's been tender-
ized.

You care about conversion, commission, revenue, going city
to city selling new releases to ease off the pressure from the
clan at home, but you've got a weakness for Monica, even if
she sucks at sales. The warm press of her chest when she does
a kiss-hug greeting. The apologetic smile when her husband
ignores you when you visit the store. Monica had hoped to
make up for a slow week with some late night sales; instead
you've spent two hours yelling out encouragement to try get
people to buy books. She squeezed your arm in appreciation
as you publicly shamed yourself to defend her. The two of you
together versus a bunch of timewasting old idiots.

Monica licks her finger, dabs creamy cake crumbs off a
stack of paper plates, tells you for the tenth time it's dark
out there, you ought to go home to your family. Sairi doesn't
like you coming home early, you respond. It makes her sisters whisper of failure. Makes her witch-of-a-mum mutter
ancient curses.

Monica stands on top of her stepladder while you hold her
hips. You study her calves, knees, thighs disappearing into that
skirt. You've never slept with a white girl, well, *girl* is not the
right word, considering her age. *Lady.*

Monica has taken one end of the bunting off the ceiling. She
rests her weight on your hand as you guide her body down.
You haven't touched much, before. You and her shook hands
for the first year you sold books to her store, then you began
kissing her cheek as a polite hello each time you dropped by
with a trunkful of new titles. The brush of your forearm on
hers as you reached to turn the same page. Your hand on her
shoulder.

She flaps her fingers in front of her cheeks to cool her red
skin. Eyes pink from crying, rimmed black, runny mascara in
the cracks.

Hoo, she says, sniffing. Hot up there.

You pick up a copy of the old ladies' anthology. Last Gasp, the publishers call themselves. The wannabe authors and their stiff husbands have left Monica with bills for catering, power and ads in the paper. The launch was supposed to bring a thousand dollars of custom to Monica's shop. A tiny crowd of people turned up, a few anthologies were bought, though the store only made three sales. Bag End Books needs to make two thousand bucks a week, you know from two years of selling to Monica. She's always laughed, said numbers are Peter's job. Peter the Great, genius ruler of the books.

You bend a Last Gasp book from the centre outwards. We have to make a stand, you tell her. You drizzle the torn pages on the carpet and stamp on the shitty literature. *Please laugh. Please wince and half-turn away.*

She says you're sweet to stand up for her, silly boy. Squeezes both of your shoulders. Her body fits yours. She tears a Last Gasp poster off the wall. Plaster dust powders her face.

She says you ought to get going. You've got other clients to see. They're all lonely shopkeepers, presumably, these ladies of yours. Does your wife know?

You pick the BluTak off the Last Gasp posters, pull them away from the windows. You sweep confetti into the dustpan. You tip un-drunk orange juice back into the bottle and put it all in the fridge.

It's nearly midnight when Bag End Books begins to look like there was never a book celebration. She's handing you a glass of bubbles.

You clean the glitter off her earlobe with a wet thumb, leaning in close.

But you're just a baby, she whispers, closing her eyes.

You stagger across the room to the children's corner, fall into a beanbag. She claws your back. She's telling you this will hurt. You silence your bleating mobile. You were supposed to call at seven. You promised your wife you'd read the kids a bedtime story over the phone.

After sex, you doze on the beanbags in the kiddy corner. The night descends then lifts. You creep away, stagger into your pants, belt buckle clinking. Monica pretends to sleep. Glitter in the carpet. Confetti on the bookstands. Helium balloons on the ceiling. You stagger into the blinding morning light, opening the trunk of your car, retrieving the case of books you're supposed to sell. You stagger into Paper Plus, feeling radioactive, contaminated. Your dick's dirty and reeks of latex. Your mouth is full of her spit and cells. You do your business with a fake smile and shiny teeth then drive a hundred kays home and swear you'll never let down your guard again.

2.

Walking into these shops —there are 40 of them in your sales region—you wear a façade of grinning Teflon. Golden earring on honey skin. Tight suit. Sales tongue. Just the right amount of handsome black stubble.

You tell these shop owners how to run their bookshops better, where to position the Nadia Lims, how to hang the new Yuval Noah Harari display. How to scatter the sand that goes around Sebastian Junger's Gulf War book display. Your strong young arms reposition the breath mints and mineral water around their counters. Every little bit counts, you assure these shopkeepers. Here, see on Chart Six? You've got the revenue growth to prove it. You rearrange their potplants for them, their pamphlets, their door mats and rugs. You sweep the dead moths away from the windows. You prune the ferns. One bookstore in Orewa, the owner doesn't realize her door-mat prevents wheelchairs coming in. Another place in Tauranga, it's the cluttered counter that's the problem. It needs to be shaped like a funnel, not a fortress. Customers want chewing gum at the counter, not poetry chapbooks. You move the indulgent poetry pamphlets away from the impulse items and over to the far corner. You had delusions that poetry was important when you were young and naïve and thought that money didn't matter. Even got a little book of poems published. You wrote a whole secret second manuscript, actually. Even Sairi's never seen it.

You sign up a Bay of Islands bookshop to have 5000 flyers tucked into local letterboxes once a month marketing romance only. Their sales rise through the roof. You'll get a good commission this week. Your mother in law and your wife and her biker brother Billy Khoury will get off your case for a while.

The one store you'd love to avoid, but can't, is Bag End. Your manager knows you've got that special rapport with the owners. Use that Prince of Persia charm-thing of yours, son. Monica's managing the place mostly on her own because her husband has gone cold on her. Peter is a stiff, square man in a cardigan with a moustache he can't stop licking. A man outstanding with numbers. Deaf in one ear, always grunting. Christian; ten years older than Monica. A man so conservative it's taken him a decade to decide to buy the store a website. It's wrong for him to be married to an Anastasia. She's beautiful and valuable. It's wrong not to share her.

You do the Coromandel run, the Hamilton run, you do Whangarei and Dargaville and Mangawhai and even Helensville. Lots of unpaid overtime for a chance at some good commission. An extra thousand some weeks. It's not enough, though. Sairi's mum has been whispering witchy wisdom in Sairi's ear. Sairi rolls her eyes, but she doesn't disagree. The family needs you to make even bigger numbers this month. Sairi has her essential oils to pay for. Fine. You'll build up some credit through suffering. You visit all the stores on your roster ahead of schedule and tell 'em you're positive the Silver Ferns confessional and the Prime Minister's memoirs will make you both rich. Bertelsmann have asked the price point to be pushed up near the $40 mark.

By the time you get to Bag End Books, you have to vent your frustrated secrets inside of Monica, except she blocks your ingress, arms folded, head tilted in disapproval.

Monica wants to talk about "the incident."

Incident? INCIDENT? You're really gonna call it that, Mon?

You talk with your hands, pacing, ranting, arguing for an hour before she pushes you against a wall and seizes your angry shoulders. God you're pent-up. What's the matter—wife hasn't taken you for a walk? She locks the door, flipping the Open sign Closed, undoes your buttons with red fingernails, teeth oozing over her lips.

On the carpet, on the bean bags, behind the counter you rock together, cradling each other's backs. You snuffle her clefts and crevices. Fragrant armpits and secret pleats and grinding thighs. Her rippling, pillowy body. Stretch marks and little scars to lick. Thirsty tongues on salty skin. Torn hair. Fingernails clutching your broad back. Don't let me fall, the claws say. Carry me. Your daughter does the same when you carry her to bed.

Monica's wild foot kicks a psychology textbook off the wall. You flip through it as the two of you lie spine-to-spine after you've come, hiccupping air like deflated balloons. The shiny hardback has a diagram of the brain glowing in certain spots. Your body releases feel-good drugs called endorphins after you make love, it explains. A person looks more muscular post-orgasm, feels better about flab and flaws and crow's feet. First the brain leaks testosterone then estrogen, then dopamine then norepinephrine then serotonin. Oxytocin and vasopressin afterwards to cement attachment and encourage it to happen again.

You slide the book gently back into its slot. Back to business. You can't even look at her as you pull your underwear on. A proper Leb man doesn't let ladies make him weak. Be like Samson, bro. Be like bully-biker Billy Khoury who beats up people for no reason. Strong as a pillar. You have to get back to normality. Boring-arse banter from the boys about wanting to fuck the kids' teachers cause no one's wife is putting out, yeah, that's normal. Hating your wife's evil old *amati*. Weeks without getting laid. Hours of driving, sucking angrily on your vape, swearing at the radio. Billboards telling you what your life should look like. Low carb beers and barbecues and bigscreen TVs. Movies and motocross and rippa rugby and hotdogs and juice. The same safe clique of 33 year olds at the same Wog weddings. League, trucks, rings, tattoos, Facebook, vows, hen nights, man-camps. Massive family meals with mountains of kibbeh and beef and chawarma and humus. The next ten years are written; there's shame if you don't follow. Your mates will play for the same Old Boys team, they'll set up the same charter fishing trips, they'll fly to Las Vegas for a predictable Instagram selfie at the Bellagio.

Cheating on your wife, though—that'll get you disinvited from high school reunions and Vegas and the Junior Tigers fundraising committee. Sairi's mum will claw your face. Billy Khoury will stomp you for dishonoring his sister. Better a heroin habit than a cheater.

All you can do is keep telling yourself that the thing with Monica wasn't cheating, and definitely not an affair. It was two consenting adults sharing a drug. And it'll never happen again.

3.

Monica sits up behind the counter. She wrestles her bra on, folds up the towel you've been making love on. She riffles through a box of stationery, selects a rubber band to tie her hair back. She's doing everything except look at you.

You have to talk business for a sec. You tell her Bag End's gonna go bankrupt if she lets everybody walk all over her. Sorry to be brutal. You need to get control of your losses, Mon.

Monica refuses to answer. She moves the poetry books around. You try to tell her it's pointless trying to get value from those things. Just people's bottled delusions.

Peter comes in minutes later as you're tucking your shirt in behind a stand of *Call Me Evies*. Something about looking at the accounts. Your fly is hanging open. You can feel wind on your thigh.

'Good to see you bro, um, Peter,' you stammer, 'I was just telling your wife, I can give advice on how to effect sales, I'd be happy to... y'know. Some pointers.'

Peter snorts. 'Something you learned in university yesterday's going to revolutionize the industry, I take it?'

'Just trying to be professional.'

You shelter behind a giant atlas and fix your fly. Monica's giving her fern a drink of water and humming Schubert.

'You've done enough,' she says, 'you can go now.'

'Jesus, Monica.' You glance over to see if Peter's offended. Deaf cunt didn't even hear. 'That Kieran Read book, the All Blacks one, I'm supposed to park 50 with you.'

'Is that all you came for?' She's shaking pellets of food into the rats' feed dish. 'You know where to leave em.'

Back to business then. So be it. You unlock the car, parked out front in a space she reserved for you with road cones, your name written in lipstick on the white rear of a life-size cutout of J. K. Rowling. Those cut-outs fetch hundreds if you sell them second hand, for crying out loud, don't destroy them with my unimportant name, Mon! She could sell the one she's defaced and meet this week's revenue target. Sigh. It's not that Monica doesn't know how to run a business. She just doesn't care that much.

Monica loves watering her snapdragons, walking her Cavalier King Charles spaniel Aldous Muttsley. What she doesn't love is sales. You've seen her ring up sales. She'll take a customer's credit card pinched between finger tips like a dirty needle, shoving the keypad at the customer like it's contaminated. When she was young and free and didn't have to pay for her son's MBA, her and her hippie friends lived in a village of yurts in a valley. They had a barter system, swapping eggs for dreamcatchers for horseshoes for paintings. She didn't have a job or a husband or a bank account. She was happy.

*

t happens three more times in a month. Same day, every week, and you wonder if you're the only devil in the world. You've never seen other people having an affair. Fucking in the bushes. Sneaking into a motel. Skulking around. That stuff takes place in hidden pockets of the world. Secret pleats. Two anxious adults making chemicals together in a clandestine lab. You roll the word around your tongue. *Clan-des-tine.* There's a new 600 page edition of the *Oxford English Dictionary*. It needs to retail for $45.99 so everyone can get paid. It's a challenge, that one, though Monica accepts a case of them and promises she'll do her best to sell em. She's always had faith in you. She used to lean over the counter to check your eyes. She stroked your throat with her finger, one time. Sure these things'll sell? You lying to me, big boy?

You top up her store with books twice a week. She teases your true personality out of you. You loved your mum tonnes, you miss her. She was fat and always baking and hugged and kissed you in her sticky dusty apron even as a grown man. She's the only person you've ever read your notebook of poetry too, apart from goths at the Gong Show at university where Sairi never even showed up even though her family had marketed her as a perfect match for you, Mr Sensitive Artist. She was training as an occupational therapist; you were studying English Lit. You weren't meant to cross paths, really. Gee, what else... You once had a poem in some literary journal. You have half a novel saved on your computer. When you dropped out of writing classes and went corporate, that was your first infidelity. Cheating on what the young you promised the old.

She comes around the counter with the slow saunter of an aging indoor-type. She bites your neck and comes alive. She drinks your salty skin, shrugs off her shawl. You drive to her house for an urgent shag, pashing in the car, lips locked like fish wrestling a hunk of meat. You enjoy pushing a woman as old as your mother on her back, listening to her beg for you to stop. She ruins your chance of driving through to Gisborne to get your sales up for the month. Instead you lie sweaty on Peter's side of the bed with the curtains flapping in the wind. She tries to feed you, which is a joke. You can't eat food made by a real human. Too intimate.

It's not any easier when you stagger in the door and Sairi's mum assesses you with a sniff and Sairi asks how much commission you made, shoving a plate of dinner into your hands. You're too sick with guilt to eat her meals. Too sick to concentrate on the book about ponies you're supposed to read to Dasia.

Before bed, Sairi lies with her head on your lap while her mum snores inside her sleep apnoea mask and you wish you were inside the TV. People on TV don't have dirt on their skin. You find yourself reaching for your phone, messaging Monica, setting up a time to do more business. Tomorrow's good. Maybe even twice. This thing is a funnel. You keep sliding down.

4.

Peter the Great's away on business in Melbourne. You told him his concept of ordering stacks of manga to bring in teenage customers was a terrific idea. Always explore new markets. Go for it, bro. Take ten days.

With Peter gone, his wife drags you out for a date in public.

In the black wet night she clings to your arm. She negotiates mainstreet's gum and dogshit and trees and benches, grinning giddily. You're withdrawing money from an ATM and she comes up behind and puts her fingers in your coat pocket. You stand with your face in the wind, letting her cradle your back. She's closed her eyes, buried in warm flesh like a koala cub; you're scanning the street for spies. *God, just let us get the itch scratched and be done with it all.* You watch over your shoulder, terrified one of the bros will recognize you, call your name, ask questions, spread word that you're an infidel. Tonight Monica's painted lipstick over her years. She has earrings and a sparkling rhinestone jacket and she's swinging her handbag. Jesus Christ. Is this worse than fucking? Does this exonerate the sex? That'd be nice. Your brain is wracked. She asks question after question, drops annoying little comments about your "strong arms" and "youthful energy." You give her grumpy grunts. You've agreed to a movie and some falafel and Turkish tea. You never said it was a date.

You scuttle into the cinema together. It's a terrible movie; people walk out. An hour in, it's just the two of you. You lie her on the hard, thin carpet under the seats in a middle row of an ocean of seat-backs where no one ever goes. She pulls you inside her, refusing to kiss, eyelids down, just holding your lower back like a kid she's afraid to lose.

Strolling the street, she strokes your dark black jaw, reckons she loves Middle Eastern culture. Gimme a break, you want to bark. You're a tourist, Monica. Eating mezze with your backs against the wall in the corner, she's ordering baklava for dessert and having a great time, really making the most of the night, even asking about your high school and hobbies and you want to scream, YOU'RE FIFTY ONE, MONICA. WE'RE NOT ALIKE. WE'RE TWO DRUGGIES SWAPPING STIMULUS. That's all. She tries to tug the photos of your kids out of your wallet. The photos spill onto the table. You bury them back in your wallet, growling. She slaps your wrist, goes out front, orders a herbal tea from a hippie food truck, blows on it, shivers.

To bring her back around, you agree to drive up to the top of Pine Hill. On a bench surrounded by a landscape of twinkling Christmas lights, you pash like teenagers, ripping at each other's gums and lips. You biff stones at a lamp till it shatters then flee, snickering, to the far end of the park. She straddles you on the bench. A breeze probes your stomach. You both fart and giggle. Your belt tinkles on the metal and concrete. Monica pours her head into your neck, rocks until she's calmed herself. She leaves your lap wet. Your buttons are torn—she pulled them off, stripping the fabric from your thumping chest—and now there'll be questions asked about the jacket. Sairi bought it so you could look decent in that family portrait you had photographed at the mall.

You make love on your half-wet coats and scarves when work is heavy and depressing and it's raining outside. You make love against the plastic walls of the toilet cubicle in the café where you're supposed to be looking at next month's orders. You make love when the sky is dirty, when it's clean. You rendezvous in secret little nooks and furrows and dark spots in the day. Gotta get that little squirt of serotonin. It's not happiness, but it's a distraction. Better than being just another working class wog.

You begin to spot secret sex everywhere. Pairs of people stumbling out of doorways you didn't expect. People doing things around corners. Bursting out of fields of tall grass. Snickering couples emerging from alleys adjusting their pants.

Girls whispering into the ears of men in elevators. The woman in the line at Starbucks whose fingers tuck her giggles back inside her lips as she reads some text message. The man who hauls his body out of the passenger seat of a rocking car with the seat reclined.

Conspiracies everywhere. Clan labs where people cook chemicals.

5.

You watch little Dasia in the three-legged race on a blue sky Saturday at her school gala. Dasia has to run with a boy who's younger, stronger, fitter. More aggressive, more determined, more impatient. Dasia has done the three-legged race before and knows what's at stake and why you should step with caution; the boy has more stamina, more energy, more ruthlessness. The boy wants quick results. The boy is tired of stepping in sync all the time. The problem is one person within the couple stretches the band, moves away from the cooperative. The tightly-bound couple screams at each other. The band breaks.

The Lads are here at the gala, of course, watching their kids frolick same as you. Hard slaps on the back. Knuckles on the chin, playful slaps, chest bumps. Billy Khoury plants his girl on a pony ride then winks at you. Tony Daouk shoots water into a fibreglass clown's mouth. Abe Mahfouz drops a few quiet jokes about fucking women and you have some good chuckles, standing round, arms folded, shoulders shaking. This morning, while Dasia was skipping in the yard, Sairi locked the bedroom door, pinned you down. Fucked you hard and rhythmic and joyless as a marathon. It took you forever to come. She kissed your brow and asked what was wrong.

They catch you daydreaming.

'Dreamin up another novel, bro?'

'Pantoum,' you go. You cut them off before they can say something dumb and explain that a pantoum is a type of poem.

The boys are falling about laughing, now. Billy Khoury has passed around a joint from cupped palm to cupped palm. The boys are commenting on every mum at this gala pushing prams, holding candy floss, wiping faces with spit-moistenend handkerchiefs. The back of your neck's sweating. Dasia's on the bouncy castle with her *habib*. She's safe from your radiation.

Tony's going on about some chickypie waitress he visits every lunch who's definitely gonna have sucked his cock by next weekend (whatever, Tony). Abe's saying the most he's got from his wife in the past year is second base, some sticky fingers on the couch after she put her knees on the carpet looking for the TV remote. The boys are punching each other's shoulders and shoving your chest and Billy Khoury's snipering you with his eyes, lining up a shot.

'What about you, book boy? Still writing gay love ballads?'

'A ballad is a song, by definition. Sonnets is what you're thinking of. I, I, I guess I keep a notebook but it's been years since—

'You still doin that marriage counselling with Sai?'

'Yeah man. Totally. Tuesday nights.'

'Tell us what fuckin happened. You been an infidel to my sister?'

Gulp. Quick check on Dasia. She's alive, thank fuck. 'Fidelity intact, much to my chagrin.'

The boys crack up laughing, She-grin? Course she grin, mate! Dolmio grin for that fuckin bitch when she's ragging!

Billy's looking through the laughs, though. His nostrils twitch. He smells something.

*

You do it again in the car, parked behind a dumpster to give shadow from the streetlight. It's quick and disgusting and predictable. She keeps her shawl on, and bra and cardigan, muttering, making you seem ridiculous, over-eager because you've stripped completely. She barely even smiles, just rocks with her eyes closed, thinking about something else. You get some serotonin in your system but it's a dirty batch. Contaminated with guilt. You're both frowning afterwards as you wipe up. You're counting the silver threads in her hair. They've got to total more than 50% of her scalp now, they're taking over—plus there are brown smudges you've never noticed hidden at the top of her skull. Liver spots, they're called. Like Mr. Burns on the Simpsons. Like Sairi's leathered mother.

She insists you use a condom next time.

You're not serious? You splutter that there's no way she could possibly get pregnant. She says actually, it's about protecting HER. She doesn't know how many women you've done this to.

Done this to?!

You heard me.

Like, what, like I'm some serial cheater?

Well are you?

Monica announces she wants you to return to your wife. You tell her you never left your wife, never strayed. She sniggers at that.

The arbitration spills down the street, out of the car and into her shop. You endure it only because being with Monica is one percent more enjoyable than enduring interrogations at home. You notice for the first time how decayed Monica's shop is. Every book cover is sun-faded. The carpet hasn't been updated since the 70s. And risking your safety for some Western cracker who's not even Leb? The fuck were you thinking?

Tonight is the last time you'll ever be alone with Monica, you're about to declare, except Monica has her hand on your wrist and you're sinking.

6.

Sairi throws a massive surprise birthday party that's totally not a surprise. You knew she was going to show off. That's the culture, that's the code: show the Haddads next door how much love there is in your household. Treat your man like a king even if you treat him like a flatmate soon as the last guests have cleared out. Not that you ever wanted to be a king. You wanted to wear black Doc Martens and perform poetry as dark as your beard, not be some sheikh on a throne in the light. Billy Khoury brings his girls and a keg to your party, blocks the driveway with his giant Harley and lets his Doberman run amok the yard. Abe Mahfouz has his sullen pissy teenagers in tow plus his mother-in-law, for fuck's sake. Tony Daouk brings that new bimbo he's dating. There's a structure for the afternoon—speeches, dancing, cake with candles, succulent spit-roasted lamb, honey, wine—but you and the lads start having shots of Sambuca and the shisha comes out and Billy Khoury's packing weed into the pipe and the afternoon is a messy blur.

Sairi makes it a two-day thing, this Festival of You birthday jaunt that you totally don't deserve. She drags you out to Devonport to see the history, the tunnels, the ships, the green hills, the crenellations, the brick, the ivy. The five dollar coffees, ten dollar croissants, the art deco facades, the socialites in yoga pants walking their beagles on a Saturday morning. Silk trees and cycads. Silver dog dishes out front of the café. The Rolls Royces, the private schools, the city councillors chatting with real estate agents outside the patisserie.

It makes sense Sairi should squeal with excitement when she spots the J.K. Rowling-shaped sign in the Bag End Books window. Your name's still written on the white back of the plastic. Shit.

Sairi veers into the store, pretends to study the back of the Kieran Read book, the Nadia Lim book. She messes up a display of cookbooks she doesn't even pretend to read.

'Is this where SHE works?'

'Who?'

'The old white lady that's been sending you all those stalker-y messages.'

The woman behind the counter freezes then reacts with a smile so wide her fangs stick out. You say Monica, Sairi and Sairi, Monica Martin, manager.

Sairi is so stunned she drops her water bottle on the carpet.

'Ah, the young interloper on an unannounced visit. Here to see my wife, or... ?'

Peter has white dust on his useless ears. He's saving thousands putting new plasterboard up in the renovated office instead of getting a tradesman to do it. Peter suspects people ripping him off everywhere. Taking what's his.

He says your name, tosses it up and down in his mouth while Sairi stares. 'You write, a little, so I've heard?'

You gulp and admit it.

Peter's squinting like a sceptical detective. 'I remember you now, yesss. Used to be the pride of the literary magazines, n'est-ce pas? You spoke on public radio too, if I recall correctly. Book Hour, they read one of your stories. Hang on.' Peter rummages behind a huge copy of Audubon's *Birds of America* and pulls out a poster. Your face; your forgotten poetry collection. 'Monica, she loves this book. Admires it greatly. She mentioned you've been paying quite a few visits this year. Urging us to stock your books.' Peter is a cat leering down at a slapped-around mouse. 'She talks about you altogether too much, in my opinion.'

Sairi rotates her body to face directly into you. She has zero interest in friendship with this old dysfunctional nerd-pair. 'You guys wanna get a room or what? What is this?'

Her phone pings. She batters out a frantic text message.

'It's work, honey.' You clear your throat and reach to take your book out of Peter's hands. 'Caaaaan I take that thing off your hands?'

A flash of mirth lights Peter's stony eyes. He tucks the book inside his cardigan. 'You just keep on taking from me, don't you, son.'

On the way back home you and Sairi stop at a gastropub. You do not have money for lobster—it's going to fuck up next week's budget—but there is a storm brewing in Sairi. You want to buy your way out of this, so lobster it is.

Sairi's uploading photos of the spread of seafood and salad to her Instagram. She takes ages choosing the filter that'll make the food look most impressive for the girls.

'She was checking out your butt, that old lady.'

'She's only 51.'

'I'm not stupid. I know what's going on.'

Sairi begins frantically texting.

'What the fuck are you writing, Sai? You reporting to the fucking CIA or something?'

The waitress sets down the crayfish, the potato skins, the garlic butter, the finger bowl, the wine. Sairi's ordered a whole bottle to herself. She pours most of the bottle into her glass, tosses it into her throat looking everywhere except into your face.

Sairi adds another few words to her phone then locks it again.

'I am doing my utmost to convince that brother of mine not to bash you. He's got mates in the fucking Comancheros. God knows why I—why I even... ' Sairi catches a few tears with her fingers then sniffs snot back up into her head, shakes your hand off her. 'God knows why I *bother* defending... hang on. What's this?'

It's a text message from a number that makes your heart sprint.

We need 2 talk about your husband pls. ¯_(☺)_/¯.

7.

You park opposite Bag End Books and walk slow lunar steps across the dark road. You cannot avoid this meeting. There is no other place for you in the world.

They've cleared some displays out of the way. Sairi and Monica have a stool for you to sit on.

'So I messaged my brother,' Sairi says.

Oh fuck. Oh god. This is it. She's set you up. Arranged an ambush.

You spin, attempt to leave the store.

Monica is sliding the bolts into the ceiling and floor. Locked in.

Sairi is fumbling her phone, spinning it, tossing it.

'My brother's babysitting till nine so you better make this quick.' She jerks her thumb at Monica, who has by now retreated to the back of the store and has her arms folded like a watchful waiter.

'Your *eahira* friend here told me I need to support your poetry so... .' She pulls her handbag onto her lap then makes a show of dumping it on the carpet. Her knees are firmly folded. 'I don't know this thing you do. Go on, then. Show me.'

There is a pallet for you to stand on. Monica has draped on it a black sheet.

Monica moves from something in front of your eyes to a speck at the end of your vision, then she's gone.

The store is yours.

Sairi is fidgeting, chewing. She wants you to know her time is precious.

But she doesn't take her eyes off you.

You clear your throat, slowly work the wet pink muscles, pull words up from the mines. You lick your dry lips. You look deep into the eyes of your audience and begin. The sonnets flow like cool water from a spring.

On the drive home, Sairi struggles to find adjectives. She's never seen poetry on TV or movies. She doesn't know how to understand poetry well but promises she'll try from now on. You promise you won't make fun of her Diploma in Massage Therapy or her yoga classes or her DoTERRA essential oils on Shopify.

You check your watch, fretting that it's past nine o'clock, fretting that Billy Khoury's brewing up reasons to kick your ass.

She tells you she'll put in a good word for you. Long as you're ready to come home.

CASINO KIDS

1995

Sam watched his dad place his black case and pouch and filters on top of a barstool that was, like, as tall as Godzilla. The humongous stool said PROPERTY OF HORNBY WORKING MEN'S CLUB on the stickers on its legs. Murray rolled a cigarette and lit it with his shiny silver Zippo and blew two snorts of dragon smoke into his moustache and told his son to get him two JD and Cokes. Sam dragged a stool over to the bar so he could get up to the counter and Stella roared DON'T EVER LET ME CATCH YOU DRAGGING BAR STOOLS ON MY NICE CARPET AGAIN, SONNY. Sam said sorry and hopped until he was high enough to toss twenty bucks over the counter and Stella gave him his drinks for Murray and he brought them back and Murray nodded at his boy without looking. There was some real important dogs running on TV. Murray had fifty bucks on Red Baron to win at Newcastle. Sam fingered the edge of the tabletop. He was itching to hang with his mates.

Someone called out 'Mister Fixit,' and Sam's dad replied 'Blake-o,' and the men shook hands then tucked their hands under their armpits and frowned at the TV. Finally they creaked off their stools and tossed their beers down their throats and opened their long black cases and screwed their pool cues together as they talked about Murray putting a new hard drive in Blake-o's PC. Murray could fix any engine, any electronic system. He spent weekends welding and building and demolishing without saying a word to Mum or Sam.

Sam was hopping from side to side. 'Can I get some chips, Murray?'

'Ask your mother.'

'But I don't know where she is... ?'

'Only one place you'll find that woman.' Murray pointed his beer towards the gaming lounge.

TELL YOUR BOY TO QUIT RUNNING IN MY GOD DAMN PUB, MUZ, Stella called across the bar, but Sam had already made it to the dark cathedral of the gaming lounge and all he could hear was dinging bells and chinking coins.

The slot machines almost reached the ceiling. They were covered in gold. Their screens were shiny diamond. Three cherries were spelled out in red pixels then the cherries disappeared and there were three bags of gold. Coins tumbled into someone's cup and overflowed onto the metal drain and Sam looked around corners till he found whoever had just won. It turned out to be twin uncles with towels around their heads who were transferring the coins into a gym bag.

'Mum!'

Mum pulled down her sunglasses for a moment and said, 'Hello, trouble.' Mum's back and sides were a black shadow. Her face was glowing. Same with Gina's dad Donald Duke to her left. Same with all the other statues perched on their stools.

Mum held her cigarette out to the left. With her right hand, she pressed the shiny red button. Fresh pictures lined up. One harp, two harps... FUCK. Lemon. Mum pulled another two dollar coin from her cup. It didn't even scrape the sides of the slot as she fed it into the machine. Two dollars was how much Sam got for folding the laundry. Mum wasn't around home much anymore and even when she was, she was always too mad at Murray to do laundry for him. Sam was being asked to do more and more mum-stuff, lately. Vacuuming, dishes. He even had to tuck himself in.

'Can I get some chips, mum?'

'Yeah yeah.' Mum took a sip of her black stinky drink, rummaged inside her jacket pocket and pulled out three white plastic circles. She pushed them into Sam's hands without looking at him.

'Like, salt and vinegar, I mean.'

Mum fingered the pineapple button ten times then punched the machine. 'SHIT.' She caught up on her cigarette, tapping an inch of ash off the tip.

'You seen my friends, mum?'

'Thataway.' Mum pointed her smoke left and it went straight into the tattoo on the sweaty shoulder of Donald Duke.

'Oh my GOD, exCUSE my manners!' Mum said. She tipped her stool till her face splatted against Donald Duke's fat wide ginger arm, then caught herself. Donald Duke was the biggest man in the world. His shoulders were round as basketballs from hauling cray pots and tuna fish. Sam smelled his fat burning where he'd been scorched by Mum's smoke, but he didn't flinch. Mum must've been drunk, the way she licked the little burn on his mermaid tattoo and stroked Donald Duke's beard while he chuckled and told her it was nothin'. Sam watched Mum licking the big man's arm to cool the burn.

Gross. He walked away to find his friends.

Down the corridor with all the names of the old men who died in the war painted on wood, past the kitchen with its clanging pans and swinging saloon door and noisy fans and men in white, through another door, across the polished floors where the DJ was saying 'One-two, check one-two' through the speakers. There was a banner big as a sail reading LINE DANCING HO-DOWN FUN-RAISER and people assembling underneath dressed like the Marlboro Man. Beyond it, almost at the end of the club, Sam found the Casino Kids. They were in a quiet corner of the dance hall, bending the plastic screen off the Coke machine. There were six kids tonight. The biggest the group had ever been was eleven. That gathering was the second bestest night of Sam's life. The first bestest was the time of the blizzard when the city bobbed in an ocean of snow and school was cancelled for a whole week and you were an extra metre tall if you stood on the right mound and the streetlights steamed orange and Murray's home-made heat pump exploded and from out on the street he could hear his mum screaming I BET THEY'VE GOT HEATING AT DONALD FUCKING DUKE'S PLACE.

Standing outside the boys' shoulders as they probed the Coke machine, Gina Duke had her arms hunched in one of those farmer shirts with a pattern like the grid in Sam's maths book. She looked like her dad, tall, thick arms, fire-colored hair around her freckled face. The lips nibbling on her fingernails contained secret naughtiness.

'Hey dudes,' Sam said.

Govind Singh, arm buried in the Coke machine, rolled his eyes. 'Don't you know dude means a camel's diddle?'

'Coke's dumb, anyway,' he said, speaking towards Gina. Everyone in the gang was a blur compared to her. 'I'm a Pepsi man.'

'I like Dr. Pepper,' Gina said, 'My dad gets caseloads of American stuff.' Painful seconds limped until Gina added, 'But Pepsi's okay too.'

Sam and Gina watched the boys rock the machine, finger its guts, put the power plug into the socket, pull the plug out, and press its buttons in the magic Fanta-Diet-Diet-Diet-Fanta-Sprite combination one of the boys said would make it spew free Cokes 'cause he read it in Mad magazine.

'Put this in.' Sam held out a casino chip.

Nobody breathed as Govind Singh forced the chip into the slot.

It got stuck. None of the boys could pull it out.

'Thanks a lot, Sam-*not-wise* Gamgee.'

'Here,' Sam said, giving his second to last chip to Gina, 'I don't want it anyway.'

'Thanks.' She squinted at the chip through the black glasses covering up her dark brown eyes. Sam had accidentally been pulled into those eyes one time and a big exclamation mark had gone off inside him.

'Want a smoke? I stole some off my dad. He's got, like, a hundred cartons. They bring 'em in off the boats.'

Sam took a smoke from Gina and stored it in his left fingers but didn't put it anywhere near his lips. They watched the Casino Kids punch the Coke machine, swear at it, wipe boogers on its sides.

'I saw your dad,' Sam said. 'My mum burned him accidental. She's kissing him right now. Kissing his burn, I mean—hey—where we going?'

Gina was walking away from the group, drifting towards the cowboy people, propping her sunglasses up with one finger. Sam caught up and jogged alongside her. Mum and Donald Duke appeared down the end of the hall with a tide of incoming cowboys, tucking their guts into their belt buckles as the DJ invited them in to dance. Gina and Sam veered into the nearest toilet.

It was quiet inside and the machinery dripped.

'Wanna see my pussy?'

'Okay.'

Gina positioned herself with her back against the big metal thingy that Sam's dad had taught him to pee into, watching the door. She tugged her shorts down over her bare feet and kicked them away and squatted over the big green buttons of soap. A ribbon of gold suddenly twisted out of her pussy like a drill blade. Everything was exactly like when Sam peed, except her knickers had unicorns on them.

Sam wasn't really looking at her pee-pee, though. His eyes were on the wrist holding her right knee open.

'You got an owie on your wrist.'

'I know,' Gina said, pulling her knickers up with one hand while holding the sunglasses against her eyes, 'My dad's got, like, the strongest hands in the universe. You shouldn't vex your dad. It could give him a heart attack.'

'What's vex?'

'I dunno. My dad just says it.'

'Can I try your glasses?' Sam had already pulled them off her eyes when Gina clawed his arm and forced them back above her nose.

'NO.'

'Gimme a turn, I said.'

Before her orange curls slid over her face, he saw a flash of purple and green around her left eye the color of the concert lights in Murray's old videotapes. He wasn't sure if it was makeup.

'GIVE EM BACK!'

'What happened to your eye?

'I'LL SCREAM. GIVE EM BACK, I SAID.'

'Did your dad punch you again?'

'GIVE EM BACK I SAID.' Gina slammed Sam against the wall and Sam was pulling her hair and crumbling and surrendering the glasses when Gina speared the air with a sharp scream. Sam watched her tonsils dance.

The door smacked her as Big Donald Duke and Mum filled the room. Gina was in her knickers and shirt. Sam had her hair knotted around his knuckles.

'WHAT IN THE NAME OF CHRIST ARE YOUS TWO DOIN?'

'Easy, now.' Murray arrived, breathing hard and fast, lips chewing behind his moustache. 'I'm sure there's a perfectly good—

'YOU. You and that fuckin kid of yours.' Don Duke turned and got his knuckles ready.

The women watched.

2000

Sam emerged from the black winter parking lot. Before the club entrance were rows of shiny motorbikes. Govind came up beside him in brand new Adidas track pants and a t-shirt with skulls on it. He checked his hair in the reflective chrome of a parked motorcycle, adjusted his spikes.

'Kids,' nodded the bouncer.

'Not kids any more, bro,' Govind said, pausing to let Sam haul the door open.

'13's still a child to me, son. Where's your parents at?'

The bouncer was old-ish with craters on his cheeks. He wore a tie holding his neck together, a long coat and black leather gloves. The Epitaph Riders had stomped some people last month and Stella had fired a shotgun in the parking lot and the old fogies in the granny flats had complained and the club was gonna be shut down if they didn't get security on the doors. Everyone had talked about it, non-stop. It was the first fight since Big Don Duke had knocked out Murray Simpson five years ago.

Sam and Govind went past the bouncer as quickly as they could. He was too new and wasn't part of the family yet. Shit, they'd been coming here longer than he had. They couldn't wait to piss him off. Steal his walkie talkie, let down his tyres. Something like that.

Sam and Govind slapped their hands on the bartop and asked for Smirnoff Candys.

'Nice try.' Stella gave them a jug of Coke each. They could drink only if their dads and uncles bought it for them, except they weren't sure where their dads were. Tugging on someone's elbow while he played the slot machines was not cool. Asking anyone for any kind of help at the Club was not cool.

The boys struggled to get on top of tall bar stools not designed for thirteen year old butts. They struggled to enjoy the trots on TV without any money on the horses. Finally they agreed to go and play pool. No one could tell them off for that. Govind ripped the cloth with his cue and told Sam that if he told anyone, Govind would get the mafia on him. It was true— Govind's uncle had paid for protection for their laundromat empire. Govind was being taken out of school at least one day a week to help with accounting and management. He'd probably get his school leaving certificate at 14 and finish up. He didn't have a choice.

Past the line dancing hall where Sam's mum had her hands on Big Donald Duke's hips they found the Casino Kids huddled around the kitchen doors. A chef had filled a pot with hot chips for them and they were kneeled around the pot scoffing steaming fistfuls.

There was a girl with short spiked hair, dyed the color of the amethyst crystals Sam's mum rubbed when she needed good luck. Gina. Thank fuck. Sam hadn't seen her in forever. He'd heard her Dad had taken her out to work on the lobster boats or something.

Gina let go of her fistful of chips, stood up, wiped her hands dry in the hair of that new eight year old kid, the littlun. Gina, with her spiked pink hair and dog collar and Rancid t-shirt and cut-off denim shorts, swayed as if she was about to lean in and give Sam a kiss on the cheek.

She punched him on the shoulder instead. 'Sup, faggots.'

'This guy's the faggot,' Govind said, 'I'll fuck you any time.'

Sam was about to say something when Gina said, 'I'm thirsty. C'mon. I got a plan.'

Gina walked ahead and Govind forced himself behind her so he was ahead of Sam. They grabbed a few chips and checked on the wee Casino Kids before they departed. Someone had put down a beer jug full of Fanta on the ground with ten straws in it. They seemed fine.

Gina veered left and they entered a service passage Sam had only been in once, when Govind had locked him in it while they were playing hide 'n seek. There was almost no lighting in the passage. There was a disused toilet, a pyramid of boxed photocopy paper and lots of mops and buckets and gallons of chemicals. At the far end, Gina pushed against the wall and it swung open and the kids found themselves in a black room with automatic teller machines lined up like Easter Island heads. The ceiling sparkled and flickered and there were robotic CHOOOOPs and WHIRRRS and DING-DING-DING-DING-DING as somebody's cup filled with coins.

They'd spilled into the casino.

'I never knew this entrance,' Sam began.

'SSSH! Stay low if you wanna get drunk. You wanna get drunk, right?'

Sam gulped. 'Definitely.'

Gina led them through the black and they arrived at the first row of zombies. One Chinese woman with two handbags under her right arm had a tall slender sparkly drink with a little umbrella in it. Gina drank that one herself and slid the glass back without the woman noticing. They crept along to the next people, a pair of sisters with arms covered in swaying blubber. These women had six cans of Canadian Club and Ginger Ale. Three were unopened. Gina divided the cans between them and they retreated back out into the supply corridor and drank the sweet spice until they melted down the wall and sat on the carpet grinning.

'Canadian Club,' Govind said, nodding at his almost-empty can, 'Kinda sounds gangsta. I'm in the Canadian Club, yo.'

'Are you guys drunk yet?'

'Yeah, I'm so drunk. You?'

Govind had a flick knife in his hand and was twirling it. 'Yo, Ham-Spam: you know what scarification is?'

Sam's blood froze.

'Leave him alone,' Gina said. 'Oi: gimme that.'

She swiped the knife out of Govind's hand. The big white oval of her inner thigh poured out of her shorts as she bent her knee under her chin. She scratched an angular S into her thigh, then an A, hissing. Tiny red dots rose around the letters as she finished the M.

Gina tossed the knife into Govind's lap.

'Keep it, I got another one at home anyway,' Govind said. He yawned and flexed his muscles and pulled his gold chain out from his collar. They listened to bass pounding the walls. Distant coins clinking.

Sam slammed his empty can against his forehead. It left a circle above his eyes and didn't crumple.

Govind began singing, 'G's in love with a looo-zaaa, G's in love with a loo-zaaa.'

'Am not.'

'Your old man's a loser.'

'Least I got an old man. I heard they wouldn't let yours into the country.'

Govind's eyes went red and his mouth turned to a horn and Sam was beginning to lose control of his laughter when Gina reached between Govind's legs, snatched the knife and put it in her pocket. 'If I go to third base with you, will you leave him alone?'

'Whatever.'

Gina took Govind into the haunted toilet. Sam watched the minutes tick by on his wrist watch. He read every word on his empty can. Then Gina came storming out.

'I'm goin back in the casino. Sam, you should come.'

Govind jumped ahead of him as they left the corridor. 'I highly doubt this shrimp can come, Gina.'

Gina looked back over her shoulder. 'I can make any boy come.'

They stole five Pall Malls from Mr. Blake-o and some salted peanuts from Murray, plus a whole jug of something stinky from Gina's dad and Sam's mum. Big Donald Duke was way slower since he had his heart attack last year. Fatter, too, and Sam's mum couldn't move quickly without coughing up black stuff. By the time they circled back on their starting positions, the people they'd robbed were getting off their bar stools and frowning and patting their pockets.

'They're onto us! We have to split up!' Gina bailed and cut through to the restaurant. Blake-o was rattling his box of smokes and shouting so Sam and Govind ducked into the cleaning corridor, circled round and emerged in the steaming clanging whiteness of the kitchen where they collided against the huge tits of Stella.

'I THOUGHT I TOLD YOUS NEVER TO—OI! OIIIII! WHERE IN THE NAME OF CHRIST D'YOU THINK YOU'RE– '

Govind shouldercharged the far door and found himself in a pool of circular tables. Women in dresses were carving up mountains of pasta salad and watercress from a buffet.

They scurried to the black margins of the room and Sam scanned for Gina. They finally found her near the window. As they came up, they heard the silver haired man she was talking to say, 'I suppose forty bucks is reasonable for a massage, but it's gonna need to have a little somethin extra,' and Gina was tapping her foot as she tucked his money into her pocket and pulled the man away from his steak.

'Move, you guys. Playtime's over.'

The boys parted to let her through as she pulled the man out a door, Gina's eye briefly catching Sam's, stopping his heart. Gina and the old man passed the restaurant window in the dark with the bouncer calling 'Have a good one.' There was a glimpse of the old man's silver hair as they vanished into his car, possibly a flash of white thigh as her legs moved, possibly a vision of Sam's name scratched into her. Sam prayed she'd come back into the club where it smelled warm and she could get a ride home with her dad at closing time.

When Gina emerged ten minutes later, staggering into her shoes, Govind was away with his uncles, feeding dollars into a slot machine, but Sam was still watching through the window.

2005

It's Christmas and Stella has got out the can of snow spray and blasted all the windows powdery white. She's sprayed fake snow on the rugby players on the Super 12 poster too, whitened the All Blacks, the Warriors, David Tua and Lennox Lewis. There's a plastic wreath of holly over the doorway leading inside and fried turkey on the menu with cranberry sauce.

Not only is Bing Crosby crooning through the speakers, it's fuckin loud in here cause there's a 21st going on in the corner. Associates of Govind. Dudes that wear jackets all day long in the heat, gold chains and caps and white shoes.

Murray's been humouring Sam over some snooker, letting Sam make foul after foul and only calling him out on a couple. Even when Murray tries to fuck up shots, he sinks the balls. Pointless trying to act like he's not South Island regional champ.

Murray winces as his hearing aid picks up something it doesn't like. He goes to drag his stool under the panel of TV screens so he can hear his ponies, realizes he's about to get a growling for dragging a stool on old Stella's carpet and lifts it instead. His crimson face wrinkles as he strains. Sam easily carries the stool for his old man.

They watch the Ellerslie Christmas Derby in silence, sipping their beers occasionally, rolling smokes. Sam may have failed at snooker but he wins twenty bucks on the race.

'Look, Mum's here.' Sam sticks his thumb and forefinger in his lips, whistles then waves Mum over. 'She can keep you company.'

'I don't need no one to watch over me,' Murray says, 'Specially not that woman.'

'Easy, tiger,' Mum says, pointing her chin at the ceiling, trying to be classy. 'We're all friends here.'

Murray glowers. 'You got some extra-close friends, don't ya, Pam.'

'I'm worried about you, Pop, seriously. Your lungs, man. You shouldn't be smoking.'

'Takes one to know one.'

'You're gonna give yourself another stroke. Eh, Mum? Says right here on the packet. Smoking fucks up your brain.'

Sam tries to walk away to quietly replenish his own smokes from the cigarette machine when the sliding doors part and something beep-beep-beeps and in drives a big barrel stuffed into a flannel shirt stuffed into a mobility scooter, followed by a gust of wind and a skeletal thing with a ginger clown wig.

'Christ, this guy,' says the man who almost became Sam's stepdad, pausing his vehicle briefly beside Sam as he looks for an avenue between tables. Big Donald Duke has a cylinder of oxygen in the front basket of his scooter and tubes in his nose.

'Oh,' says Gina, arriving after her dad, straining to carry a baby capsule in one arm, 'Hello, you.' She charms the frown off her face and wobbles over in her pumps and miniskirt and sequined singlet. Gina's either been out scoring or she's planning on scoring after a quick drink at the club. It looks like the baby will come with her on whatever mission she's got planned.

Gina's thighs are fishbelly white. Sam is sure he can see the purple *M* scar on her skin. She tugs her denim skirt down and clears her throat to say something that'll cut through the awkwardness when the barrel man bellows, 'THE FUCK'S HE ACTIN ALL LOVEY-DOVEY WITH HER FOR?' and Donald Duke drives over to the table where Murray and Mum are having a conversation, beeping as he interrupts.

'Those two, man,' Sam says, unwrapping his Marlboros, 'Those three, I guess.'

'Your dad could've easily found someone else,' Gina says, hoisting her baby capsule onto a stool and preening over her baby.

'Nah. See you're wrong right there. A wife ain't a machine. Murray can fix any machine in the whole wide world, but like I say—

'-a woman ain't a machine, gotcha. Except this little guy thinks I'm a machine, don't you just? Don't you won't you justy wusty think mummy's a machine!' Gina plays with her baby's Play-Doh cheeks. Sam grabs a couple of Smirnoff Cruisers from Stella, tells her to put it on his tab, sets a drink in front of Gina.

They watch Donald Duke haul himself onto a couple of bar stools and thump the table and poke his big thick sausage finger into Murray's face and howl with laughter and slap Mum so hard on the back she stumbles. Their conversation could descend into a fight shortly. Murray's mates are strewn across the walls, Blake-o and Piggott and Judge, all bleached and drained these days. White hair and saveloy skin. They'll step in if there's trouble, but Don Duke's still got danger in him.

Sam opens and closes the lid of his box of smokes ten or twelve times, shuffling his feet. 'So I thought your baby might come out with a little rag on his head, y'know.'

'Is that supposed to be funny?'

'Kind of. I fucked the joke up. Sorry, Geen. Haven't seen you in yonks. Just nervous, I guess.'

'Ech. It's called a *dastār*, the towel that goes on their heads. His fuckin' uncles, Sam, they kidnapped Govind and locked him in the boot of their car and told him he had to marry me to bring honor to the family cause he got me pregnant and all this shit. Can you believe that?!'

Sam is looking at a 19 year old with a boy's name scarred into her flesh who turns tricks and used to get hidings from her dad and dropped out of school in Year 10. There is nothing about Gina he can't believe.

Bellowing erupts again. The way they're pointing at the TV screen, it appears Murray and Big Don and Sam's mum are arguing over the Lotto numbers. Everyone in the club is watching Donald Duke shouting and climbing into his scooter for a ten second drive down the wheelchair ramp to the lakes of green felt.

'ALRIGHT THEN, SMARTARSE, WE'LL SETTLE IT ON THE POOL TABLE THEN, YA CUNT.'

Donald Duke pulls the tubes out of his nose, sets up a game of pool, tossing colored balls and triangle and cueball onto the table then driving up to the head of the table to drive a hard shot that scatters the balls, sinking one solid and one stripe.

Murray arrives, calmly opens his black case and screws his cue together before doubling over and wheezing pink spit onto a napkin. Murray hasn't lost a game since the 80s. He sinks two balls then scratches his eye on a spiky wreath Stella has hung above the pool table. He misses his shot.

'Paaathetic,' big Donald Duke goes. Mum gives him a hand getting out of the scooter. He rests his huge pillar arms on the table and stalks up and down it until he decides on a suitable shot. 'I'll let you be solids since I feel sorry for ya.'

'Solid's what I am,' Murray says, 'I'd hate to be anything other.' His mates are getting their arms perfectly folded, beers positioned in the crotch of their bluejeans. With Sam and Gina and Govind and his entourage, plus Govind's uncles and Stella with her Fosters towel on her shoulder, there must be 20 people watching.

Big Don Duke thocks the blue into a hole, then the red. He gets flustered and starts sweating as he works to make the purple go down, then the orange quickly follows. He's enjoying himself as he works on sinking the green and maroon, taking a big gulp of oxygen.

'I'm putting out a meal shortly,' Stella says, 'Don't get too distracted now.'

'This is important,' Govind growls at Stella.

'Man stuff,' Mum adds.

Murray fumbles shot after shot. Often his white ball hits nothing. Don chortles and yells for the audience to witness as he pots balls from every foul.

Don took Murray's marriage years ago, and his honor and dignity with it, and he's one ball away from taking Murray's status as Hornby Working Men's Club pool champion in front of a huge crowd.

Finally Don sinks the maroon and shakes his head with astonishment at his own brilliance. All Don has to do is sink the black ball now.

'You seein this, Geen?'

Gina confirms yup. She's seeing her dad destroy Murray's dad. She squeezes Sam's arm and gives him an I'm-so-sorry-about-this look.

Sam just winks. He watches his dad tip up off the bar stool where he's been quietly studying the situation. Murray would have to sink five balls in a row to merely even the game, let alone getting to the black before Don.

'Y'all want food?' Stella calls through the crowd, 'I'm tryina serve Christmas lunch if yous'd kindly... .'

Everyone's attention is on Murray, who chalks his cue and puts the tip behind the white ball and drives it hard into the yellow solid, which collides with the blue solid. Both balls disappear soundlessly into their pockets.

'Lucky,' Don snorts.

'Red, corner pocket,' Murray mutters. He doesn't seem to register the creeping grins of the crowd. Murray sinks the red then mentions the purple is going into the left side pocket, the orange into a corner, and the green hits the maroon and both balls disappear after knocking the black close to a hole, with the white settling in front of it.

'Bit fairer now,' Murray says, 'Your shot.' His moustache covers his lips.

Don curses and grumbles as he rests his fat and muscle on the edge of the table. There's a thin whine leaking from his lips as his lungs wheeze.

Don lines up an unmissable shot and hits the white. The black jars against the hole then rolls away without going down.

'Have another go if you want,' Murray says.

'DO I LOOK LIKE A MAN WHO CHEATS?'

'With people's wives, yup.'

Don is speechless for a moment. Then he lunges. Five people leap up to hold him back. Don drives them all forward while Murray retreats against the wall. Mum gets between the men, screaming. Five of Govind's gangsta friends push the fat man back, then a couple more, then there's a shick-shick and everybody parts.

Stella is in the middle of the room. Her shotgun is pointed at the ceiling. Her finger is curled around the trigger.

'CALL IT A DRAW, YA FUCKIN BARBARIANS. NOW YOU'LL COME AND HAVE SOMETHIN TO EAT AND THAT'S FINAL.'

She levels the shotgun at Don's face. He shows her his sweaty white palms and ten fat fingers. Stella swivels around and aims the gun at Murray, who has backed into the shadows. Murray puts down his fistful of sharp darts.

The crowd follows Stella up the wheelchair ramp towards a grid of ten tables pulled together. Stella has set out a steaming turkey, deep fried so its skin is as crispy and brittle as pastry. There are five dishes with new potatoes, steaming gold balls. Stella has lain out Brussels sprouts on a drinks tray, beer jugs full of gravy, a dish of buns, knives, napkins, candy canes, peas and parsnips, a pile of streaky bacon and fifty tiny packets of butter.

Everybody brings their stool to the table. They press their warm plates against their chests while they wait for Grace to be said. Govind, his goons, Blake-o, Murray's mates, and

Murray, with Don Duke parked outside the ring in his scooter, and Sam with his arm around Gina and her baby capsule in the middle of everyone.

'Dear Father, who art in heaven,' Mum says, 'We thank you for this food.' She takes a cigarette and plays with it while she tries to think of the ending. 'For bringing us all together... '

When she can't think how it's supposed to end, she says Amen.

Everybody eats.

BROKEN WINDOWS

1.

A window smashes, tinkles. Party music punches the air. You sit upright in bed, afraid to breathe. There's a lull, for a silent second, then your neighbour is bellowing at his woman over the bass.

Doof doof doof. Like somebody stamping on the floor in boots.

You speed-dial the council, checking on Felicity as you wait to be connected. Your wife's eyeballs twitch under the sleep mask pulled against her chubby soft face. She snorts, turns, mumbles. She's had an exhausting day setting up the gallery. Take control or Felicity will direct her frustration at you. Don't neglect your duty. This used to be a good street before the uncivilized moved in. *Regain it, man.*

Noise Control, please. Me again, ha ha, I know, I know, terribly late isn't it, ha ha, and on a Tuesday, I fully agree, but listen, there's a situation I'm hoping you can help me resolve… .

You give your details and clarify, yes, you're THE author, of the Dan Drayton action thrillers, yes yes, studying her tone as she reads your name back. You're insistent that noise control officers intervene to silence the doofs and roars at 148b Calcutta Close. Gazza Hendrix and his uncouth tribe cannot be allowed to ruin the neighbourhood. It's not even his house—the man has the privilege of renting the place. You inform the phone operator about the decibel breaches you're registering with the app on your phone and insist she shares your complaint with next door's seldom-seen landlord. You email her a copy of the spreadsheet on which you've been recording the date of each noise crime over the past year, decibel level of each infraction, notes on associated violence and damage and rubbish pollution. You send in video of the framed diplomas on your wall rattling. You add for her a description of Gazza's reprehensible so-called music, a vile electronica sampling *Pachelbel's Canon* with periodic pauses to lull one into a false sense of security before a robotic DJ says 'Let the bass drop,' and drop indeed it does, like a piano crashing into your bedroom.

Since bringing his boys home from school and putting on a smoky sunset barbecue, Gazza has spent the night blasting his apocalyptic soundtrack while guzzling bourbon and cola, throwing empty cans at your fence, pacing the verandah, making endless calls to cousins yelled into his cellphone. There has been six hours of Gazza's racket so far, plus pops and shrieks from the Hendrix children as they destroy bottles with a BB gun. At one point Gazza mated with that woman of his on the trampoline. You zoomed in with the video recorder on your phone and made sure to capture the evidence up close, the blue droplet tattooed under Gazza's eye, the empty bowl of his partner's starved stomach. Her flimsy knickers dangling off her big toe as she rocked and kicked.

After the noise complaint is officially received by the council, you follow with a strongly-worded email. You then spend an hour taking photos from the safety of your double-glazed windows. At 1:16 am, you email Parking, Barking & Noise photos of broken glass which has fallen into your property from the garage window shattered at 1:08 by Gazza's elbow. You supply photos of garbage sacks on your berm, a photo of an oil slick leaking from a rusting hulk under the fence towards your stormwater drain and, perhaps most ghastly of all, photos of two shirtless brats on the deck, lit by a security light, having fun far past bed time. All this on a fucking Tuesday night—well, Wednesday, now.

It's 2:15. The thinnest part of the night. Insanity is near. Madness. Social breakdown. Five millimetres of glass protects you from the chaotic air outside. In bed, you pull noise cancelling headphones over your ears and listen to a podcast. Lisping liberal Malcolm Gladwell is discussing the 'Broken Windows' policy enforced in New York. Radical when introduced, Broken Windows punished even the most minor crimes, dissuading offenders from letting their sin pollute the population. From Gladwell's cool lips spring sage statistics. Within two years of citizens being encouraged to report violations as minor as a broken window, neighbourhoods measured 78 percent decreases in noise pollution, graffiti, muggings and assaults.

Your eyelids settle. Your thoughts wobble. At 4:22 there's a wet *PLAP*, and *PLAP* again. Fists hitting meat, meat hitting wood. Red and blue lights lick the ceiling. Gazza begins bellowing at the cops. His woman is sobbing. There's a squeal from Gazza's swing set. The gasps and giggles of children.

Nearly dawn, now. They've been partying all night. Their obnoxious noise has invaded your home. As treebirds begin chirping, you email property manager Neelam Gurunathan the name of your solicitor and inform Ms. Gurunathan that unless she gets rid of Gazza and his feral family, Mr. Graham G. Baigent, LLB, will be launching civil proceedings on your behalf.

Drained, zombified, you stagger down the hall. Slippers and coffee.

Lots of coffee.

2.

The services of solicitor Graham Baigent cost $295 an hour. From 9:13 to 9:43 am you give him as much pre-prepared information as possible over the phone and email him six times, handing over photos, your spreadsheet, your audio and video recordings of smacked flesh and cracked glass and outrageous fornication. He promises to send a letter to the property manager forthwith. The letter is dispatched at 12:01 pm. The end begins.

Mr. Baigent's legal notice summarizes the Residential Tenancies Act, its laws regarding the right to peaceable enjoyment of a property, penalties of two years imprisonment or a $100,000 fine. The letter concludes by encouraging Ms. Gurunthan to research Broken Windows policy and neighbourhood renewal. First step in renewing the neighbourhood: the immediate eviction of one Gareth Mason Hendrix. Your solicitor has checked Tenancy Tribunal hearings from the past ten years. This isn't the first time Mr. Hendrix has broken rental rules.

It's 1:08 pm when Neelam Gurunathan telephones and apologizes and promises to take immediate action. She didn't know "all this" was happening, she swears. Her words have a forced, grovelling tone. A higher-up has leaned on her.

You put two Sulawesi statuettes on the windowsill to hold your bedroom curtains open, kneel against the wall and watch as, 20 minutes following the phone call, Ms. Gurunathan parks her BMW convertible with a squeal and trots up the rubble of the driveway in clopping heels, stumbling as she navigates potholes. Gazza comes to the door in a singlet, camouflage pants and a blue paisley scarf wrapped around his forehead. His boys run among his legs, even though it's a school day.

Neelam's body contorts meekly as she hands him an envelope and attempts to walk away. Gazza opens the letter, understands he's been given 48 hours to vacate the premises, and begins hurling bourbon cans at his property manager.

Homo pauperis can read! Astonishing, really. Not so astonishing is Gazza's reaction to the upset. He biffs a toaster down the driveway. It thuds against the door of the convertible. The boys chase after the toaster and play with its spilled springs and filaments. More troglodytes emerge from the house, men in caps and singlets, cousins or uncles, then follows a long period of drinking and smoking on the deck, the men muttering while the children frolic in a car wreck. Gazza then begins hauling rubbish onto the curb—a couch, a boxing bag leaking foam, some tyres. Bottles, cans and crates: he and the children simply throw them from the deck towards the road.

Gazza's common law wife is seen, briefly, carrying small seedlings out from the woodshed and loading them into the family's van. You watch the sashay of her buttocks moving up and down. A firm bum, hard and ripe despite her pilled grey Warehouse trackpants. She's slim, the wife, and with her hair sequestered in a messy bun that makes her chin looks elegant. Cleopatra-esque. You can see the knobs of her spine. Every ounce of fat smoked away. It's a shame she's wasted on a man who spends his final moments doing pointless loops around the driveway on a BMX. He could have made something of his life, perhaps. When they first moved in 18 months ago, there was a friendly-enough conversation over the fence and you ended up lending Gazza your copy of *Rich Dad, Poor Dad* and assumed, since it never came back, he might have been studying it.

The boys carry armloads of shiny orange metal out. They've stripped the copper from the hot water cylinder, it appears, and you begin dialling the police before they scream away in some vehicle and it's over.

You've fixed the broken windows problem! *You!* You're a superhero of sorts—a real life Batman. You message your wife, ask her to pick up dinner and wine on her way home from the gallery. You squeeze in a couple hours of highly productive writing, fizzing with glee. Covert ops mercenary Dan Drayton finds himself on shore leave in Bangkok and isn't sure if he should trust the advances of a sultry Saigon siren who lures him into a grotty flat full of Thai ruffians with black plastic sunglasses fixed to their eyes, baboons in tank tops who beat the stuffing out of the hero.

The scene is making you anxious. This isn't the outcome Dan Drayton deserves. You put your computer to sleep and lie down on the couch, flipping on the telly for some comfort.

Felicity arrives home with some good sirloins. You dine quietly with a tablecloth and candlelight, Brahms on the stereo, and outside, silence like snow.

3.

He shows his face, the landlord does—well, he visits his property, though his face is concealed under black Ray Bans. You're summoned next door for a handshake and a chat.

Ms. Gurunathan introduces you to the owner, inflecting the introduction with apologetic little notes about 'the tenants,' then backs away to let the men talk while she tallies the damage on her tablet. It feels wrong to stand on Gazza's turf. It's a contaminated place.

You're astonished to find yourself dealing with a landlord who's cool-headed, professional, courteous. A late 30s gent with the physique of a yachtsman and the polo shirt to match. Behind the aviator lenses, his skin is well-stretched over his skull—he pays for a good chemical, perhaps, or a great surgeon, or maybe it's just the sun which really smooths a man's frown-lines. He says he splits his year between sailing the South China Sea and tending to his investment properties in this country.

Once you're done chatting, he's given a tour of the run-down bungalow by Neelam—seemingly for the first time. The owner of this half-a-million dollar asset appears never to have seen his own building. He takes cautious steps around the verandah, perhaps imagining he's on the deck of his boat. He steps over a sun-brittled plastic buggy lying on its side, kicks a dog dish away.

At the end of the tour, the landlord leans against your broken fence and pulls your ear close to his lips.

'By the way,' he says, looking down his nose so you almost get a glimpse of his eyes, 'I could use someone like you to check my assets for me, if you're needing work. You're not, like, agoraphobic or anything, are ya?'

'I edit a financial magazine; I also publish action thrillers... well, I *will*, so long as my publisher gets off her behind and.... Anyway, I'm gainfully employed, but thank you.'

He pushes the sunglasses back up his furrowed nose. 'I just assumed you didn't have much goin on, since you've been monitoring these guys 24/7… .'

'When you say check your assets for you, d'you mean keep an eye on tenants? A secret agent, of sorts?'

'Tenants come and go. Bricks and mortar's the part that stays, my friend.' He hands you his business card. It's thick and white and the corners are sharp. 'Spies like us, huh? Hit me up if you wanna go pro. I need a kicker-outer. You do renos too?'

'Beg your pardon?'

'Renovations. Fix things. Like these windows here on the garage. Whack out the busted panes, chuck a new bitta glass in. That sound like you?'

'I'd imagine that's best left to the professionals.'

'Well my friend, think about it. You'll be saving me tonnes on a glazier. Paneless. Get it?' He winks, makes a clucking noise out of the corner of his mouth. Ms. Gurunathan opens her convertible for him and he hops in and disappears. Onto the next property, presumably. Or the airport.

It's settled, then. Gazza the window-breaker, the polluter of neighbourhoods, is moving on. Gareth Hendrix, whose last name prickles you with its non-traditional spelling, its pretentious X as if he's trying to make a political statement.

Be a kicker-outer. The world needs people like you. You're pretty sure he said it like that.

You set the alarm and lock the gate and phone security to tell them to monitor your home, even though you're only popping down to Deli Delight. You pick up a kilo of salmon steaks, dill, unsalted butter, choux pastry, portobello mushrooms. Your Range Rover is parked in front of the laundromat. Amongst the dark den of washing machines there is music erupting from a portable speaker and people chattering. You see them and freeze, acid rising up through your groin. Gazza's mob are draped across the laundromat like a still life painting, some sitting on washing machines, others lying on the floor playing games on their cellphones, spending a pointless day there in the dry warmth. You hoist your canvas shopping bag onto your shoulder to hide your face and scuttle past.

At supper, the vol-au-vent with truffle and fennel sauce tastes heavenly, garnished with praise you recite to your lover. *The world needs people like you. Be a kicker-outer.*

Felicity throws down her knife and fork. 'Is that what he said?!'

'Words to that effect.'

You lean your chair back from the dinner table to dip your ears in the ambrosia that is the Jean-Francois Paillard chamber orchestra performing *Pachelbel's Canon* distributed through a Dolby Atmos 5.1.4 wood panelled surround sound system. You stroke your wife's hand as the third movement climaxes then put your fingers under her wrist and tug her to the bedroom.

4.

With the ability to concentrate on your work, you ascend through the peerage of publishing. You get manuscripts completed and sent away, you get correspondence dispatched, you get acceptance, and cheques, and bylines. First there's your longlisting in the Tom Clancy Awards for Action Thriller Writing. Then there's a two-page spread in Saturday's paper covering your six published novels, your biography of von Tempsky, not to mention your academic papers. What really accelerates your ascent is the telephone call directly from Penguin managing director Ferguson Chen, who says he has a talent acquisition manager looking for more titles specifically within the veteran-turned-mercenary action thriller genre you specialize in—so long as you can bring more spies into your books.

Indeed you can. The advance which Penguin pays you is a profound motivator to get more manuscripts completed. You purchase a Herman Miller Executive Size B Lumbar Support Aeron chair so you can truly write in style. It doesn't fit in the boot of your Range Rover so you stop in at the dealership on the way home and upgrade to a roomier 2018 Tesla Model X.

That night, you and Felicity celebrate with tapas and a show—Puccini's *Madama Butterfly*, a 2.5 hour return trip to the city centre and home, cringing as the car slows when you enter Calcutta Close. That prick neighbour's probably having another party. That's the night ruined.

You exhale with relief as you realize there is no sound on the street. The smashed windows of 148b are black and silent. You will never see Gazza again.

5.

A van comes by one Wednesday. The vehicle hums and rumbles on the lip of the driveway. Perhaps workmen have been dispatched to clear away the car wreck and—hang on, who's this—it's the female, the fuckable wife, scampering inside the house, re-emerging with some bundle of fabric in her arms—the curtains?! The filthy devils have stolen—no. No, she's spreading the big square cloth against the side of the van. It's a quilt, yes, a quilt with gaily colored trains and tractors. Eager hands reach from the rear of the van and snatch the quilt.

The vehicle honks twice then disappears.

A honk aimed toward your house... and a *wave*. What could it mean?

You contact property manager Neelam Gurunathan hoping for advice on whether you need a restraining order. Your guts are a pretzel of twisted angst. Ms. Gurunathan no longer works for Asset Advance, you're informed. The new property manager, Jitesh Johnson, informs you the decision has been made to keep the house empty for a year to "increase its value."

Mr. Johnson breaks it down for you. It's a formula known as TRA, or Tenant Risk Algorithm. The decreasing value of a property caused by suboptimal tenants is plotted on the Y axis of a three dimensional graph. Rising prices for the property are plotted on the X axis. The Z axis shows the rental payments of the tenants, which restore some balance to the force tugging down the price of a house once it is no longer pristine.

'It's like when you drive your car off the lot, it loses half its value the moment it hits the street, sometimes better to leave a property empty, 'specially when there's heaps of demands from the rental crisis and stuff, know what I'm sayin'?'

You tell him that as the owner of a 2018 Tesla Model X you indeed know what he is saying.

Jitesh Johnson drops round to check the water meter at 4 pm and shakes your hand, strolling the driveway with you, tutting at the cracked fence, the crushed cans and glass crumbs tangled in the bushes.

'Honestly, don't worry about him getting revenge, these people are used to getting kicked out of places all the time,' he explains. 'They know it's nothing personal. Listen, we got some seriously bad TRA scores with our applicants at the moment. If you know any good tenants needing a place, please send 'em my way.'

You inform the property manager you don't mix with renters. Anyone with half a brain years ago got a deposit for a mortgage, signed up for the Reserve Bank newsletter and watched house prices push up from underneath like being on top of a fountain of spurting oil.

The TRA thing is fascinating, though. You discuss it with Felicity as she tucks forkfuls of beef Wellington into her mouth, ruminating over the haves and the have-nots and how you can understand why sterilisation is offered to certain families and it's really doing them a favour. After the main is cleared away, she moans over a delectable lemon gelato.

You squeeze in a quick three hours of writing before bed. There's a rather wooden subplot about a vindictive villain your publisher has insisted you put in your latest novel. You stay up writing while Felicity snores, wearily adding a backstory about your Ukrainian baddie becoming enraged by a brutal landlord's oppressive Tenant Risk Algorithm score when he was a young man. The score turned him into a remorseless anarchist. It's a humane detail, you feel. Something about his mother being chucked out of her apartment into the gutter of a snowy Kiev December. A realistic motivation. Half-realistic, anyway. Next time you're on a panel at a literary festival and you're asked how you get inside the heads of such disturbed characters, perhaps you'll reveal your genius.

Or perhaps you'll chuckle quietly to yourself and play coy.

6.

With the Laundromat People long-gone, life goes from strength to strength.

It's not just being shortlisted to ghostwrite the new Jack Ryan book *Explosive Decompression*. It's being asked to write a guest column for the *Wall Street Journal*. It's the A+ from your cardiologist. It's spinning your chair to face out the bay window and feeling powerful within your walls. It's the limited edition *Pony of the Penines* 2000 piece puzzle from Berslfärne. It's a matinee film at Rialto Cinema Deluxe watching Anna Netrebko sing *Aida* at the Met while you sip a tiny bottle of champagne and enjoy a choc top ice cream with pecan nuts. It's the smiling faces and sensuous smells at Divine Deli on the way home. It's gouda cheese and a macchiato and managing to walk past a family of beggars outside the exit without treading on their wet blanket, quilt, rag, whatever it is.

It's the way your wife points her nose in the air as she hot-glues wires onto her sound installation. Felicity is about to display an exhibit at the art museum about how the eruption of Krakatoa in 1883 inspired artists worldwide who mixed real volcanic ash into the pigment, creating an ephemeral movement known as Emergency Art. She bites her lip, strains her biceps to connect the wire to the diode and.... Light! She has light!

You wrap your arms around her flesh. She snuffles with nose and lips, asks you what makes you think you're worthy of her donating her body to you.

You're happy, that's what. You've succeeded in demonstrating to deviants that anti-social conduct will result in punishment. It's safe to have visitors round for dinner parties again.

And you've become a lion of publishing. It's hard to put it in words for Felicity, though you're sure she senses it. A don, a silverback. A hero. You want her to join you in celebration of yourself. Happiness rediscovered.

That happiness begins with a good hard shag on the carpet, changing position four times so your backs and thighs don't hurt too much. Your kisses afterward are wet, sloppy, careless, your lips smeared on her eyes, her lashes on your tongue, her hand on your hammering heart.

7.

On Pier Four, overlooking wrinkled green water, a photographer is taking photos of you with the wind flicking your scarf so those who check out your book jacket photo know you live in moody tempest.

The angst becomes real halfway through the shoot. You smell cigarette smoke, hear cans crinkled and dropped on concrete and a distinctive belch. He must be near. Your suspicion is confirmed when your ears are alerted, mid-photo, to a certain phlegmy hacking of the throat coming from the playground. They're here—the riff raff. The ferals. The Hendrix child's vile cough is followed by the mother telling the child to shut up. The boys are riding a roundabout. No coats on the children, despite the drizzle. The family is amongst a pile of suitcases and laundry bags parked on a picnic table, Gazza pacing and smoking and talking on his phone, hunched in a hoodie, evidently waiting for someone to take the family somewhere.

'YO, NEIGHBAAA!' comes the spear of noise. It lands between your shoulder blades, pinning you. Creep away, pretend you haven't heard and you may receive a blow to the back of the head. Escape is impossible. Besides, Dan Drayton wouldn't run.

'Oh, hi,' you say, and swallow. He comes jogging over, surprisingly sprightly, as if upbeat. Happiness derived from, what? Intoxicants?

'Mr. Hendrix... .'

'It's Gazza, bro. I seen you doing your camera shit. Lookin flash, cuz. Just wanted to say laters, cheers for bein neighbours and all that.' He's short, up close, and what appeared through your binoculars to be muscle is simply bosoms and chubby arm fat. He sticks out his hand to shake. There are three watches on his wrist. 'Might see you round, my bro.'

What does the inflection on *round* mean? Is it a promise? A threat? A plea for shelter?

A child's face appears between his thighs as if he's just given birth. The boy crawls through Gazza's legs, runs excited laps around the man. 'Can we stay here and play, daddy, pleeeeease?'

'Course, son, course,' he tells the boy, 'Got four hours to fuckin kill. Shelter ain't open til dinner time.'

He looks at you hard, squinting, cocks his head like he's just been insulted or surprised. He reaches out, smears a knuckle across your wet cheek. Stray raindrops appear to have landed on your eyes.

'Don't worry bout us, cuz,' he says. 'Snot your fault. Dry those eyes, my bro.'

Your photographer is loading his gear into the car. He dithers, keeps his back to you as he slams the boot shut. He says he can't photograph you if you're crying.

He's utterly mistaken about the allegation of supposed crying, but the shoot's over. Your face is flushed red, your eyes pink, nose raw. Not tears though, you insist. Just a cold.

8.

You've spent all week researching the protocol for an authentic Japanese degustation. After drinks and gossip and stowing everyone's coats, you begin with the *kaiseki*. Each item of food is served on the dining table so everyone can sit up properly. You can hardly expect yourself or your guests to kneel Oriental-style, what with Gladys's steel hip and your slipped disc from years hunched over the desk.

It's freezing outside. The trees slap wetly against the windows. Leaves stick to the glass. The fireplace grunts as the wood shifts in the flames. Your guests enjoy a shokuzen-shu of fiery sake. After a sakizuke of oyster follows the hassun, grilled tofu with wasabi, then a takiawase of simmered soy beans, carrot and bacon.

Maura Sanders, unimpressed with the slow reveal of the ten courses, makes a joke about starving to death, which causes Felicity to lament that news report surely everyone's seen about that DREADful famine in North Korea. Richard Sager postulates we should hear the dictator out and that this Kim Jong-Un must be a satirist method actor of unrealized genius. His riposte gets you all chortling, your warm humour topped up with spicy liquor.

Between the mukozuke, futamono and yakimono courses, a playful argument brews with indignant snorting, explosions of laughter, refills of bubbles. From the discussion of global concerns arises a debate over the threat of climate change. The inability of low-lying nations to respond is discussed. The fate of uneducated poor people is lobbed about the table like a beachball, which reminds Maura Sanders: whatever became of those reprehensible redneck neighbours of yours?

You begin telling the story with a disclaimer that Gazza Hendrix has had many options. He was privileged to have had civil neighbours who allowed him an extremely long leash, considering the dole bludger didn't have to get up for work any day of the week. What's manifestly unfair to taxpayers is 44 percent of supposedly poor people actually collect benefits which, added up, give net income greater than that enjoyed by legitimately hard workers. You cite your sources. Everybody's nodding, except James Boxleitner, who counters that in his eight years on the board of Salvation Station the divide between middle class, working poor and benefit-dependent shrank every six months until there was no divide left whatsoever. He cites his own sources. Our world is unfortunately choked, in the centre, by economic forces pushing aspirational families back down the ladder to keep them from receiving wealth re-distributed from the one percent, he claims. We see it when good people can't get houses and have to live in neighbourhoods full of broken windows. It's not their fault they're forced into conditions of hopelessness.

'Economics is the answer, not eugenics,' he says, staring at you hard till you're forced to look away.

Felicity stands in front of you and informs Boxleitner that actually a certain Malcolm Gladwell not long ago addressed these very same concerns and sided with you. So there.

'GLADwell?!' James Boxleitner sniggers, '*That* flip-flopper?!'

By 2008, Malcolm Gladwell was, at every appearance, publicly accepting that Broken Windows was a failure whitewashed by a mayor who sold it as an effective system when it was in fact the opposite, Boxleitner explains. Broken Windows policies caused naïve juvenile window-breakers to enter the criminal justice system and become convicted felons, permanently altering the course of their lives, destroying their chance at getting a career, a mortgage. No right to vote or get a business loan or lease a place to live.

'So effective council monitoring of bylaw breaches is all that's needed in disadvantaged neighbourhoods, you understand?' Boxleitner continues. 'Not crucifying people for blowing off steam now and again. Jesus Christ, that broken windows thing's been discredited for a decade. You oughta get out of the house more.'

The table laughs. Your collar burns.

'It doesn't change anything,' Felicity interjects, shielding you with her middle. 'Have some more Chianti.'

'This stuff is $200 a bottle.' Boxleitner has to peer far around Felicity's waist to look you hard in the eyes.

'Auction it; let me auction it. I'll give the proceeds to Salvation Station. You said you had two in the cellar.'

'Boys!' Felicity lays the su-zakana loudly on the table then hurriedly fetches the shiizakana and naka-choko. Sasha Gould changes the subject. She has eight days in Kyoto booked for the northern spring. The Sanders talk about their 10 day cruise of the Alaskan fjords. Felicity dishes out the tome-wan then the mizumono. Everybody groans with delight, pausing periodically to wipe their lips with silk napkins and gush compliments.

As coffee and brandy are being served and you're stacking plates beside the sink, Boxleitner pulls you conspiratorially into the laundry. There's a load of washing on; the room is warm and smells comforting. Boxleitner says he's doing his Ph.D. in social anthropology and would be delighted to get in touch with that nasty neighbour of yours for a research interview. You're happy to help, though when you go to write down where to find the family, you're stumped. All you can do is describe the rainy playground, the wet quilt on the cold concrete.

DOC BE DOWN

'How often have you been bothered by feeling down, depressed, irritable, or hopeless over the last two weeks?'

Doc's mouth smiles but his face still looks sad. He didn't spend his whole life healing people to end up reading some boffin's bullshit questions off a list prompted by his computer, fiddling with cup of tongue depressors all distracted.

'I felt down, shiiit, I guess the day after I snorted all that molly. Can't sell it if I can't vouch for it. Comedown was epic, Doc, epic.'

'I'd sure love to meet Molly some day.'

'Doc, I know you're a Straighto, but Molly is... it's not a girl's name, know what I'm sayin? It's street. You ain't heard of the streets, have you, Doc.'

Doctor Downes is nodding, but his mind's not registering me. He's reading off his computer screen like a robot. Just like those slaves at Probation. Totally hypnotized. Totally corporate, hoping to get to the next miserable poor person needing a flu jab before the computer system records some fuckin' penalty.

'Have you experienced diminished pleasure in doing things you ordinarily love over the last two weeks?'

'I had minimal pleasure coming here, Doc. Hell, I popped in to get a fuckin' haemorrhoid cut out, not to get my head shrunk.'

'I'm required to... Please bear with me till the end of the questions, it's a requirement of our funding. Have you had trouble falling asleep or staying asleep?'

'The gear my Mex connex get me? Damn, nobody sleepin' on that. Score me a ten outta ten. I'm in the clubs all night every night. No time for sleep, know what I'm sayin?'

'Working men's clubs, presumably?'

'Doc, you a wack mother... Listen: *club*-clubs. Like itty bitty titties jigglin all about-clubs. Security, earpieces, champagne, DJs rippin' beats... I guess you more of a tennis club cat.'

'Badminton, actually.' Doc has a file on his desk with a lawyer's logo on it. He winces as he lifts the stack of legal papers away from his keyboard so he can peer at the screen closer. He's wearing a yellow boat shirt with short sleeves, except he ain't on no boat. No tan, no muscle, and the doc's about as stylish as a bean with glasses glued on it. He's in an office where everyone's pissy and grumpy and bitches kick in his door to tell him off for taking too long with patients.

'Now, have you experienced poor appetite, weight loss, or overeating in the last two weeks?'

'Me, I eat garbage. That's how come I got the haemorrhoid, like we were discussin before you started getting all Siegfried and Roy on me. I live offa bar snacks, know what I'm sayin? I eat at work.'

'Sigmund Freud I believe is the name you're... regardless: We'll talk about your diet momentarily, plus your other... consumptions. Now: how often have you been bothered by feeling tired, or having little energy, let's see here... Feeling like a failure... Christ. Really one ought to turn the questions one's self... never mind.'

I give him a hard look, like What up? A look he knows he oughta respond to. 'You got the blues, Doctor Downes?'

'You can go now. You're not depressed. We're cutting your haemorrhoid out this Tuesday, 11:30 I believe is our appointment. Can you endure the pain for two days?'

He pulls a paper bill from the printer. I rip it out of his skinny chopstick fingers. Thirty bucks for him to look up my ass at a throbbing purple grape? Pfft. I got Special K that'll make me forget the 'roid pain. Shouldn't've even come here. It's not like I can't find meds.

'Y'know you oughta take a look at yourself sometime, you hypocritical-ass motherfucker. You depressed as shit. You need a potplant, B. A fuckin' fern. Somethin' to nurture.'

I have the Exit door to reception halfway open when I hear the sound of, well... just background chatter. The sound of nothing. The doc's holding his door frame like he's watching his son leave to go off to college or some shit. Silent, defeated.

I pause, turn around and wink.

'You know I'm playin, doc. It's just... we need to cheer you up, is all.'

'You'd be depressed too if you had the Medical Council bullying you. They're saying I've had a complaint lodged against... never mind.'

'Bro: fuck that highfalutin bullshit. Yo: hit the clubs with me any time. Those stuck-ups can't get you on the dancefloor.'

Doc snorts like I've just mispronounced the huberus bone or something. 'A kind offer, but not for an old fuddy duddy like me. I'd stick out like a sore thumb.'

I'm this close to walkin off, except I know it'd crush him. I've been seeing the Doc for years and his depression's not, like a choice or nothin. I've seen my own life go up and up while Doctor Robert Downes has gone the other way.

I pinch the bridge of my nose and make a little growling frustrated noise.

'Listen, if I swing by here bout 9 o'clock, ten, you gon' be here?'

Doc looks like a raccoon caught raiding some garbage. The light reflects in his eyes.

'I don't—I don't know if I should—'

'I'ma swing by. It's a sin to waste a Friday. We hitting the club. I'ma cheer you the fuck up, old man.'

*

The air tonight is warm as a blow dryer so we're down to our singlets and shirts and we have the windows open and it's tickling our ears. The stereo's thumpin, we have a cold beer each in the cup holders and I have a mean-as joint burning in my roach clip. We're feelin' lucky—well, I'M feelin lucky at least. Doc Downes, he's brought his nervousness with him tonight. Doc's gripping the grab handle as I shave corners and drift across roundabouts.

Hell, Doc, I try to tell him—I'm drivin a Mustang here. It's practically illegal NOT to blaze the fuck out of it.

He tells me he couldn't possibly do this in his Kia and I spit laughs like an AK-47 and that's us: conversation killed for two solid minutes. To shake the awkwardness out I crank the bass on my Beats by Dre speakers. I swear I can see Doc's thin silver hair flap with nervousness. Jittery motherfucker, this guy.

'So your kids ever take you out for Father's Day and shit?'

'No, oh no no. No, my son, he… .' He begins a sentence, drops it, stares out the window.

'Me, I lost my dad when I was like eight. If he was around, shit, I'd never let him go.'

The doc's doing that far away nod again.

First part of the night is about getting a decent chilli dog down us. There are 30 clubs on The Strip for me to hit tonight. Any customer that's serious about buying a decent portion of product off me will want to take his time and enjoy a beer, cause if your dealer is itching to get away from the transac, you're almost certainly being sold something which is only 10-20% effective, which is how come I need to work on a full stomach. You let yourself get intoxicated, you're gonna end up saying Yes when niggas try to haggle and that's gonna depreciate your bargaining power.

I'm only telling all this to Doc Downes because I've finished my chilli dog way before him and I'm trying to hurry him along. First deal's scheduled for 9:30. Second one is 9:45, then they're every fifteen minutes until 5 am when people are needing their uppers so bad I get to—how do I say this—*UP* my fee.

Across the laminated table of the café, Doc's giving me some speech about how he can tell from the color of the chilli that it's swimming with saturated fats and apparently every ounce of satch-fat takes ten minutes off your life expectancy. I've been watching the street behind him, there's certain gangstas I have to avoid, and I'm getting edgy then I'm up and yanking him by the collar of his weak-ass Hawaiian shirt and throwing Doc up the line and bumpin' the bouncers and we plunge into Loco Parentis. Loco has an island in the middle with a channel of water and everyone's got their shoes off and the DJ's up top of a tower shaped like a palm tree. As the Doc strokes the rope and fingers the sand and kicks the water, hypnotized, I take a backpack from my flashy British bro and as soon as I've hit the Transfer Bitcoin button on my screen, he's gone, melted into the crowd, and I'm left to babysit twenty grand of chemical compounds plus a depressed doctor.

After forcing a Malibu and Coke down the doc, next place along is Vida Loca.

'Single people,' the Doc says, as if he's spotted a rare mammal on the Serengeti. 'Happy people.'

'Ain't nobody lovin you, Doc?'

'Love isn't the only way to achieve… ' he begins, and trails off.

The Doc's silver hair is ruffled and the top couple buttons of that gay-ass Hawaiian shirt are down.

'Y'know you oughta take that thing off,' I tell Doc as I yank him into the cool night, along a few queues of people, then into the tiny black stairs of Tango, 'The shirt's taking points off you,' I'm yelling. 'You ain't fat or nothin. Get crazy, I reck-rnrnrnn…. .'

My words are evaporated in the steam of a club so loud and hot and greasy that when a fat woman stands on my toes, I scream ten swear words at her and all she does is flash a white smile. Nobody can hear anything at the bar. Our ears are numb with a hellish pounding of noise. I have to reach over the counter and grab the bottle of Jose Cuervo then slide a twenty at the bartender. Jesus Christ. Luckily these big country bumpkin triplets spot me before I have to search for them and we go to a corner to talk—that is to say, their bellies squeeze me into a corner. These fuckers are so fat their clothes are tryina get away from them. The Bumpkin Brothers are three huge farm boys in flannel shirts, jeans and boots. The biggest, Darrell, is six feet five; his two brothers are only a little less. They have chubby red cheeks and hair as blonde as hay. I try to introduce Dr. Downes who's limping behind me like a lost lamb but the music is jet engines in my ears so all I do is elbow Doc in the ribs and he gives a Wassup chin to the Bumpkins and they Sup him back so we cool. I sling my laptop backpack onto the circle table in our booth, unzip a pocket, pull out a little something. I watch their blubber crease as they press the drugs to their noses and sniff. These porkers have arms as thick as my thighs. They hold entire jugs of beer like pints.

I make two grand off the sale. It's 40 mollies I have to cough up—and I could get $2300 for 'em if I seriously shopped around—but I want to get on with my night and get the hell away from the Dukes of Hazzard. These country boys grew up protecting one another, bullying women into sleeping with them, intimidating bartenders into giving them discounts and freebies. They're shameless and stupid and fat and fearless. They have eyes like starving sharks. The mollies have a hell of a lot of powdered sugar in the mix, the purity's down around the 50 percent mark and they're only worth a couple of bucks each, but I'll make it up to the next customer. We just have to keep moving.

We conclude business and beeline for the bouncers. It feels safer on the street. Those bumpkin boys scare me. I lax a little bit at Calendar Girls. There's this one stripper, Sofia, who's tiny and skinny and she gets pushed to the edge of the stage like a sick puppy. I like her skinniness cause it makes her purple hair looks longer, more luscious. I like the sharpness of her ribs. The dancers point their nipples into the pink light and stare up at some kind of heaven above the crowd of black silhouettes holding beer bottles. Doc's caught in the deadlights, seriously hypnotized, and I can see a boner struggling to escape the cheap outdated 1993 white cotton pants he's wearing.

I drag him into Pzazz and move a few cheeky joints, 18 of then at $20 each. Speedballs, Adderall, Coke, Xanax. Quick, cheap, disposable cash. Next club is called Mermaidz and the girls swim around in tanks then dance on towels with their titties all dripping. I know this dancer called Brittany and I slip her forty bucks to grab Doc by the ears and plant a kiss on him and we're all laughing while I slap palms with this sky-high Samoan soldier named Tevita and within a few synchronized bumps and shakes and pats on the shoulder I've negotiated a hundred Viagra at $30 each. He has the cash straight up—no tick book, no bullshit. Seamless business. The pills are in a milkshake sippy cup this Persian gangsta slides along the bar at me and I'm handing it to Tevita and he's pretending to take a jokey sip and we're all laughing and the only thing about to burst my buzz is the Doc muttering, 'I could just walk off a bridge tonight and nobody would care' and I'm rattling Doc Downes's shoulders and going, 'Yo! Shake it off, doc! We here to party!'

We're buried in a pool of elbows and hips and women are running their fingers up and down Doc's midriff. Then there's a couple of guidos whose fight spills into our group, and I look across the room and make eye contact with Tevita and just as one of the guidos' fists scrapes the Doc's cheek, Tevita is grabbing each of the fighters' round heads and cracking them together like rocks and a cheer goes up. I make a couple of time-wasting fifty dollar sales at El Greco and Hunters, then my appointment doesn't show up at FoundingFather, then I move some excellent meth at GangBang as bluey-orange dawn is starting to finger the clubs and I'm shutting down the night, clicking the tiny padlocks on my laptop bag and burying the keys in my pocket.

We end the night with bacon and eggs at Jonathan's Café with two honeys who are telling Doc allll about their pre-med classes in biology and Doc's so engrossed it's ridiculous.

'I'm stealing your bacon, Doc,' I tell the old fart to get his attention.

'Bacon has a 93 percent chance of causing bowel cancer,' he mutters, not even looking at me, just floating in a pussy-induced hypnosis.

I bite into the chewy ribbon of pink and brown fat.

'You'll be the one going up my ass to fix it if I do get bowel cancer. Actually, I almost forgot: we're a day closer to our date.'

'Oh,' say the college honeys, 'You're dating someone?'

'Doc's opening up my ass and putting a scalpel in there on Tuesday,' I go.

The girls bray laughter, spitting chewed-up eggs into the air. The doc's looking shellshocked.

'I'm just joshing. Had yourself a good time, didja?'

Doc bursts into tears and I stand up and chuck some cash on the table, ready to gap, when he reaches across and seizes my knuckles.

'I'm repaying this. Every expense you've entailed, Karl, all of this—the petrol, the beverages—it won't be forgotten.'

'I don't need your money, Doc –

'Supper—59 Kinnaird Place, Hillmorton. Sunday, 5 o'clock. You WILL come, won't you?'

The girls are eyeballing me. The doc looks like a little boy who's been told Christmas might be cancelled.

'Fine, okay. Whatever.'

*

Soon as I pull into the street a dog starts barking at me, like as if to say 'You don't belong here, bro.' I can't tell which house it's in because it's buried behind a tall fence of great wood. There are redwood and cherry trees, berms with no garbage on 'em, and none of the fences is made of that chainlink hurricane wire shit.

The doc's house at number 59 has a flag on a pole. I guess he's grateful the country treated him good. Him and every other upper class white motherfucker.

I open the little hip-high gate (the fuck's the point of having such a little-ass gate?) and shake out a cigarette then pause. There's a fountain chuckling, fairy lights glowing on the trellis, and God damn the roses are immaculate here. Red, orange, pink… I make a mental note to steal some and give 'em to Sofia. Or maybe Brittany. Hmm. Not wise to invest too much in a single woman.

I wander around on Doc's lawn for a minute smoking my cig until I step in the wrong part of the lawn and the security light hits me.

The front door opens. Inside is a woman in a dress and cardigan. She's so fat, she fills the doorway, edge to edge. Her hair is above her ears in some frilly arrangement I ain't seen in decades.

Behind her, peeping through a little gap between her fat, is Doc.

'*This* is him?' the wife asks.

Jesus fuck. Off to a bad start.

They beckon me in and I put my gift on the Downes family breakfast bar and shrug my windbreaker off. I've got my finest Adidas tracksuit on, the red and white striped one, Manchester United colors, plus my red Ferrari cap to match. My trainers are designed by Tesla. They cost 600 bucks.

'My wife's telling me I ought to offer you a drink,' Doc says, rolling his eyes. He's got black dress pants on and shiny black shoes. On top, a Pink Floyd *Dark Side of the Moon* t-shirt with a hole in it.

'You always do what your wife tells you?'

'Don't joke about that,' he whispers. 'Simply wearing this shirt is a privilege I don't want to lose.'

My gift thunks as I plonk it on the counter.

Doc cradles the wine bag with two hands like a newborn baby. 'I'm touched.'

'What did you say your name was again?'

I flinch. Filling up the doorway behind me the wife, Kath, has spooked the shit out of me. Since I done a stretch in jail it's been a rule of mine to never let people creep up behind, but god damn.

I tell her my name.

A young man puts his fingers on Kath-the-wife's shouders. Dude looks about my age, similar height, same fat-skinny body from living off fried food.

'And what do you do for a living?' Kath-the-wife goes.

'I'm in sales. You must be—'

'Richard Downes. Rich.' Doc's son steps forward. His arms are folded. His button-up shirt is tucked into his pants and there's a scarf around his neck even though we're indoors.

'We look about the same age. What school'd you go to? You look like a Hillmorton type. Something low decile, anyway.'

'Damn, dawg. Good guess. Yeah, Hellmortz.' Three Downes is more than I can take. The room is burning me. 'Ummm, so I brought you guys a bottle of kombucha infused with THC and hops. It's some seriously handcrafted shit. I get my mushrooms off these Swedish hippies and, you know... barter system and all that.'

They're all looking at each other. Finally the Doc comes round from behind the breakfast bar. Now it's us two against the rest of his family.

Doc puts a hand on my shoulder. 'Why don't we eat.'

First to come out is home baked bread, with butter, and drinks. Doc slaves over platters of lamb and potatoes. Kath-the-wife licks her lips and rubs her fingers watching her man work.

I take a bite and tell 'em it's fuckin divine. 'Y'all got sauce?'

'What for?' asks Good Boy Rich, who's cut his lamb into perfect cubes exactly one inch on all dimensions.

'Tomato sauce. For the meat.'

'This is top quality lamb. Grass-fed; 9 months old. Tomato sauce'll ruin it. Hey! Is he allowed to do that?'

I'm up out of my seat with my hands on the door of the fridge. I'm looking into Doc's eyes to see if he's got his balls in today. He does a single soft shake of his head and I leave the fridge and the sauce alone.

We crawl through the most awkward dinner in history. They all talk about Doc's failure and shortcomings and I can see the doctor has drowning eyes. Rich is a manager at the city council. He's in charge of 30 people and a budget of $100 million. He tells me all this shit, dropping in two, then three references to the Engineering Society before he finally goes, 'You weren't in EnSoc, I take it?'

'Bro, I skipped university. Got my education on the streets.'

Rich Downes looks at his dad—except I'm already looking at Doc, and so is Kath-the-fat-wife. Everybody wants a piece of him.

'Y'know medicine's a waste?' Rich says after Doc's cleared all our plates and started boiling some coffee that can't come fast enough. 'It used to be a prestigious thing, sure. Today though, you're a sucker if you're in healthcare. Slave hours, corporate bullying, governmental whims out to destroy doctors for political advantage, all sorts of immigrants chewing up healthcare services when real genuine citizens need it. If you ask me, doctors need more respect for themselves.'

'Well I got plenty of respect for doctors,' I say, shrugging, 'Specially this one.'

'He lacks confidence,' Kath-the-wife goes. 'Pass the gravy, would you, Robert. Come on. While we're young.'

'Nah, he confident as fuck. The Doc be down,' I tell the haters.

Everyone goes silent.

'What? You down, Doc.'

Dr. Downes looks miserable. He probably thinks I've outed him for being depressed.

'Like, y'know. You're down for partying. You cool. It's a compliment.'

Rich the son's squinting at his dad cause he knows I'll crack his jaw if he claps back at me. 'Why'd you even bring this guy around, dad?'

Doc Downes swallows and says, 'Well, it's…

Kath-the-whale takes a coffee out of Doc's hands. 'I assume you're working on having better relationships with patients and this'll be a weekly thing until this whole… investigation… is through.'

'Better relationships? Fuck happened, Doc?'

They're all pale and speechless.

'He has a disciplinary hearing next week,' the fat wife says, filling another plate with roast food.

'Does that sound like he's doing the right things, Karl, hm-mmm? Frankly, I think his chances are slim.'

'After you, ma'am, the doc might enjoy somethin slim for a change.'

The words have fallen out of my mouth and onto the table.

They're all speechless as I get up, say cheers for dinner, and let myself out.

*

It's a Friday night and I'm walking up and down the Strip while the sidewalk shakes. Cars are for people who WANT to sit back and let the cops jump them. Me, I walk up to my clients then I walk away. I got a little jail and some probation for some dirty deeds last year but I haven't had a straight-up drug bust.

The night goes fairly routine. Good vibes. Hardly any cops. I'm up four thousand bucks within an hour. Chilli dog, Jose Cuervo, Calendar Girls. Pills at Pzazz; speedballs at Soda Lounge. Bath salts at Bathory, the dizzying club built into a cathedral. I bump into sky-high Samoan soldier Tevita outside Oasis and he's shambling away in a hurry, limping on the right side.

'TEVITA! Slow ya roll, cuz! What up?'

Tevita's jumpy and flinchy. The collar wings on both sides of his neck are torn. He's missing a shoelace and there's a foot sticking out that looks like it's got gout. Even in our blacky-orange half light, I can tell it's sprained or broken.

'The fuck happened to you... I was gonna see if you wanted to catch up.'

Tevita gulps, looks flustered, casts his giant head side to side. He's about to hobble away without talking to me when he goes, 'Look, I don't want trouble. You're a troublemaker; not for me, thanks. G'night, bro. Don't follow me.'

'Troublemay—but Tevita, bro—'

'I'M NOT YOUR BRO.' He stabs my chest with a fingertip. 'Those fuckin Deliverance motherfuckers are lookin for you. Hayseed and Dixie. You ripped 'em off; they're lookin for a scrap. Guess they'll swing on all your friends. Busted my fuckin' ankle, those cunts. Three on one.'

As he jerks his head back, I notice he's had his bottom teeth smashed out. I'm about to apologize when he shakes his head like my dad disappointed in me and strides away.

'Karl!'

The doc falls out of a queue of people outside Fortitude and drapes his tentacles all over me.

'D'you know I love you, Karl? D'you actually realize that? It's oxytocin, that's what my thyroid's secreting right now but hey, listen—listen—shssshhh: I love you, Karl.'

'CALM THE FUCK DOWN, DOC, JESUS!' I peel him off me. 'I'm working a half shift tonight. It's not safe out. Fuck you doing in town, anyway? Is that... ' I pull apart the flaps of his shirt, which is black silk, tonight. On his knobbly chest he's had somebody etch in ink a snake circling that pole that shepherds use.

'Don't tell me you got a tattoo, Doc.'

'It's the staff of Asclepius. Got my nipples pierced, too. See?' Doc pulls his shirt off his head. A trio of girls wearing sashes reading Bride 2 B whoop as the Doc flings his shirt at them. They sniff it then the bride shoves the shirt down her top and everyone laughs till their faces glow.

We have another night of indulgence, though I do what I can to get Doc to go his own way. The night's chequered black and white—Doc'll blacken our night with some inappropriate shit, like talking about how he can't make love to his wife and how the disciplinary tribunal is hauling him over the coals to set an example, and how his son called him a failure and forgot his birthday and how he's in trouble for trying to force a mum to vaccinate her kids. Between his whiny, open-handed pleading and laments about how his father always told him he wasn't competent to practice medicine, we have a laugh dancing with a pair of gay models, sink tequila shots and pash some seriously young girls who don't look 18.

We dip into the Asian spa pit and get a rub down and the dirty Thai girls finish me off while the Doc seals thighs and clutches his knees and begs the girl to stop trying to masturbate him. I whip out my phone and grab a video just as Doc rolls off the massage table and lands on the floor. The old man insists he's fine but he's given me a heart attack, the prick.

We still have some horniness in us so we hit Loco Parentis. The dancefloor is so thick we have to turn side-on and slide our way through the crowd, sucking in our bellies, pointing our slicing hands towards an empty square metre where we can dance. Doc has this little Filipino looking chick grinding against him and he's showing her his tattoo when another guy grabs her hips and tries to waddle away with her while grinding her ass. I grab the prick by his sticky gelled hair and I'm about to ram his face down into my knee when the interloper whirls around and it's a student overachiever, a preppy guido painted tan same size as me.

Rich Downes. Manager by day of 30 corporate clones.

He's stunned to see his father in the club, and me? I'm stunned the bouncers are wrapping their arms around me and yanking the backpack off my shoulders while I shriek no and claw towards my baby and beg them not to take her.

A bouncer tears off the tiny padlock (stupid, STUPID) and begins reaching inside my backpack, pulling out a fistful of cash.

'Stop, stop, it's mine!' Doc shrieks. Valiant, sure, cheers Doc, but stupid. The bouncer grabs us both by the wrist and pulls us towards the door where four more security pin us against the wall. The police are waiting outside. I'm thrown into a van and driven to the police station.

Before I can even tell him in a holding cell that I'm sorry, they drag Doc around a corner and I'm reaching out towards him and he's cooing 'Well now, this is something different'—giggly, giddy, excited.

I'm put in a cell, alone for the first ten minutes before the door is opened. Three massive white boys with beards and bellies and bloody knuckles saunter in, too large for the cops to shove them.

They have purple splotches on their blue jeans. The splotches were red just 30 minutes ago, I'll bet. Red from holding the bouncers in headlocks and kneeing them in the mouth.

The door closes behind them. They crick their knuckles, slap me off the steel bench with a backhand and begin stomping.

*

At the end of a black corridor there's a square of yellow in a door. This is meeting room 5. A sad little room buried under a twenty storey high hospital tower. Basement level 1. No daylight reaches down here.

I rock up to the door and put my hand on the 1950s style painted wood (fuck this place is old fashioned) and I have my hand pushing but I only get it open a crack before I freeze. I can see a sliver of the hearing. There's a panel of three doctors with their backs against the window and a pull-up banner with that, fuckin', what do you call it—the snake curling round the popsicle. Exodus or Asclepius or whatever. Doc Downes is on the far side of their big curvy desk. He has to stand with his hands and notes on a little lectern.

I take a gulp, nudge the door open just enough to slide my body in the crack.

The Health Practitioners Disciplinary Tribunal is fronted by an unimpressed-looking Chinese man with a black beard and droopy jowls. He wears a blue suit with a pink tie and has a name triangle saying Sir Selby Chan, MD. On one side of him is an Indian woman with a stick up her ass. On the other is a young white goody-good who looks like he probably doesn't make it to the other side of the street unless there's a zebra crossing. There is a projector screen in the corner. The humming projector fastened to the ceiling beams a picture of six other cunts in a meeting room. All judging the fate of my friend.

A sexy, mousy little secretary comes over. I get a decent look at her tits as she crouches and adjusts her white shirt and short grey skirt.

'Hi! You're here for the disciplinary tribunal yeah? You'll need one of these. He's almost done.'

'Done?' I whisper, 'What do you mean he's done?'

'His time's almost up.'

She hands me some paper listing the charge against the doc. It says the location of this place, and the day is today and the time now. The charge is listed as, 'One charge of negligence resulting in professional misconduct and likely to bring discredit to the profession for prescribing paracetamol to a patient found by a review committee to be in need of dihydrocodeine.'

'Doctor Downes,' interrupts the Tribunal chair while Doc is turning over pages and muttering some lame defence.

'As we've heard this morning, the complaint alleged you refused to engage with the patient when he requested a prescription of painkillers. The complainant has told us he asked for what he called DHC and you snorted and responded, "What you need is Weight Watchers, my friend." The patient was deeply upset by this and endured a week of pain and discomfort. You've told us this morning you're not sorry for your actions and that you would do it again in a heartbeat, to quote.'

'Those are my words, yes.'

'And you are aware that without a valid reason to refer the patient to secondary care or another primary care physician, you don't have a choice but to treat the patient,' Sir Selby Chan goes. 'Every citizen has the right to be seen by a public health professional. It's Article Two of the Code of Rights for Health and Disability Services Consumers. Do I need to read the code out to you or can you repeat it back—knowledge of the Code being condition 4.1 of your licence to practice medicine.'

Everyone's silent.

'You'll tell me articles four to six of the Code of Rights or I'll have your registration cancelled by lunchtime, Dr. Downes.'

Doc's about to crumble. He looks over at the two meagre rows of spectators. There's Kath The Fat Wife wiping her eyes with tissues, and his son Rich texting someone and jiggling one Hush Puppy as it dangles off his toes.

'Very well,' the Doc begins. 'Article Four: You must be treated with reasonable care and skill and receive well-coordinated services. Five: Service providers must listen to you and give you clear information that you can understand. If you don't understand, you must feel comfortable about asking questions. Six: Your treatment must be fully explained to you, including the benefits, risks, alternatives, and costs, and your questions must be answered honestly. Seven: You must be able to make your own decisions about your treatment, and be free to change your mind. There. I give up. I'm broken, now. I'm a broken man.'

The Indian grump goes, 'Any other submissions we've over looked?'

Doc's looking over at his lawyer, who's busy typing something on a tiny laptop the size of a novel.

'Doctor Downes,' Sir Selby Chan says, rising from his chair and cricking his joints as he stretches. 'You DO want to continue practicing medicine, do you not?"

The doc looks to me for an answer.

'You're receiving a written warning. Next time a patient asks you for a prescription and you're tempted to decline, do get a second opinion. Case concluded.'

'This is bullshit,' says the complainant, over in the corner... the complainant Darrell—nooooo.

Darrell the Barrel. A whole chorus of bumpkins mutters the same complaints. Fuuuuckin' Bumpkin Brothers. I should've seen it coming. The big barrel-bellied buttheads are mad because the doc wouldn't prescribe them heavy drugs.

They get up and shove the pews aside so they can squeeze their fat asses out of the room.

Wincing, hobbling, I pray they don't spot my crippled ass.

The Board of Review asks me if I'm a patient come to see the doctor punished, or a friend.

I'm speechless, I don't want to embarrass the doc, before the doc blurts 'He's my friend.'

*

I can't help stroking the furry leaves of his plant, nodding at the walls, muttering, 'Okay, okay.' On the yellow-painted walls of the room inside this villa are posters for Asia and Rush and Pink Floyd and Genesis. There are a couple of barbells on the floor, and empty boxes of KFC and soft drinks and lollies, plus some fruit flies. This is a chilled-out doctor who set up in this sweet-as villa a couple weeks ago as a private medical practitioner and doesn't have to be force-fed shitty patients by the government. Nah, this doctor ankled all that. A chilled-out doctor in sandals. Not like that bundle of live wires I used to have.

'So I've just enrolled to study counselling and social work,' I tell today's doctor. 'You probably didn't know I'm all about that shit. But I care about people. It's true.'

'Show me your ankle.'

The doctor today is full of energy. The doctor takes my ankle, bends it right, then left, then stands up and puts pressure top-down on the tendon. The doctor is watching my eyes. I've had guns pointed at me in the past. Not much makes me flinch, especially not this marginal pain.

'It's healing well. You must be looking after yourself.'

I peel my lips back to let a grin out. My right front tooth is a jagged shard. The bottom four are completely gone and I tongue it when I'm nervous—when there's an exam or an appraisal.

'Kind-of, I guess. I walk places. I took the bus here today. Sold my Mustang. It was costing me like two thousand a month anyway.'

'I can check your ribs. Stand up. Take your shirt off, if you wouldn't mind. Put your hands on the wall.'

I do the whole lineup turnaround pat-down thing, hands on the wall, butt out.

The doctor's fingers probe between the white zebra stripes of my ribs.

The doctor checks the effects of my beating one by one. Yes, I do have a sprained rib that was bent so badly it nearly snapped, but the pain's not acute anymore. It's a dull tickle, and only when a doctor puts their fingers on it. The doc prints out a prescription for penicillin for the scrapes on my knuckles which ooze mint green pus.

My teeth won't grow back. That's something I have to get used to.

'Anything else?' the doc asks, printing out a receipt with the bill.

I don't want to get out of the chair. I make a big show of stretching and pretending to wince about my fucked-up ankle and ribs. Truth is, when the Bumpkin Boys were stomping me, I rolled across the concrete right then left, north then south, so only one in four hits connected properly. The boys got tired dishing out the beating and sat down on the bench panting, the unfit fucks. Me, I hugged my knees in the corner, waiting for bail.

'You have your antibiotic; the teeth we've talked out. And I have Quitline organized to ring you once a day while you're weaning off the cigarettes. I have a cure to keep you in perfect health, if you'll hear me out.'

I've got time. I put one hand on the door handle and tell the doc to go ahead.

'You want to be in perfect health, you need to get out of your line of work entirely.'

'I am out, Doc. I'm studying. I told you that.'

'Then what's that on your back?'

Damn it. Cringe. I unsling the backpack, dangle it over the seat.

'I got a student loan to pay off, bro. Come on. Lighten up.'

'It's not good for you. Is it. That lifestyle. You could die on the job. You almost did.'

'So can you, man. Don't old white people get, like, heart attacks and shit, from stress. Hypertension. Bro, I saw on the fuckin' breakfast news: Loneliness is now the number one leading cause of death.'

'Well I changed all that. I got out. I healed myself.'

'Bro, listen, the point is I need start-up cash so I don't get crushed by a student loan. You wanna pay my student loan, huh?' I shake my sack of valuables. 'I can't afford *not* to move this product.'

This doctor in front of me is completely different to the doctor I had a month ago. Relaxed, confident, unafraid to say what needs to be said.

'And you need a little cash for it all to pay your student loan.'

'Zacly.'

'What's in the bag, anyway?'

'A good time. A party. And plenty profit if you know how to deal.'

I have the door open now and I'm just about to slink out. There isn't even a reception here, just an unattended TV and some bean bags.

The doc's question stops me in the hall. He's interested.

'What price might we be talking?'

THE FLEMISH BOND

My flight from Christchurch up to Auckland is supposed to land at 3 pm but delays push it back to 4, then 4:30, and by the time I'm squeezing into the back of this Uber fella's souped-up boyish Honda outside the terminal, I'm seriously watching the clock.

If I don't get up to Warkworth for the show at 7:30, I don't get paid. It's that simple.

I chuck my overnight bag in the boot, not that I'm even staying the night. We have to get out of Auckland Airport and into mainstream traffic by 4:35. I want to yell at Uberman here: you could've squeezed into that gap there behind the tanker, or that gap, or that one. It's a roundabout, man: just go for it. I drum my thick blunt fighting fingers impatiently on the glass. Hopefully he'll take note of my scarred knuckles, my thick arms. These hands get results– so you need to hurry your arse.

Uberman gets the car a few hundred metres along but it's slow as fuck and every car seems welded together into a train. No gaps. We're dealing with Friday afternoon traffic here— every cunt in Auckland's on the motorway heading to their fancy bach. We can expect this one hour drive to take two and a half.

Air New Zealand made me late, the incompetent wankers. Story of my life, honestly: people taking what they want from me.

The deal is I'm expected at the Warkworth Masonic Community Hall for 7 o'clock. 7:15 is juuuust doable; 7:30 is when the actual bell rings for my wrestle. If I miss the bell, I'm in breach of contract, which means no pay, which means I've paid for a flight for nothing, which means I'll miss my credit card repayments, my rent, my child support. My car could get repo'd. Everything will fail.

We finally screech into a space and point north and I relax a fraction and get a chance to study my driver: Hawaiian shirt, gelled black hair, messy black goatee, Jesus on the dash, rasta air freshener hanging from the rearview in the shape of a weed leaf. He's my age, more or less. His biceps are interesting. Bit of muscle on him.

'Vili,' he goes, offering me an upside-down handshake over his shoulder as he changes lanes.

'Tone.'

The fella looks Tongan, I reckon, and I'm about to strike up a little small talk about Tonga's chances in the World Cup when the driver goes, 'You're Tony Timaru of the Timaru Two, right?'

'Just the Timaru One these days. My partner got himself a house and a spouse. Shoulda followed suit, really.' I snort. 'God knows why I chose to fight for a living. Cheers for noticing, though.'

'I know my fighters.' His eyes in the rearview are serious. Unlaughing. Some kind of stalker. Great.

My driver suddenly overtakes a BMW and we start leaving hotels behind us. He's 20 kays an hour over the speed limit but it feels good to dodge the traffic.

My fight is strictly 7:35 to 8:05pm. After that the Warkworth Community Hall is being used by the country music club at 8:30. I'll need a ride back to the airport to fly home to Christchurch at 9:50 pm because the $110 flight is cheaper than paying for a meal and a mattress in Auckland. Wrestling, kickboxing, Muay Thai, bareknuckle, MMA—none of the disciplines pay much so I have to haggle to find a taxi driver who'll do the drive cheap and fast to cut down my costs. Being a journeyman sucks.

Auckland is oozing by my window now at a good pace. The driver tells me he's taking the route past Middlemore. He's gonna connect with Highway One then we'll be sorted. I relax one percentage point but I can't trust this motherfucker completely. I learned a long time ago never to let your guard down even when a man seems solid.

'You said you know your fighters?'

'Hard. MMA, UFC, bareknuckle, Golden Gloves. I keep up. This fight tonight's AAWA, right?'

'Aotearoa Amateur Wrestling Association indeed. These jokers are a lot less prestigious than they act, I gotta tell ya. Bastards wouldn't shout me a flexi ticket for the plane.'

Vili flits between lanes then zooms up an onramp and settles in the centre of the motorway where the flow's pretty good. I look at the cars on either side to gauge whether we're slipping. I notice us lose a couple places when Vili veers left, races up then veers right again.

Vili stares at the car in front's bumper, deadly serious. 'It's all bullshit, behind the glam. Oi: you see this right here?'

We're passing a new housing development called Mangrove Waters that doesn't seem to end. Linked by new black asphalt are all these McMansions held up by pillars rising up from freshly-poured concrete sitting in brown dirt with sprouts of grass. At the end of the subdivision is a brick house on a tiny paddock with a dozen cows. It's completely circled by new roads.

I don't know why the driver's singled out some standard brick build.

'Typical Dorkland expansion?'

'Nah, G,' my driver tells me, 'Brick, bro, brick. Built to last. And you know how come? No plaster, no steel– '

'Flemish bond.'

'Damn, Tone,' he says from the front. 'How'd you know about the Flemish Bond?'

'You lay the bricks, fuck, what's the word... perpendicular. Looks like they're goin different directions but they hold together better than anything.'

Vili the driver gives me deep eye contact in the rearview. 'My man. You lay bricks?'

'When I was a kid, a bit, yeah. Couple of my stepdads were bricklayers. Made sense to go to work with them after I dropped outta school. Guess Mum had a type.'

Driver Vili is nodding deep and long and slow. He cuts to the right, across two lanes. I watch the needle creep up and hit 140. I don't care if we die. My life started off shit; let it have a symmetrical end.

'You got the government tryina vaccinate little kids, you got homos gettin married: while the rest of society crumbles, decent masonry holds tight, my brother. I wish more people appreciated it.'

My driver is positively grinning into the mirror now. He thinks he's found a friend.

'One brick watches the other brick's back,' he continues. 'That's why it's strong. Get a brick on its own, it can be susceptible. But two united, nothing can hurt it.'

'You married, Vili?'

'Nah. You?'

'Used to be. I was an arsehole to live with.'

'I'd live with you, bro. Watch fights on YouTube all day, am I right?!'

He's getting a little serial killer-y for me now. Vili punches the dashboard, steps harder on the gas. I study the fascinating billboards we don't have down south. Wendy's, St. Pierre's Sushi, Rainbow's End... .

'Bro, layin bricks was meeeean money when I was tryina get out of the hood. Wasn't much else work in Aranui, eh.'

'Aranui? Mate, I went to Hornby High. I'm old school Christchurch too.'

'So you're a westside whiteboy eh? East Side Bloods over here.'

He passes his hand over his shoulder again for a fist bump while he holds the wheel with his pinky finger.

We blaze past a city-sized shopping mall called Sylvia Park, then a bend in the road where there's a Tip Top ice cream factory, then a Mercedes dealership and a gigantic church and this smokestack billowing melted Pink Batts, then my driver's pointing out brick buildings left right and centre as we put Newmarket behind us.

He won't stop running his mouth, this guy. Tells me his whole life story—after his old man got shot by the Harris Gang he tried to find an alternative dad in church elders, Scout masters and rugby coaches before settling on boxing pretty much because he wanted to punch people constantly from the age of 14.

It's gotten a fraction colder in the car. I put my bag on my lap for warmth. We're in a tangle of curled concrete bridges now. Traffic is bunching up and the Sky Tower appears between buildings. My driver looks for a different lane but everything's slowing.

'FUCKIN' SPAGHETTI FUCKIN' JUNCTION.' He thumps his door.

'So you like to get some punches in,' I chuckle, 'I used to box at Dutchy's in Cashmere, dunno if you know the place.'

Vili hauls the steering wheel left and settles in a nicely-flowing rapid. He's got an anger management problem but my man knows how to hack traffic. My phone tells me it's now 5:05. We might actually make the venue on time.

'I was a Dutchy's boy myself,' Vili mumbles. 'Don't recall seeing your photo on the wall.'

'I don't let anyone take my picture less it's marketing shit. How old are you? Maybe we were a couple years apart.'

He tells me he's 34; I tell him I'm 37. *About 17 years too old to be fake-fighting for minimum wage*, I want to add. *Couldn't stick with boxing though, not after what happened.*

We reach the top of the Harbour Bridge. Halfway. I've got white noise in my ears.

I've hardly thought about Dutchy's Boxing Gym in ages. When I was 18, 19, I doused my brain with so much weed and crack and bourbon my memories of Dutchy's got pushed wayyyyy down. I found myself smashing people on Colombo Street, jumping on the bonnet of some cop car in Cashel Mall. Can't even remember how half the fights started.

Dutchy's was so refreshing at first. We used to have Fight Club at school with a few uppercuts and kinghits but Dutchy's was a hundred times more disciplined. My mum drove me there one afternoon just before dinner time cause her boy-friend had pinched my ear and I'd busted his nose and my mum was shrieking if I wanted to fight so bad I could at least get some exercise while doing it.

She dumped me on old Coach Dutchy's driveway. Coach Dutchy came out in his white singlet and flip flops. Springy curly white chest hair stuck out around his tits. His eyes were 100 percent on me. Didn't ask to meet my mum or anything. No fees, no paperwork, no names, no nothing—just shoved these sweaty, manky leather gloves in my arms, tossed a roll of cotton bandage on top and told me to glove up and get in the ring. We'd sort out money later. He didn't have a wife or kids anymore; we didn't have dads.

The boys at the gym were skinheads, Crips, gingers, Māo-ris—the only thing we had in common was Dutchy was like a father, punishing our arses, making us soldiers. We had to do sit-ups while he dropped heavy leather balls on our stomachs. He made us skip for 10, 15, sometimes 20 minutes. He blasted these corny Irish resistance songs with violins and big rousing choruses and cause Coach's ears were warped and puffy like fungus he wouldn't hear his shitty 1980s CD player skipping and all us boys would be haemorrhaging sweat, looking for sympathy from the photos of shirtless graduates smiling on the wall, praying for the skipping and the CD to end so we could snatch a quick sip of soothing water.

When we got in the fuckin ring though, by God: we had incredible leg work from all the skipping. Plus the combos he'd force us to practice a hundred times paid off. I was shit-scared going to my first Golden Gloves but a 1-6-3-2 combo won me my very first fight. My mum was at the casino and didn't see it but the boys were all hugging me and shit. It was all thanks to the fitness—Dutchy's people had gone through famine around the Second World War and he was obsessed with self-denial. Pain makes you strong, he'd tell us. The first dude I fought saw right from the ding of the first bell I was in for a long, hard dance instead of a quick knockout. I made him drain himself chasing me round the ring till he let his guard down then I pummelled the cunt and got me a medal.

I started to love Dutchy's after that. He offered three sessions every week and I took them all up. Other fights in life had brought me only trouble but Dutchy's was a place to turn your anger into gold. Every dude that turned up for training was from a different clique but we all bowed down to the god of discipline.

That discipline took a lot of forms not even related to boxing. We weren't allowed to smoke or drink or eat pizza. He'd use forceps on your stomach. He whipped you with a skipping rope if you had any fat on you. If we wanted an energy snack it had to be sunflower seeds. Some days there was zero boxing and Dutchy had us laying bricks. We built something called a heat wall where the bricks face north to catch the sun so Ol' Dutch could grow kumara around his house, which was on the same section as the gym. And he was proud, don't get me wrong. For a few minutes a week he'd be all mushy, nuzzling your hair and telling you he loved you. Then he'd whack you in the guts for not standing up straight.

I boxed all through 14, 15, 16. At 17 I was still going hard. Partly I was waiting for a chance to earn a one-on-one session with Dutchy on some rainy Friday night when he'd get all fatherly, dust off the camera and take a photo for the Wall of Fame. Dutchy didn't give all the boys the honor of being photographed with their medals dangling between their pecs. His head was as banged-up as his ears and he'd go months forgetting to take a new photo before quietly leading a boy aside to arrange a photo sesh. *Kom met mee, jongen,* he'd always go. A few days later there'd be a picture of a boy on the wall, freckled with sweat, neck flared, chin upthrust. The heroes. The favorites. I woulda given anything to have my picture on that wall.

One night we witnessed Coach Dutchy face down a whole carload of Road Knights out in the blue and orange woodsmoke of a Christchurch winter night. The gangsters were calling out little Hori for a one-out and our coach, bro, he mighta had vegetables in his head but he knew how to win a scrap, woo whee. It was obvious Hori wasn't being called for an actual one-out—a buncha bearded 40 year olds were planning to stomp his face into the gravel. Dutchy went over to the car, cocked his finger like a gun, pointed at the passenger then each of the two goons in the back of the Holden and shouted, 'YOU FIRST, THEN YOU, THEN YOU, JA, COME OOOOOOOOOOON.'

The little toerag prospect calling out Hori got the fuck back in the car reeeeal quick and disappeared. Dutchy hadn't even thrown a single punch.

That was one of my last memories of Dutchy, actually. I dropped out of the gym not long after then.

'Dutchy died real sudden, eh.'

'That he did,' Vili says.

God, I've drifted off. We've moved up the map. We're passing a huge glittery spire sticking up out of Takapuna. The motorway is wide and generous. Saints be praised, we may just make it to Warkworth on time.

I'm about to ask what happened to the gym, how long it kept going after I dropped out, when Vili goes, 'How much you weighing these days?'

'Eighty. Reeeeal good fighting weight. Lets you be nimble if you keep yourself at 80 kilos. You?'

We're passing a KFC beside something called North Shore Stadium. God I could go for some fried chicken. I hate having to stay paleo.

'Me, I don't weigh myself any more,' Vili goes, swearing at a Mini as he moves around it. In the mirror I notice Vili gritting his teeth. He's pissed about something.

I'm getting a flashback of when Coach Dutchy used to weigh us boys. Dutch started doing weigh-ins at 7 am. The gym was always cold, nobody moving, nobody speaking. Hardly anyone showed up to the before-school sessions, actually. I would've appreciated some of that Irish music but the first half of the day was just warming the air up. Wiping the dribble off the windows. Dutchy'd told me we were here to scrub the gym clean. After I'd mopped and hung the knuckle-bandages on the clothesline to dry he had me strip naked and stand on the scales. Coach Dutchy then asked me, 'Do you think you are weighing more if you are having a piece of wood on you, yes?'

'What wood?'

Dutchy reached between my legs. I froze. Dutchy peeled the foreskin off my diddle and started stroking it. He was close enough a few of his chest hairs tickled my arm. I felt static electricity. He got down on his knees and put his crusty lips on my cock and moved his tongue and his gums. Then he pulled his mouth off and told me to jack myself til I got a "schtiff-cock." I said I was scared.

'Son, I will knock you out lickety split. You are doing what I am tellingk you, ja?'

I did what he said. I could've smashed just about any cunt in Christchurch back then. Anyone except Dutchy.

*

The car is silent as we put Auckland behind us. We gobble up farmland with mist settling on it like bedsheets. Overpasses, roadside turkeys, sheep, Snowplanet, Silverdale. I grab the headrest of the passenger seat that's in front of me and crush it, fingers digging into the foam. Maybe I'll dig out an eyeball in my fight tonight. I'm pissed about everything. These McMansions we're hooning past? Fuck those people. Fuck their luck. They never got pulled out of the mainstream for a private photo session. All them homeowners in Millwater, Auckland's most expensive development, all them cunts had daddies and mummies to hand them a fuckin' chequebook and say *Here ya go, son. Take as much support as ya want. It's bottomless.*

Me? My life is layin' bricks and takin' hits. I can't get a straighto job. I've got convictions for, God, you name it, GBH, assaulting a female, assault with a blunt instrument, armed robbery, drug utensils, you name it. Put your body on the line for a dime. This fuckin' world didn't give me many alternatives.

As we come up to some tunnel near Puhoi, we pass under a bank of cameras.

'What's with all the photos?'

'They snag your licence plate. Government's always watching citizens, bro.'

'I fuckin' hate being photographed. Dutch, the bastard, he took.... Never mind.'

I don't say anything while we're in the tunnel. We emerge and race past the Puhoi turnoff. There's a billboard saying you can get oysters and chips for ten bucks. I could use a feed. No time tonight, though. Pay the driver, fight, get dressed after, scoff some sunflower seeds, hop a taxi to Auckland Airport.

Catch the late flight back down south. Eat white bread and margarine to balance the books. Keep my phone in hand til the next gig lands.

'He took photos of you, I'm guessing,' Vili the Uber Driver goes, 'Said he was weighing you then started taking your photo and shit?'

'Mind your business.'

A sign says Warkworth is 35 kays away. The time is 6:49 and the sky is indigo. *Hurry, driver, hurry.*

'I quit the gym, god, 2003-ish,' Vili goes.

'Good for you.'

'Lemme finish.' He's looking at me hard in the rearview now. Can't be long til we hit Warkworth. May as well hear the weirdo out. Dude seems to think we're some kind of equals.

'So I dropped out of my apprenticeship. Drinking, burgs, fuckin' gangs, Tone. That was the life. Anyway one night I got really wasted on BZP. Member that shit? That was just after the 90s, cuz. I used to pushbike everywhere back then, I didn't give a fuck, and if my bike got nicked I'd just boost another one. Anyway I wound up at Dutchy's house when I was real baked. This was like four months after I'd stopped showing up to training cause Dutchy'd taken those bloody photos of me, on the scales of course, butt naked, as ya do—and he tried the old "got wood" trick on me too, the unoriginal cunt—so anyway, it's summer when I bike round for a catch up, I'll never forget that. Cicadas in ya fuckin' ears. Bugs crawling on the light on his porch. And I'm high as a kite, right, and I pedal from Aranui all the way to Cashmere on autopilot. It was 8 o'clock on a Saturday night, I remember cause they were drawing the Lotto and one of my aunties had my birthday as her numbers. But you don't wanna... ah, sorry man. I shouldn't've... never mind.'

'Bro: finish.'

Vili matches my eyes in the mirror. I can feel the car slowing slightly. This better be good.

'Anyway I bang on his door and Dutchy's real happy to invite us into his warm lounge, even though I'm looking rough as guts. I've got an NBA singlet on and gumboots. Dutchy lays two cocktails on the coffee table and sits beside me on the couch zif we're on a date. The movie was *E.T.*, I'll never forget that. Classic Saturday night family shit in front of a roaring fire, nice drink, everything's happy endings.'

A sign says Warkworth is five kilometres away now. The clock has just spilled past seven. We're going to make this.

'God knows why but Dutchy got a stiff from *E.T.* He was real engrossed in the movie, the fucking paedo, and it was only when the ads came on he put his hand on the back of my head and kinda nudged my face down towards his cock. I whacked him with a left hook to the jaw, of course, all while sitting down. He was stunned, right, sitting there in his old man robe. I didn't wanna get a hiding so I put the cunt in a sleeper hold. Lights out, old man. Then I kneeled on his shoulders and held a cushion on his face. Musta choked him for a good ten minutes, eh. Made it look like a accident. Then I went through this box under Coach's bed and I found all photos of diddles and boys crying and standing on the scales naked and shit. Burned those fuckin' photos in his fireplace, eh. Oi: here's Warkworth. We did it.'

We bend through a couple streets and find a parking lot. The Warkworth Masonic Community Hall is a brick building beside a low muddy river. Palm trees and wrought iron lamps and paving stones. Cars everywhere. Bass and treble and voices on the breeze.

'I'm a good guy,' I tell my driver, 'A babyface. Just so you know. In the ring, I mean. Not one of the bad ones.'

I pay my driver, pull my gear from the trunk and head for the green room. 7:13pm. A respectable time, all things considered.

'I'll find a taxi back,' I tell Vili as I slam shut the trunk of his car and prepare to go put my body on the line. 'I don't expect you to wait for me, man. Laters.'

The small crowd cheer and whistle as I stride through them. Amateur wrestling brings joy and escapism to their lives. I realize that now. I replay a charade I've done over and over—Tony Timaru the superhero. People rip my epaulettes off, firstly, then the cuffs of my shirt, then some of my buttons. Souvenirs. People have always taken a piece of me.

The Beehive is a heel in a beekeeper suit whose signature move is The Sting. Backstage we plan our battle, synchronizing a couple of choke slams then go out and smash each other round the ring for half an hour. After our fight, everyone poses for photos with me. I escape after four minutes, sweaty, struggling to breathe. I've knocked fans unconscious in the past. I can't always control my fists when I get anxious.

In the parking lot beside the salty river, a shitty Uber is waiting for me. An elbow is pointing out of the driver side window. The radio is playing Bob Marley. Vili is giving the Eastside with his fingers and grinning, waiting to take me home. This hall is built of 120 mil bricks. I knock on the masonry and wink at him. Call it shitty, call it shabby, but the Warkworth Masonic Community Hall has stood since 1895 cause nothing can bring down the Flemish Bond.

SILENT RETREAT

Me and Mickey are under the moon in the freezing mountains above Delhi, awaiting permission to enter ten days of silent retreat in a golden temple. The silent running-away thing is just in time, honestly, 'cause if I don't find shelter I'm going to scream.

Standing on tired legs in a queue of shivering backpackers watching the vultures and the squirrels, I squeeze my fiancé's hand. Mickey, the big lanky wildman with his dirty mullet, ignores me as he chews, bouncing his big shoulders, fidgeting, wishing he had a bump of coke or a piece of ass. He's in a singlet; I'm the only one who researched the weather up here and brought Merino and Gore-Tex clothes. I lean into him to share my warmth, stamping my feet, puffing into my palms. My head tucks into his armpit. He rubs my scalp then pushes me away. I need my man 'cause I'm super-vulnerable right now. I should be with my Mumsy but she's two and a half continents away. I Skyped Mumsy a week ago and she told me she'd been given one month to live. She reached through the webcam to stroke my fringe away from my eyes and my face melted cause she told me FLIPPING LYMPHOCYTES are making my precious Mumsy's flipping BLOOD dissolve into runny clear pus, totally degrading my mother, all this while me and Mick are having the time of our lives, romping around Asia.

Unfair doesn't even begin to describe it. *GOD.* My Mumsy is a saint. She captures spiders with a tumbler and a piece of paper and shakes them out the window. My Mumsy puts music on for pot plants. She's been a primary school teacher for 39 years, on her feet for 6 hours a day, she's only just got her pension and you know what that jerk in the sky gifts her? Leukaemia. No words in the universe can express my frustration so here we are, beginning ten days of vipassana so I can at least learn to control my feelings.

Dhamma Salila Vipassana Centre of Light is a group of concrete huts painted gold with a quiff of snow piled on the some of the domes. It's a 10 kay trek north of Shivpuri, this cluster of huts on a cliff over the coldest, northern-est gorges of the Ganges. Uttarakhand is this state held up on the cold shoulders of mountains north of Delhi. The Beatles hung out here, apparently. Did they last ten days? Me and Mick have to last ten, though I'm not sure if this induction counts as a day, since it's 6 o'clock in the morning. It's actually rather important to have control over precisely when this experience will conclude as I'm expected to telephone Mumsy in Bolton as soon as I return to civilisation, and I would return a lot sooner if these silly volunteer henchmen guarding the door would let us get on with it. The sahayaks, as the volunteers are called, are half a dozen pimply Indian young men in button-up shirts. They take their job way too serious. They roam the line, reminding people in accented English that this is a non-denominational centre. Religious symbols must be put away. I see a Malaysian-looking girl unfasten her headscarf and fold it up. Some Sikh guys shake their heads and trudge back down the driveway. My silver cross necklace goes in my pocket.

Keeping 100 French and Germans and Japanese standing still on stone steps with heavy luggage while the sun rises over the Garhwals is part of the vipassana spiritual journey, apparently. It's all emotional highs and lows until we get to ask a question on the second to last day and get a profound answer. Maybe I'll ask if these sahayak wankers get off on torturing Westerners. Mickey's stamping his feet to some private rhythm, looking around for some action, his huge shaggy head towering over everyone. Our whole OE, our whole trip around the world, it's been one big party to Mickey. Cape Town, Patagonia, Rotorua... we've worked in orphanages, ranches, organic farms and offices, hopping from visa to visa. Mickey guzzled and snorted our wages, spent thousands on football bets, Champion's League tickets, gifts for his female "friends," some of whom felt obliged to hit on him right in front of me. Urgh. I brought in most of the money. Sometimes we were students, sometimes apple pickers; a couple times I was an au pair. Mickey got us deported out of Monaco for weeing in the street and filming the snake of urine wriggling downhill, *Go piss, go!* I told him he was a foolish child. He got in a tizzy and embarked on Operation Globetrotter, having little affairs in four or five countries, four or five jobs, Sri Lanka, Agra, Nepal, and now we're here, we're engaged to be married a month from now once our troubles are behind us and, hurrah, the line is finally moving, shuffling away from the sucky world outside, away from all the friends criticizing me over Facebook for sticking with Mickey. Away from my Mumsy's limp voice and wet cough and letters that smell like her.

We file inside a concrete temple painted white and decorated with pollen, bunting, prayer flags, pink and gold paint. A cow watches us enter, chewing a stick. We settle on a floor of flagstones polished smooth from a hundred thousand bums. We face the front like kindergarteners, adjusting our spines. One Norwegian-looking girl, a metre away from me, has hair as bright as a lightbulb and sharp breasts. Mickey shunts his bum away from me and whispers something to Miss Pointytits and I'm about to break my silence to interject when our guru-ji shambles out of some side-passage and hauls himself atop a cushion on top of a barrel. He is a little Indian man with a black afro scorched white. He wears a three-piece suit wide around the shoulders. The cuffs of the suitjacket are too long, but he's by far the neatest-dressed here. I spy the gold links of a pocket chain. He also has gold circlets around his long white wizard-beard, and gold rings on his fingers. Jeepers. Considering all the gold our money is sponsoring, there'd better be a good breakthrough at the end of this thing.

Parking themselves in positions around the hall, guru-ji's *sahayak*-helpers drizzle their hands downwards and give us the SHHHHHH gesture, though they make zero sound. The rules we've agreed to are no talking, no mime, no sign language. No reading, no writing, no texting.

Our guru-ji launches into a monologue, rubbing his heart and smiling. He has a poster of himself behind him, explaining his name: G. G. Nirmal, *Escort To Peace*. I'm amazed the people down the back can hear his subtle, moist voice, the clacking tongue, the tiny emphasis on every fourth word. He's telling us to scan our bodies to identify what pain we're going to address over the next ten days. I'm tuned to Mickey more than myself because Mickey's pulled his big sweaty brown bear-paw off my buttermilk hand and he's leaning towards the Nordic-looking woman. About to stray again, the bugger. We went to Antarctica on this protest boat and he managed to pull this girl from flipping Korea who didn't even speak flipping English. Mickey's always been my rock, though. I used to be fat; he gave me a chance to improve myself. I still have my stretch marks. I'll forgive him a thousand times.

I try to listen to the front, get my two thousand Euros' worth. I paid for Mickey to attend; he really ought to get his money's worth too. It's not as if our relationship will automatically heal and this is some hotel: we have to sleep in separate male/female dorms. I need to let him go for the next week and a half. He'll come back a better man, surely.

It's agony, at first, listening, straining, feeling the sulphur in my throat, stinky hungry breath, sore vulva, petrified thighs. I'm quietly trying to keep track of the time. I guess our guru-ji's been talking for 90 minutes by counting one Mississippi sixty times a minute, sixty times an hour... We pass the two hour mark—no break—and I keep losing track but judging by how the sun's baked the blue night away, we're three hours deep into noble silence. Guru-ji hops down off his barrel, reminding us we're allowed to prepare a single essential question for the afternoon before we leave on the tenth day. I'll ask why my life is amazing while Mumsy's life has broken down and which God I can scream at.

*

I am in Mumsy's arms. Her frizzy Christmas jumper tickles my nose. Her boobs warm my face. She carries me like a basket down the hall from the Christmas party where I've fallen asleep watching telly with a coat for a blanket.

A cry of agony. Squealing car tyres and fingernails on a blackboard. The dream disintegrates. Someone's bleating for hel.... Roosters! That's all: you're on a farm on top of a mountain, girl. You paid to be here, far from Christmas. Get up. Get hurt. God's unhappy with you. That's why he's taking Mumsy. In this discomfort is a lesson. You'd better listen.

With finger gestures and tilted heads from the sahayaks, my tribe of sleepy backpackers is invited to shuffle—in our pyjamas and singlets—towards the temple. The air is cloudy and wet. Someone's chasing a stray goat. My teeth tremble. Men file along the path first, women after, and I intentionally step towards Mickey, hoping to brush against him, though I notice he's preoccupied with some Russian-looking boy and has his fingertips under the Russian's nostrils and the boy is smelling Mickey's fingers for.... DAMN IT.

MICKEY, YOU ABSOLUTE KNOBHEAD. Mickey's fingered that lightbulb-haired harlot, presumably. I sidle up to him and kick his ankle. He makes a show of squishing a mosquito on his hand then winks at me and wipes his fingertip on his shorts.

After a long sitting-session with another unending speech, this one describing the life of a breath, we have a lunch of porridge and jam at wooden trestles in the dining hall. Everybody winces, trying to adjust their spines and tailbones. As soon as everyone's had a bowlful of prison food, the sahayaks beckon us out onto the lawn. Geese mutter and waddle away. Guru-ji Nirmal leads us in a long sprawling tour across the estate, a flock of 100 of us corralled by the *sahayakon* keeping us in line while guru-ji, wearing a white suit for a change, points to the sky, the mountains and talks about the atmosphere. There are thin paths which are sometimes just planks of wood over springs of cold water murmuring between the pebbles. Out the back of the farthest corrugated iron shack I can see there's a dull grey glacier. Apparently China is three passes over. You can see its mountains if you climb the cherry tree.

I turn to Mickey. 'A *glacier*, honey, how cool is that?'

A sahayak puts his hands on my shoulder. It's a gentle scolding.

Silence, Amelia. Don't waste your words.

*

Around noon we're sent out across the fields to collect firewood, bundle hay, pluck handfuls of spinach. We sweep the cobwebs out of sheds, scrape moss off the bridges. This place is the size of a small country. I listen to the birds talk. I watch a rumour of wind run through the wheat. Cicadas chatter in the trees.

Later, we return to the stone floor. Guru-ji is demonstrating how to swallow food more slowly each time we eat, going forward. He strokes his fancy suit-buttons as he mimes ingesting a spoonful of imaginary porridge, chewing like a baby. It's insulting, demeaning, and I pick up Mickey's hand for a sympathetic squeeze but he pulls out of it. Looking across his big chest, I can see he's busy with his pointy-titted side-project.

The two of them are giggling discretely into their cupped palms, trying to duck the attention of the sahayakon. Probably they sneaked out of their dorms for a midnight rendezvous. God Mickey's a bastard.

G. Nirmal chews through a few more hundred of my 2000 Euros while I fantasize about coffee. I descend into a half-asleep trance. I'm feeling fundamental changes trickle through my veins, into my toes, my fingertips. Guru-ji talks about 'butterfly thoughts,' how when a person is truly relaxed and receptive, thoughts will settle between our ears and we should simply stand back and admire those thoughts without pouncing on them.

'...A thought is merely a thought,' Guru-ji Nirmal tells us. 'A thought is not an order, nor is it a command.' *My rotunda, July 15 2020, my bridesmaids, Jasmeet and Ashley and Deeya, the catering, my chocolate cheesecake with truffle butter.*

'A thought has no substance. A thought is made of wind.' The thought that settles on me is the little receipt with my bank balance, Mumsy's fifteen thousand bloody quid she popped into Western Union saying she couldn't use it, but Mumsy, you can't talk like that, you can't give up, Mumsy, I need you, you're my MUM.

'My cheeldren: blow on the butterfly. Let this butterfly alight into the weend and dreeft over to China.'

I listen to the air flow in my nostrils, and out, and in. Mumsy's laughter, unwrapping the photo frame I made her with popsicle sticks and glue. Spice Girls on the stereo. Iraq on the TV. I hear the engine of my heart. I watch vultures climb columns of warm air. Mumsy fainting on the far end of the phone. Dialling an ambulance from eighty countries away. I hear the crick of Mickey stretching some cartilage. I hear the gloop of blood swimming through my arteries. My pulse vibrates in rhythm with the cicadas chirping in the bamboo. I smell the salt leaking from my man's armpits. Whatever's not quite right with my Mickey, we'll mend it. Couple's therapy. Spend the last of Mumsy's money stifling the animosity.

Time is a river, children. Dip a toe; let your consciousness flow. Do not stick a stake in the riverbed.

My river, the Wharfe, ebbing past the abbey, cool bronze, liquid shade. Stinking summer. Lawn baked brown. My Mumsy is excited that exams have ended and she gets to hang out with me, not realizing I only want a boy. I can't have an old lady killing my cred. Mumsy yanks her dress over her head and runs, cream knickers, faded bra, into the river and I'm aghast with embarrassment, but no, there are couples, families, toddlers all piling into the river under the spell of the Bolton Priory ruins looking over us, and I'm still refusing to go in, I'm far too cool, I have to bury myself under the picnic blanket and text back this crazy Irish boy I met at this disco and my Mumsy hauls her wet laundry body out of the river with a whoosh of dripping hair, her eyes stretched with glee and she's collected water in her dress like a dribbling bucket and she dumps water all over me and I scream YOU SLAG, YOU ALMOST GOT MY PHONE WET and she's trying to drag me into the Wharfe and I can't help laughing and scratching and fighting as she forces me into the river and dunks my head under and I'm sure, amongst the gold and olive bubbles, I'm sure I spot a stickleback and a flurry of tadpoles, little beads of joyous life to match the happy miracle of Mum.

We should BE like a river, actually—Derren Brown said, that, weirdly, on one of his specials. Derren Brown, mentalist philosopher, yeah, his show used to come on after *F*R*I*E*N*D*S* and I always wished my relationships were like Rachel and Ross, and that weird coffee guy who's obsessed with Rachel who looks a bit like an albino Derren Brown, that's right, I remember his specials about the power of the mind on TV as I watched the screen upside down on the sofa out of one eye, texting the apeman from Muine Bheag whose boat was ashore and needed a bed for the night, telling him my bed was his and

I'd leave the back door unlocked for him, yeah, Derren Brown talking about the stoics and my Mumsy putting down a nice cuppa tea and asking me if we'd studied the stoics in Greek and me responding with a PFBBBT, blowing my fringe out of my eyes.

This ancient Greek grandpa called Seneca—or was he Roman? No, surely Greek—said you should envision losing everything to make you more appreciative. Picture your house being burgled and you'll appreciate your assets more. Envision Mickey being run over by a tram. Picture me howling sorries in the street. Imagine Mumsy's eyes closing forever, her funeral, everything she carefully collected summed up in a so-called estate, her teaching pension, one hundred grand all for me, money I'll take to a bioresearch company in Oxford and beg them to clone my Mumsy back from that clump of hair I picked up off the bathroom floor when she could pull out her hair without scissors, the hair I've always kept in my purse, my purse in a suitcase in a locker in a temple in the Himalayas.

A butterfly thought settles then it's gone again.

Mickey shagged our wedding planner in London. Huh.

Mickey beat up that poet boy in Tangier, the sensitive kid who massaged my feet on the deck of our lodge overlooking the ocean.

Huh.

Thought here, thought away. I am not judging the thoughts. I am a conduit for the universe, as Ross said in that joke to Rachel with the barista who looks a bit like Derren Brown leaning between them and .... what was his name, the coffee creep.... *Shit*.

Thunderclap. Purple storm in the distance. Spears of heaven stabbing the mountains. Burning mosquito repellent. Citronella tang. Pollen in my nostrils. The tickle of a cockroach running up my leg. Swallowed shriek. I hold the wriggling cockroach up against the sun. Its body is bronze. I look through its wings. They turn the sunlight gold.

A voice, coming from the cassette player on the barrel beside Guru-ji, is telling me to think of my nostrils as passages from heaven to earth. Breathe the infinite into you. There is no life without breath. Controlling other human beings doesn't matter. Money doesn't matter. Food, sex, sports cars, mobile phones, sitcoms with gorgeous New York singles sipping coffee and laughing: all pointless detail without breath.

Stop doing everything in life except breathing, Amelia. That's it.

*

We eat rice and dhal and ghee-fried vegetables for dinner. It's all delicious and desperately-needed. I try to hold each vegetable on the tip of my fork and appreciates its green, its yellow, it orange, though I'm starving, too, and I gulp it down. My senses have become sharply attuned. I listen to my stomach kneading the food. Steaming lentils being slopped into little bowls, and we're given plastic jugs of water decorated with frangipani. Mickey bends down and gives me a quick peck on the cheek before going over to sit with the good-looking people. I appreciate his tiny gesture. I have resolved to tuck my ego away.

In my dormitory, I sleep next to the Nordic beauty with triangle tits. Everybody sleeps easily—except Miss Norway. I listen to the tiny slap of her feet on the concrete as she creeps to the toilets to suck my fiance's diddle while I stroke my boring brown hair.

*

Days pass, days of roosters, cold bucket showers, porridge and potatoes for breakfast, mushy soup, sweet tea. I pass Mickey in the food hall. He tries to high five me like I'm some comrade.

At the trestle table where I eat, Mickey has scratched into the soft wood of the breakfast bench, with his spoon or his fingernail, 'Ur on the rag I dont blame u 4 angry. Mick xoxo.'

And it's true. No need to take it as an insult. My period makes my guts churn like a washing machine. Occasionally, my vulva itches and I need to scratch. I'm destroying my good knickers, the peach ones. Let things flow, Amelia. Don't stick your stake in the stream. I want to vomit and smash, rage and cry. Understand the thoughts knocking on your brain are just that: thoughts. They're not premonitions, not instructions. They're just butterflies.

Unfurl your fists, girl. Eat your breakfast. Meditate. Accept that today is a day of breathing, and tomorrow. Don't anticipate leaving, Amelia. Don't wish you were somewhere else.

During today's sermon someone mutters 'Black Hole of Calcutta,' and there's giggling from the back and the sahayakon get in a flap. I ignore it, study the mosquito bites on my calves. They are annoying and itchy. I accept this without judgement. Just as cows are a source of food for me, so I am a source of food to a tinier life. A big old cow, girl. Cowgirl. *You can ride me sometime if you want, Rach.* Canned laughter. Who said that? Jennifer Aniston's in Central Perk coffee shop and she's talking to... SHIT! Who's the interlocutor? That's a word I haven't used since I took LAW101 eight years ago. What the heck was that barista guy called ... Geoff? Gareth? SERIOUSLY, BRAIN, YOU'RE GONNA FAIL ON ME NOW? It's on the tip of my tongue...

Back to the Nineties when I used to rest my head in Mumsy's lap, Y2K, 9/11, Gulf War II, Seinfeld, Frasier, Ally McBeal, E.R., Ross, Rach, Monica, Chandler, Pheebs, Joey and, um, what's his name, all those outstanding minor characters like, SHIT, white hair serious guy... Chandler.. no, that's been taken.

Buried in the back of my brain is a video of me and my Mumsy weaving Celtic promise knots. Our gran was from a farm in a valley-crag between two cliffs outside Donegal and she would take Mumsy there when Mumsy was my age to 'Learn The Ladyness.' I can feel Mumsy's calloused palms as she comes behind me, teaching me how to tie a Celtic heart knot to capture my love, sealed with a rhyming spell.

I promise I will find a man / broad of chest and strong of hand

My husband, faithful, never strays / I boil the beans / he rakes the hay

She has passed, a voice says, Your Mumsy. She's dead. Just now; today. A red light glowing in my brain. An urgent message from across space.

I beckon a sahayak aside and whisper I'm pretty sure I need to phone my Mumsy.

'In Rishikesh there is being telephone,' he says. 'You may leave. You are walking and this bus, it is taking you.'

I ask for my suitcase, go to my room, sit on my mattress, pull my knees up against my chin. What's a suitcase? A stone on wheels I choose to drag around. For four thousand Euros, Cancer Research UK treats women to a late-life pampering. Women are matched with top quality wigs made from real human hair. My Mumsy, who had to throw away dresses kids spilled ink on, my Mumsy who was sworn-at by council estate rat-people when she dropped off their homework after hours, my Mumsy could have gotten her nails painted with the money I paid for this place. She could have had a Thai girl file the corns off her feet. She could have had cocoa butter rubbed into the grey flesh of her forearms. The money could've made her a queen before she died.

Things we hold to be top of importance—life or death—are only as important as rainfall, or the drop of a rotten branch, or a feather falling from a vulture.

I cry til I'm dry, then return to the meditation hall.

*

A rooster pierces my dreams. My spine complains. The cold stones prick my feet.

Today is not a day of Mississippis. Today we are allowed to line up and one by one ask Guru-ji the most important question in the universe. Our lives are jigsaw puzzles. Restore the missing piece, our lives will be complete.

When I made him put that ring on me in Corfu, did Mickey really promise to be faithful or did I only imagine it?

Did my mum lie about how long she has left to live, or did I mishear her, preoccupied with Mickey?

He's ahead of me in line, that man of mine is. He's asking guru-ji for—*seriously?!*—the email address of that pretty girl. I'm astonished that the helpers actually bring it out to him, written on paper. Mickey high fives the cool kids in line as he passes.

I'm not astonished. He has shamed me, and yet he has not. I let emotion pass through me without sticking.

He sees I'm not high fiving him and pauses his celebrity tour.

'We'll catch up soon, derlin,' he whispers, all confident. 'Have a hert-to-hert. Fix things b'twain us.'

I ignore him and shuffle up another few flagstones. 39 people have gone before me; there will be dozens after. I am a drop in the ocean. Unimportant.

'I have to ask you something, Guru-ji.'

'Please, child.'

This is your chance, Amelia.

'What was the name of the barista in *F*R*I*E*N*D*S*? It's been seriously bugging me.'

Guru-ji nods to his helpers. They disappear into an office, return within 30 seconds with the name written on refill paper.

'GUNTHER! Thank you!'

I float away, full of helium.

Mickey finds me at the back of the line.

'Babe, I'm thinkin after this we'll book train tickets tae –

'Mickey, shut the fuck up.'

OUR MEESHA NEEDS MONEY

1.

Our Meesha arrives as we're at the dining table holding a toast to the Vanuatu cruise we've booked for the four of us this summer. She enters through the side door leading in from the garage, carefully wiping her boots on the doormat like a good girl. Our wineglasses pause in midair. Our mouths hang open. Meesha has new tattoos visible on her exposed shoulders, a piercing through her collarbone, of all places, a plaited rat's tail slapping the back of her singlet. Our Meesha has transformed herself into a revolutionary, a Hizbollah, a punk, well, she looks that way to our guests at least. To me, she's my baby, my sheereen, my aziz-am. The squirming little cherub I used to spoon-feed applesauce.

We're all dazzled by the updates in her appearance. Our Meesha's tummy is tired and bulges over her belt buckle. Her arms, which used to be covered in lovely brown babyfat and unicorn stickers, are twig-thin and spattered with scabs. 'Just dropped by to let you know I love you tonnes, mama,' Meesha says, and gives me an extremely large embrace.

Keith and Lupinda Taylor shield their wineglasses as Meesha moves around the table, extending a hand to greet our dinner party guests like old friends. Lupinda pulls her Nur Donatella Lucchi handbag into the safety of her lap and excuses herself to use the bathroom, shimmying along the table-edge.

'How's tricks, Dad?' Meesha says, scratching some pustule in her sandpaper armpit. Eyeing up the plates and candles, Meesha tells us she has somebody waiting and she can't stay long. Indeed, we can hear a sputtering engine and the squeak of metal springs.

Davoud mutters a response. Glaring at me, he accepts a kiss from his daughter. The counsellor, he said we're not supposed to indulge our Meesha when she's overly affectionate. Our counsellor, though—he never held our Meesha in his arms.

I pull out a chair for her to sit but our Meesha declines. She taps her foot like a woodpecker and gives a quick update on her life. Meesha is no longer running her import-export business with the scented candles. She had to file for bankruptcy in May, which she tells us was actually a strategic financial decision because it wiped her student loan and other debts. Floating on the stock market would've been both a gift and a curse, she explains. Meesha Ghorbani was TOO successful. She wouldn't wish that stress on anybody.

'Family comes first, eh you guys,' our Meesha says, 'Oh, speaking of which, could I borrow a couple bucks? Just say nah if you want.'

The engine outside roars like a trumpeting elephant. She double-checks that we've heard her request for a so-called "couple bucks."

Davoud apologizes to Keith and Lupinda, clears his throat. 'A couple, in this language, it is meaning two. You are wanting two dollars?'

'Forget it, shouldna fuckin bothered,' our Meesha mumbles, walking over to the refrigerator and opening the double doors and studying the contents of the fridge and humming and tapping that silly foot of hers. She shakes open a padded wine bag and begins stuffing it with raspberry cider and Chablis.

'Just gettin a drink, ma,' she calls out, then picks something off the breakfast bar. 'This your chequebook?'

She's flapping the black rectangle of my bank book and clicking a pen. Our Meesha begins writing herself a cheque. Davoud and I have learned from experience that to decline our only daughter a few thousand here and there will result in us not seeing her for another six months. It is important to restrain our selfishness and to help our child.

'I'll come and sign that for you,' I offer, and approach.

'No need, all done,' our Meesha says, tearing her cheque out with a crisp rip and tucking it in her back pocket. She pulls a picture on the fridge and studies it, taking a photo with the camera on her phone. Her smile creeps out, secret as a midnight mouse. She was always good with cameras and such gadgets, our Meesha was. Top of her class in chemistry. She programmed Lego Technic and was a finalist in her school's Tech Week competition.

'That photograph, moosh-am, holiday in Persepolis, darling. 2000. You remember, neh? The statue of Meesha? The marigold, the flower angel, areh?'

'And this photo of you two, it's your guys's wedding eh?'

'Obviously,' Davoud says. 'What of it?'

She rolls the picture of us newlyweds in her palms then fastens it back on the refrigerator. 'Cheers for the cheque anyway. You really oughta change your signature, it's way easy to copy. Oi: laters. Gotta roll.'

The door leading to the garage is allowing in a smoggy, diesely draft. I pull my bones out of the chair and follow Meesha out, rubbing the crags of her spine. There appears to be a patched wound in the plane above her bottom where I used to kiss Meesha's tiny tailbone while she squirmed, giggling. Some fresh tattoo covered with a bandage.

'HURRY YOUR SHIT UP, MEESH,' calls the man in the garage. I glimpse him. The man is straddling a motorcycle the size of a horse. The arm which twists the throttle of his beastly bike has portraits of African-American rapper-thugs tattooed on it. Strange, this Western method of honoring one's idols.

Our Meesha hauls her bag of bottles off the linoleum, dumping it in her driver's lap as she prepares to climb aboard.

Davoud appears behind me and puts his velvety hands on my neck. I notice the Taylors checking their cellphones, whispering in one another's ears. We're about to lose them.

'Just quickly, my dear,' Davoud calls before our Meesha departs for another half a year, 'What's the latest on your Scentsy investment? These scented candles, neh? You promised, what was it, triple our money back, neh?'

Meesha's friend revs the engine, pushes back, revolves on the driveway.

'I ain't doin' that no more,' our Meesha says from the back of the motorcycle, patting her man's leather flanks, 'Epic scam.'

'But you insisted,' Davoud calls over the growling engine, standing his ground. I try to tell him to shush but he holds up a big stubborn palm.

'No, no, you will not silence me, Mev: we were promised 300 percent returns, were we not?'

'I didn't come here for a lecture.' Our Meesha spits on the driveway, clamps a black visor over her face and hoons away.

'I HOPE YOU'RE HAPPY.'

'*Mehvesh Ghorbani,*' Davoud says through gritted teeth, '*You will compose yourself.*'

We return to our dinner party. Where were we? Toasting our cruise, yes. We open fortune cookies and a nice Gewurztramïner. I find a smile to match my black dress with the meesha flowers on it. Still, our conversation is diminishing.

'Haven't seen little Meesha since Girl Guides,' Keith mutters after a few seconds' silence. 'I hope rehab did the trick.... ?'

Nobody responds. To fill the hole, Lupinda produces from her handbag a coffee table book of family photos her kids have had printed at Harvey Norman on Colombo Street South. We pass it around and remark on how thoughtful the photobook was and how good Lupinda's boys are to send exquisite gifts home from Macau whenever they're there on business. The conversation surges over us and washes Meesha away.

2.

This Canterbury winter night is chilly enough to warrant slippers, a hot water bottle and a blanket—not to mention a steaming cup of Lady Pārsa chai. The cool is ideal for viewing something exotic on the telly before burying oneself in bed—if we could get this damn blasted Netflix thingamajig to behave itself.

While my Davoudy-am hectors the television, I step out of the warm lounge and into the black, promising Davoud I'll telephone the cable expert from the Yellow Pages. Instead, behind the closed laundry door, I dial our Meesha in the dark. When I hear her voice, my stomach settles. I'm surprised she's retained the same number—she does have a habit of changing her phone number monthly. There are strange honkings and beeps and zooming around her. She says she'll pop round and sort out Netflix for us and with a generous discount on her fee.

I return to the couch with a secret smile and let Davoud know someone will be here shortly.

'So be it,' Davoud says, peering down his spectacles at a collection of spiral-bound tenders for the concrete for the hydroelectric dam his company is designing.

Our Meesha is soon hovering on the street in a car full of friends. They have hoods and caps darkening their faces. Shy, I expect.

It's been forever! Half a year! I lean into the smelly dark car for a kiss. It reeks the way Davoud's *peshāb* stinks up the en suite after he's been eating buttered asparagus. Compost and bleach and sulphur.

In the passenger seat Meesha rears her head back and squirms away from my kisses.

'You are just in time,' I tell her.

'In time for what?' Our Meesha's eyes shrink to suspicious slits. 'You didn't tell anyone I'm here did you?'

'The jug's boiled, dear. You can have a cup of chai while you work on your Netbox.'

Finally she says, 'Ohhhhhhhh, true, forgot,' and tells her pals she'll be right back.

From the trunk of the car, our Meesha fetches a garbage bag of technology, slinging the sack over her shoulder like Father Christmas. She comes up the drive, peers into the bushes for some reason, then comes inside.

From his lamplit armchair, Davoud nods at her. He even puts down his book. 'Moosh-am.'

'Baba... .' Our Meesha shivers then steps too-quickly into the lounge. Her fingers are tense, clenching. She must have the flu.

Meesha upends her bag. An obscene amount of mechanical treasure spews onto the carpet. Headphones, cameras, one of those Kindling devices people read books on, cords and wires, a thin white computer, a pink Samsung photo frame-shaped thingy with unicorn stickers on it and the name *Robyn* spelled in glitter. Also in the bag is a diploma in a glass frame. Our Meesha tells her father she can easily print his name on the diploma for just forty dollars, although she's running a special this week and can do it for thirty-five, 'Or thirty if that's all yous've got.'

'So our Meesha needs money, surprise surprise,' Davoud says, rolling his eyes, shifting his body out of his armchair. I pinch his wrist. *Shame on you, Davoud.*

Our Meesha drops to her knees and begins rummaging in the pile of black and grey plastic. Each time she shifts, her hooded sweatshirt lifts off her bum and I try to glimpse a portion of the covered wound on her lower back. Finally she holds some device aloft, sings 'Haaa-le-lujah' and installs what she calls a 'Stealth Box' in the back of our TV. Strange waves of static sweep across the screen. I spot Davoud's fingers tensing and I swat his hand. Have some faith, Davoud. Finally a grainy ghost materializes, then Meesha connects Robyn's tablet into our TV with a strange gold cord, enters a long chain of numbers and letters and ajji majji la tarajji: Netflix is live.

Welcome, Robyn, the screen tells us.

'Fuck I'm thirsty.' Our Meesha disappears to the fridge and returns with a bottle of bubbly with a straw in it. She sips her bubbly and strokes the gold-rimmed china plates on the dresser. Meesha won't sit. She can't stop pacing.

We're confused about where to find *Midsomer Murders*, and for a while, the language of the programmes becomes Arabic. We need a further device to un-Arabize the Stealth Box, apparently, and our Meesha generously offers to sells us a remote control for what she assures us is a competitive price. We accidentally select an American documentary and the first words on the screen read 'Are your kids on track or on crack?' and there's the image of a distressed mother finding drug-smoking paraphernalia in her daughter's sock drawer. Meesha rips the remote control out of Davoud's hand and stabs it with her fingertips until *Midsomer Murders* is at last selected.

Ready to relax with our show, I bring out a tray of artichoke hearts and caviar and salmon with those Ferrero Rocher chocolates my baby girl has always adored and I beg her to spend the night but our Meesha slings her black bag over her shoulder and insists she has to go.

Pausing in the doorway, reluctantly accepting a cheque to cover the costs of her service, plus an extra $3000 for that DJing course she's on, we hear a static-y crackle from the car out on the street and the whoop of a siren. Her friends yell urgent words at her.

Our Meesha rummages deep in her black sack and at last produces a strange black box with a digital screen. 'Y'all ain't got a police scanner, do ya?'

'I'm not entirely... the Kia's rather new, I'm sure it comes with—

'SHE DOESN'T NEED YOUR BLASTED POLICE SCANNER.' Davoud's lips are twisted into a beak. He's trying to force the door closed, the brute, pushing our *dodar* away with his big thick arrogant spiral-bound booklet. 'Leave us alone.'

I walk my moosh-am to the car, my little mouse. Her face is ruined with the cruel words of her foolish father. I try to get her back but Meesha's friends politely decline my invitation to a nightcap and a slice of fruitcake.

Meesha drives into the frosty night.

I don't know if I'll ever see my jigar again. My guts. The core of me.

3.

We're at our holiday home on the coast overseeing the extension of the verandah so it will feel like the water is lapping at the house. Davoud seldom raises his voice, but he will debate the costing of each piece of wood, each screw until he has exhausted the builders. Davoud makes structures stronger and invests the savings into the things that really matter. Salmon, figs, comfortable armchairs. A verandah with an ocean underneath.

'These 150 millimetre adjustable support foot,' I hear him lecturing two Western men, 'You are telling me you have thees part for next week, but a little birdy is telling me you have insufficient quantity, neh? You will have to use 180 millimetre here, here and here, yes-neh?'

Once the verandah can take our expanded holiday home, we'll reach that little further out onto the cliff and truly over-look the Pacific. We're having an infinity pool put in which I'm told will allow the water to flow over the edge, producing a visual effect suggesting the pool has no boundary and flows into the sky. I'm anxious about the renovations, truth be told, and I feel the bank bullied us into accepting the extension on our mortgage, as if we're nothing but moneybags. Still, we cannot have Keith and Lupinda Taylor disappointed when they come for dinner.

I squeeze my soft Dina Nayeri novel, thumb page 239. The ups and downs of Princess Anya's fight for self-confidence in the ballrooms of the Kākh-e Golestān kept me awake until 2:30 last night. I pace the orchard, reading pages, listening for changes in Davoud's voice. Listening for that certain tone that means he is happy and we have saved another six thousand dollars.

My telephone tinkles. I have a text message. An anonymous writer at an anonymous number claims to be... to be waiting in the bushes? MY bushes?! My anonymous friend doesn't want to see 'baba' and is asking me to meet her in secret.

It has to be my moosh-am! My jigar!

I race to the clearing by the water tank, following Meesha's texted instructions and there, standing on a tree stump, buried in a puffy jacket despite the heat, is my *dokhtar*.

'Sup, ma.'

Our Meesha looks weary, frustrated, grumpy. I offer a cup of tea and some baklava and artichokes, plus there's some biry-ani and mast-o-khiar in the refrigerator the builders wouldn't touch, yes, I'm certain, and if not that, we have almonds, we have balal, we have gerdu—

'I need somewhere to cook. I was just hoping, since no one's around and it's kind of stinky... .'

'Of course, moosh-am. You can have the spare room.'

'But, like, only when you and dad aren't here... listen, it's, like, it's not cooking food, okay? It's, like, chemistry. Making crystals. Cooking, kind of.' Meesha thumps her chest. 'I just need money, okay,' she says, 'Straight up. Gotta pay for this.'

Without warning my girl turns around, bends, lifts up her jacket and points her *koon* at me.

I need Davoud, this is ungodly, she's come all this way, all this way just to insult—just to— .

Words escape me.

'It's almost done. Just need a bit more shading.'

There on Meesha's lower back is a portrait of two newly-weds looking out at a bright future, hair shiny as toffee, eyes bright as metal, Davoud's lips wet from singing, my veil lifting off my face as I shriek with joy.

The tattoo just needs a little more rose-red in the cheeks. Meesha wants to make our faces happy.

'Of course you may stay here and cook, darling. You may stay here as long as you wish.'

OVERNIGHT

1.

When it started, we were drunk on anger, drunk on poetry, drunk on each other. Si, Harriet, Todd... we'd been up all night, getting more and more anxious, anxious about our English and Lit grades. Anxious about our creative writing efforts. Anxious that our literary reputations were under threat. We paced the dawn campus, unable to sit down. The birds were making noise as the blackness thinned to a watery blue and the streetlights bowed out. Finally a goon in denim overalls pulled up on his moped and unboxed 100 copies of *The Student Guide* into a rack.

We straightaway flipped to the most important literary news of our lives, page 6. There it was: our public humiliation. Disgrace immortalized in ink—our ambitions of being the leading poets on campus had been publicly mocked. Wounded, we dripped disappointment as we limped back to the flat along early morning George Street, clutching every copy of *The Student Guide*. We had three copies for ourselves, 97 to be destroyed. There would be more magazines put out for public consumption, yes, but we could help ensure that 100 fewer people read the printed attack on us. Every one less embarrassment was important.

After a long march down George Street, we crossed the Octagon and staggered to the top of View Street where our mansion looked down on Dunedin. After dumping the traitorous magazines in the recycling bin, we clomped up three flights of stairs to the top of the Eagle's Nest and arranged ourselves around the room. Harriet planted her bottom neatly on the edge of the bed; Todd spread himself across the two-seater like a quilt, taking up space, taking up attention. Si aligned himself with the wall, upright.

We had one essential question to discuss: how to respond to the *Guide's* literary editor disrespecting us.

'Revenge,' Harriet said, mashing her knuckles into her palm.

'That guy deserves to die,' Todd added.

'A dish best served cold, I believe is the recipe,' Si said. 'But the question is, do we destroy our nemesis through success or subterfuge?'

'Subterfuge,' said Harriet from the bed.

Todd rolled onto his back and laced his fingers behind his head. 'Definitely subterfuge.'

Si, the godfather of our radical writers group, took off his glasses and folded them, pacing the floor, nearly bumping his oversized head on a beam. He had to duck to avoid the ceiling light as he summed up our predicament in a lecture.

'As if it weren't bad enough that the wanker routinely rejects the poetry we send him, Literary editor Jean-Paul Fernandes has published what he calls The Top Ten All-Time Poetry Fails list, spanning the centuries. We've been regrettably bundled together on that historic list at number 2, between Byron's *Candida Sonnets* and McGonagall's Tay Bridge Disaster, which is upsetting, granted. But could it be that his little list is no more influential than a letter to the editor from an elderly conservative?'

'Letters to the editor don't get reproduced 10,000 times in *The Guide* so everyone on campus pretty much has seen it. He literally humiliated us.'

'Correction: gratuitous use of *literally*.'

'If *Student Guide's* gonna make fun of us, we have to start our own publication,' Harriet said, listing the process on her knobbly fingers. 'Put out a call for submissions; set up an editorial review board; get a website; get an email address with a—what do you call it—that professional thingy... .'

Todd flailed towards the ceiling, making a choking gesture as he envisioned squeezing the neck of Jean-Paul Fernandes, the arrogant beast who'd overlooked his genius.

'They print ten thousand *Guides* each week, right? We've got to put out 40,000 of our one. 50, maybe. Fuck it: 100,000 copies will drown the bastard out. I'll get a cement truck and one of those chutes that pours the cement. I'll tip every magazine right into his fucking bedroom and immolate the motherfucker.'

Si was nodding as the speculation burned and settled.

'Immolate him, yes, I see. You have sufficient tinder, do you?'

Todd squinted at our old, speccy leader. 'Grindr, bro. Tinder's too binary.'

Si peered down his nose at skinny, neurotic Harriet, who was writing a list.

'Your input, Harriet, if you'd be so kind.'

Harriet stood, fingers curled in tiny fists of outrage. 'HE'S SAYING WE HAVE TO DO SOMETHING!'

WHAM-WHAM-WHAM from our flatmate through the wall.

'KEEP IT DOWN, NERDS.'

We assured our protein shake-sipping flatmate we would attempt to decimate the decibels.

'There's two hours left before lectures start and everybody'll see this review making fun of us,' Harriet pointed out. 'We can print our own pages. Paste them into The Guide over that wanker's silly fucking list with our own list. The laundromat's got a photocopier. Who's got money?'

We all turned and looked at Si, who was nodding slowly and sadly. Si's family owned printeries around the world. Of course he'd pay.

2.

High on excitement, we cobbled together our own list of notorious literature on Si's laptop. We thrice named Jean-Paul Fernandes on our roll of shame. The list spilled over the first page, so it made sense to make it a two-pager. We wanted to add some art, and some of our best poems. It expanded into a small four page zine. We had a brief meeting of our Review Board, then commenced publication.

Each carefully-folded A4 had our logo on the front: *The Reactionary*, with a hammer and sickle hacking up a crude drawing of a face resembling that of literary editor Jean-Paul Fernandes. With each side of the paper bisected, there was a page for the homoerotic haiku of Todd, a page for the rage-against-the-pharmaceutical-industry mini-essay of Harriet, and the final page was an essay by Si comparing the management of the *Guide* to the management in Orwell's *Animal Farm*. Combine our invectives and you were looking at something rather revolutionary.

A shortage of paper on the laundromat's photocopier meant instead of the 1,000 copies of The Reactionary we'd hoped to distribute, we printed just 263-and-a-half (as there was confusion about double-siding.) It took 90 minutes to gather the words from our blogs and journals and emails, and this cut into folding time, so that by brunch, once StationeryStation had opened and we'd got our double-sided tape and gluesticks, we were well behind schedule for gluing *The Reactionary* into the *Guide* over Jean-Paul's list. The rate with which we covered up the hurtful words of the literary editor couldn't compete with the rate in which flip flop-wearing, energy drink-sipping kids in shades picked up copies of *The Guide* and flipped through them. We watched the faces of the popular kids to see if they recognized our names, to see if they scoffed and scorned and sneered.

We didn't detect any recognition—and that's what really hurt.

*

We gathered at 3 outside the Noodle Hut to compare results.

Si—efficient, organized, almost robotic in his discipline—had inserted 92 *Reactionary*s in copies of *The Guide*.

Harriet had managed 43 insertions before she thought she spotted Jean-Paul's silhouette leering up behind her and had sprinted to the toilets where she barricaded herself and phoned her counsellor to breathe through her panic attack.

Todd had managed to paste 14 of our manifestos in magazines before a group of catty boys distracted him. We knew he'd probably just gone off to chainsmoke cigarettes and flirt.

Shovelling noodles into our mouths, our bellies burning with emptiness from eight hours of frenetic coffee-guzzling, we flinched every time our phones dinged. Could it be an email with a TV interview request? Accusations of defamation and a lawsuit? Or was it the Vice-Chancellor summoning us to a tête-à-tête to reconcile with the demon critic from *The Guide*?

The day passed, and then the week passed, and few people joined the cause except our mothers, who told us they'd love to buy a copy of our little zine, and do you need a top-up to get yourself some groceries this week, honey?

3.

At our summit in the Eagle's Nest, we made some agreements, in principle. First agreement was we couldn't make any more neighbour-inflaming noise. There were dreadful acoustics here; the sound travelled through the floorboards and we feared an ass-kicking from our gym-towelled, protein-slurping flatmate. Harriet would need to act less bipolar. Todd would need to act less of a queen.

The second thing agreed was that *The Reactionary* wasn't quite as reactionary as we'd hoped. Few of our creative writing classmates were aware we'd even published it; one asked the lecturer to ask us how we felt about getting "totally burned."

The third thing we agreed was Jean-Paul remained above us in status, and we would have to do something significant to tear him down.

'I'll honeytrap him,' Todd conjectured, 'I'll suck his cock and get photos, chuck 'em on the internet.'

'Thaaaat doesn't have much to do with kicking Jean-Paul's ass in literary reputation,' Harriet warned, wagging her finger. She squeezed her bony butt into the two-seater beside Todd, who began plaiting her hair while she sat stiff and upright as a broom.

'If we want to get ahead, we have to write some reviews of Jean-Paul and give him, like, zero out of five stars. Make space for us. Destroy the opposition, yeah. YEAH!'

'If I can have your attention.' Si took a position in the centre of the room and cricked his fingers. 'You'll recall I did endure an internship with the university press last summer, no? I carry a modicum of expertise in the basics of publishing. One: the brand. Two: the distribution. Three: the profit. Now THAT is status, my good chums.'

'What are we distributing, though? I can't fold any more A4s, honestly. My fingernail got all infected.'

'Erotic thrillers is what,' Si said, and upended his satchel, tipping a pile of racy books onto the floor. 'My dear comrades: let us begin.'

*

The first step in our plot was a day of reading. We lay on the couch, on our beds, on the floor. Harriet put her head on Si's stomach; Todd draped his legs over all of us. We gorged on erotica till we could predict the narratives of entire books without even opening the covers.

The second step was to have Todd lay out the erotic highlights of the story we were going to write—the characters shuddering passionately in a lain-back seat in the car park outside the movies; an episode in which the characters make love in the video screening booth within an adult DVD store; the characters turning a massage into a saga of anal exploration. Si produced A1 poster paper and drew a story structure plan across it. Todd cried and bit his fingernails and stormed out of the room twice, but returned to circle locations across the narrative layout where his sexy scenes would be inserted. He'd fucked more than any of us. Sex scenes were his domain.

As they were about to shake on it, Si reminded Todd the sex scenes needed to have a man making love to a woman—not two men. An argument ensued. Si was accused of being discriminatory; Todd was being blind to market realities.

Harriet, who'd been deemed our typist, had won a novella-writing competition at age 8; she'd come runner up in the National Scrabble Championship at age 11. Harriet had the nimblest fingers and the highest levels of nervous energy. We could blurt out words and she'd type as fast as we talked.

High on coffee, fuelled by resentment of He Who Shall Not Be Named, we smashed out a couple of chapters, with Si doing his Hitler strut, roaming the room wall to wall, revolving sharply as he hit the cupboard, finger up in the air whenever a descriptive detail arrived in his frontal cortex. He said every sentence in order with few corrections, taking breaks only to let Todd suggest a sexy scene. The typing began at dinner time and was winding down around ten before coffee and No-Doz got us all going again and we pounded out the words of our erotic novel til 1, then 1:30, then 3 am when the only life in the world was a street sweeper truck and a stray drunk, staggering through the night.

The story we composed concerned a quixotic fool named John Fernando bumbling around a university campus attempting to find love. Waxy-eyed and naïve, John Fernando lets loose his lust while deep-down, he searches for love. Three pages into our book, we had John surrendering to a French swinger sporting a strap-on dildo and holding his head in his hands for weeks after, hunched and stooped and agonized. In our draft, John is unable to sit on his chair and dispatch correspondence for *Granta* magazine and so is fired for failing to submit his quarterly column. Muddied with shame, John Fernando holidays in Samoa, hoping to find romance on the beach, but contracts dysentery and vomits on an attractive American heiress just as he is about to consummate. John then attempts to find love in a lonely hearts column posted on Craigslist but is violently mugged in a stranger's apartment, disembowelled and is left having to squeeze the faeces out of his colostomy bag daily.

We ended the book at 70,000 words and kicked back, slumped against the headboard, smiling and toasting with thimbles of Turkish coffee while our brute-of-a-flatmate screamed through the wall.

We'd hit our target. With an epilogue, which Todd promised to write within the day, we would have our manuscript complete very soon. The only thing we didn't have was consensus as to whose name should take attribution.

'He can't know it was us,' Harriet said, nervously fingering her blisterpack of Seroquel, 'We have John performing cunnilingus on his mother... that might, y'know... aggravate him.'

'Lust, that's our author, a Mizz Lust,' Si said, holding his fingertip in the air. 'A first name is all that's missing.'

Todd kicked his feet playfully. 'What, like T. H. S. or something? Y'know—our initials. Like a secret code.'

Si nodded, and that was that. 'We'll add an extra T to the Lust. Got to make the credentials credible. If anybody asks, it's an ethnic Bavarian name. Means turnip farmer.'

We toasted our cups in agreement. The novel was practically complete; within two days, *Sadistic Search* by T. H. S. Lustt would be couriered to University Press. We would pay to have it printed, published and promoted on campus. Even the banging from our flatmate seemed to be banging of support.

4.

Jean-Paul Fernandes was trying to get through the twenty unread emails on his computer screen, but there was a noise distracting him. Chatter and hyperbole and repartee. He pushed stacks of books and bookmarks and book vouchers away from the windowsill to investigate what was happening three floors below in the quad. There were students in twos and threes walking out of Campus Classics, all holding little brown bags. A pull-up banner rippling in the wind advertized some raunchy romance on sale. He could have sworn the banner wasn't there last time he'd looked out the window.

Jean-Paul pulled his coat on and went down to investigate. Let those beseeching his inbox with letters begging for positive reviews wait a little longer. As Literary Editor, Jean-Paul made it a point of pride to keep people squirming as they awaited their judgement. Jean-Paul had standards to protect.

As Jean-Paul tiptoed downstairs, he brushed elbows with editor in chief Leanne Hornby. Out of her arms tumbled a softcover book featuring a woman's neck being licked on the cover, apparently authored by a T. H. S. Lustt.

The title: *Sadistic Search*.

The subheading: *John Fernando must get fucked.*

'Where did you get this—what is this?'

'Ain't you heard, Jean-Paul? *Sadistic Search* is like an overnight sensation. You should grab one before they're gone. People are going nuts for it.'

Jean-Paul walked across the quad in a daze. He'd long envisioned scenes of rapture like this around his own books before he abandoned all hope of becoming successful as a writer and turned to reviewing instead.

Jean-Paul Fernandes adjusted his scarf, unfastened the button on the pocket containing his wallet, and stepped into Campus Classics. He bumped and jostled and fought through student after student clutching the same book with the same licked throat.

John Fernando must get fucked.

The stand where the books were being displayed was empty of *Sadistic Searches* but for one. Jean-Paul snatched it and clutched it tightly. Jean-Paul's day usually consisted of spending book tokens and living off chocolate bars with the change received after he'd spent each token. He reluctantly slid a $50 token across the counter and purchased his copy. The change was just $15—meaning the book was shockingly priced at $34.99. Full price! How impressive could one romance book be? The book dweeb attempted to give Jean-Paul his change in the form of a book token. Jean-Paul would have preferred cash. His student loan was worryingly high and his income from editing didn't stretch far. Every cent was precious.

He took the book up to his office, slumped into his leather chair and turned to the acknowledgements page of *Sadistic Search* by T. H. S. Lustt. Jean-Paul read over a curious mix of named influences. Those acknowledged included professors, the dean of literature, plus some names Ms. Lustt apparently relied upon.

One Harriet, one Simon, and one Todd.

Jean-Paul turned to the first page, put his feet on his desk and began reading.

John Fernando awoke from a dream about his mother, spoonfeeding him in the nude. He stepped out of the sheet and moved toward his bookcase. The woman who'd spent the night with him was stroking the spines of his books.

'You have really shitty taste in literature,' she said. 'Oh—hey—please don't cry.'

He'd been awake one minute and already John was emotionally unstable. He was bitter, hated himself, hated the world. At 31, a failed author, with a blog nobody read, and ugly, John Fernando hadn't been able to sexually satisfy his paramour the night before.

He told her to get dressed and leave.

John packed a lunch. He was going out to change his life today.

Jean-Paul chewed the corner of his lip and scanned the book jacket. Who on earth could have written the thing?

The photograph of T. H. S. Lustt didn't depict her face, only the back of her head. The author was standing on a cliff edge, facing out toward the water, her hair tumbled by the wind. Her biography said she received her education in literature at none other than this very university.

Jean-Paul brought up the Nielsen bestseller results for the week on his computer screen. *Sadistic Search* was charting highly. Not number one yet, but it was a heatseeker.

Jean-Paul opened his Takedown List and typed THS Lustt.

Something about the name didn't look right.

Jean-Paul laced his fingers behind his head and hmm-ed.

5.

We attempted to wait in the lobby of the publisher, on a nice old leather couch with pot plants and a glass coffee table, and copies of the *New Yorker*, but we couldn't even agree on how to wait. Harriet told Todd that because Todd was certain to make a pass at somebody and embarrass them all he needed to keep his randiness to himself; Todd told Harriet her problem was she had no sexuality whatsoever. Si, trying to watch the door to the office for his moment to go and pitch the manuscript, told them both to cease their yabbering.

'Who put you in charge anyway?'

Harriet pressed her shoulders against her friend. 'If you think you're capitalizing on our work without our consent, Si, think again. We're in this together.'

Si tucked his glasses into his breast pocket, moved to the end of the endless couch, clutched his weary face. He had interned here and used to tell us his plans for his book tour and podcast and his Pushcart Prize. He'd tried many times to facilitate the publication of amazing manuscripts from fiction writing students which came upon his desk, but there were only two things the directors of the publishing house wanted: cook books and "puzzle porn"—meaning books about ordinary people having to fuck their way through conspiracies and mysteries in the Vatican and the Smithsonian, which would apparently sell stacks. If we secured the publisher's backing and went commercial, we hoped to outsell all other authors and completely stun Jean-Paul Fernandes. Paralyse the prick with envy.

The door opened and head of publishing Linda Rokonadravu stepped out. Her haircut was short, black and cubic, her earrings hard and joyless. Her suit hugged her body. Her hand opened to clutch Si's.

'Which one of you's the author?'

'We all are,' Todd said. Harriet elbowed him.

'We all are in support of T. H. S., who is extremely shy and hates meetings, is what my friend here meant to say,' Si said, stepping in front of Todd to block him. 'She's asked us to represent her.'

Linda engaged Si with her eyes.

'Are your friends coming in?'

'These two will wait outside,' Si told her as he entered the publisher's office. 'I'll speak for Ms. Lustt.'

The door swallowed him.

*

The sensation couldn't be contained on campus. Sales of Lustts boiled up through Campus Books, oozed into the bookshelves of heads of department, administrators, researchers. Even the vice chancellor was seen coming out of the toilet with a *Sadistic Search* under his arm.

The city's bookshops took on Lustt's literature and added their fee to the price sticker. Sales spilled over into the thousands, then crept up and hovered around the 5000 mark before spreading to 8000, 9000, and then five figures was reached. *Sadistic Search* was on every bus stop bench and café counter, in libraries and checkouts and catalogues.

Once Si had taken care of arranging a lawyer, bank account, and a background story for the reclusive T. H. S. Lustt, we seemed well-set-up. Si even applied for a passport and birth certificate in case we needed to 'birth' our author. To make her real.

After our first royalty check materialized, we partied in the Eagle's Nest. Even our hostile flatmate with his flaring neck shared a glass of bubbles. Si reluctantly drew cash out of the account he'd set up and gave the wadded hundreds to Todd, who forced Harriet to come away from the wall and dance with him. We made the chandelier shake. For a night, we walked on air.

A day later, we were back at work. There was money to be made, success to be capitalized upon. A chapter to write about John Fernando being banned from ever reviewing a book again and drifting the world until he finds himself in Java where an uncontacted tribe kidnaps him and pours sugar up his rectum and lets fire ants eat him from the inside out. We had an enemy to be shamed.

The three-book publishing deal stamped by Linda's publishing house specified that John Fernando's character needed to follow the same narrative arc in the second novel and the third. You don't fiddle with the formula, as Linda put it in an email. Each book, John Fernando's character would attempt to enjoy whatever miserable plateau he'd arrived at in life, then some new person would enter his life, upsetting his fragile balance. John would grow, as a human, by enduring sexual experiences with a bony introvert, a promiscuous gay fuckboy and an asexual prudish professor, plus an overly-affectionate Shetland pony, drawing conclusions about his own boundaries and finally emerging at the book's end a wiser person after being repeatedly fucked.

John's character left the events of *Sadistic Search: Book One* having accepted he wasn't the smartest man in the world, and that those who fucked him were smarter than him. In book two, published as *Sadist Unsated*, John's character receives the news that his mother has died on the same day he is fired from his publishing job for receiving a low score on a mandatory staff IQ test. Upon returning to his hometown for his mother's funeral, John is drugged while drinking wine and wakes up to find himself the sex slave of a trio of evil geniuses he callously overlooked when publishing a pretentious website during high school. The trio punish John for the duration of the novel with various dildoes and it is only when John concedes he's been living a shameful life that he is set free, thanking his captors for their mercy as he shambles out of the dungeon.

The scene in which the ants tear open John Fernando's rectum was moved to the back of Book Two as an epilogue.

6.

In an all-night binge of espresso and outrage, Jean-Paul Fernandes typed his revenge manuscript. The first 10,000 words took from dinner to breakfast to create. Jean-Paul knew what he'd typed was wormholed with spelling mistakes but time was of the essence. Using Freelancer.com, he found a proofreader in Manila who could make the English publishable and format the manuscript.

Once finished, he titled the book *Harriet Todd's Sigh*.

A week prior, Jean-Paul had searched every yearbook, class photo, online forum, student magazine, literary listing and phone book he could get his hands on, without finding a single person with the surname Lustt. He'd concluded the T.H.S. Lustt books were an attack on him from some nom de guerre, and he was 99 percent sure he'd deduced who was behind the attack. He found it a little sad that the recipients of his critiques had taken his slings and arrows personally. Jean-Paul's life had been full of hurt. He'd been beaten up at high school. He'd had to beg his stepsister to take him to the school dance. Age 13, Philip Roth had responded dismissively to his fanmail. It puzzled him that others weren't accustomed to suffering.

Regardless: *Harriet Todd's Sigh* would correct the public's view of Jean-Paul Fernandes and eradicate the gnats nipping him.

The fast-paced plot he'd pressed into Microsoft Word with frantic fingertips told the tale of a loser, Harriet Todd, admitted to university due to the pity of the dean, whose other charitable ventures include homing mangy stray dogs and curing malaria. In the novel, Harriet Todd's highest ambition in life is to harass a humble, handsome campus reporter. The handsome reporter, who is busy dealing with media adulation after having been longlisted for the Pulitzer Prize for Literary Criticism, spares an hour to meet with the drooling Harriet Todd, who rolls on her back and prostrates herself, desperate to be satisfied by the reporter, whose sexual prowess is the stuff of legend.

Jean-Paul released the novella in four installments over the month of October, 10,000 words at a time. *Student Guide* followers went rabid for it, even though it seemed a bit short and written rather hurriedly.

There were furious letters to the editor, however, once the ending was published. *Harriet Todd's Sigh* wound up with the protagonist realizing she could never be anything more than a loser and hanging herself from the flagpole outside the vice-chancellor's office. The sigh, it is revealed in the book's final pages, is the sound of Harriet Todd gasping for attention as she dies.

The outraged letters began immediately. Jean-Paul fielded interview after interview. Everybody wanted to know the reason for the publication of the story. Jean-Paul said the novella was written because it *had* to be written. It demanded to erupt from its volcanic chamber and be birthed into the public consciousness.

He couldn't think of a constructive way to explain the book was written in response to a manifest unevenness. There were three people out there in the world with an inseparable bond whereas Jean-Paul had to suffer life alone. It wasn't fair.

7.

People were seen around campus reading the third instalment of the Lustt trilogy, *Sadist Struggles On*, though in fewer numbers compared to the first. There was less chatter, fewer quotes posted online. Reviews dropped to an insignificant ebb. At one point we found ourselves having to prompt a young English student in the elevator to spill her opinion of the story.

She said the books were getting boring, now. Same old predictable shit.

In *Sadist Struggles On*, John Fernando finds himself eking out a living as a writer of TV Guide crosswords, having accepted he is unworthy of literary esteem. One day he receives a courier package letting him know he has spawned an illegitimate child who has grown up wildly successful as an author. The child's lovers and friends teach John erotic lessons, once again punishing, humiliating and spanking their cruel father John. John begs the child for forgiveness. The book ends.

*

It was at a meeting of the T.H.S. Lustt management committee in the Eagle's Nest that we agreed it was time to send Jean-Paul Fernandes a taunting email confessional. It wasn't about us relieving ourselves of guilt—we had none—and more about psychologically unnerving our enemy. *Harriet Todd's Sigh* couldn't be left to influence the audience unquestioned. Our team had to overwhelm the Jean-Paul novella before it had a chance to return in some sordid sequel, or at least hack or stab or infiltrate Fernandes' computer, his inbox, his files.

We got to work on our confession. Our email, from THS. management@gmail.com, began with the first letter of T. H. S. Lustt's name.

This
Here confessional
Shows
Loser
U are
Sucked in
This made-up author lie
The new Angry Penguins hoax
I'd laugh, but
Shame on you
Finking you were better than
Any other
Kommon writer.
Ern Malley is too good for you.
Xoxo
HarrietTodd'sSigh

A little stiff and awkward, sure, containing crimes against grammar, but it was genius the Avant Guardians would have been proud of. We had a couple of glasses of brandy afterwards, to celebrate, then Si reached inside his jacket, put his hand on his heart and produced cigars for each of us, a neat little family in his fingers.

When we awoke in a daze at 5 am as our energetic flatmate slammed the front door to jog to the gym, we all suffered simultaneous heart attacks.

That gloating email—the acrostic poem, the taunt, the obvious reference at the end—was far too lacking in subtlety. It could destroy us.

We had to delete it.

8.

The offices of *Student Guide* were at the top of a four storey building, which used to be a fire station before the university swallowed it. A spiralling iron staircase took us to the top. The rooms within the *Guide's* office were dark grey carpeted boxes on random levels, descending a foot here, rising a foot there, with creaking floorboards and low ceilings and a corner in which a poster of Ernest Hemingway glowered down on an empty chair walled in by stacks of books.

In the gloomy Hemingway hollow lay the computer with which Jean-Paul Fernandes had ruined ambitions and broken spines.

All of this, we saw peering in through the dark glass at 5:55 on a Monday morning. We had no way inside without breaking the glass in the door and reaching down to the handle.

The handle depressing by itself as Todd squeezed Harriet, biting his fingertips.

The handle wheezing, all the way down.

The door wide open, with a man standing there in a beret and corduroy jacket.

'Enter.'

Jean-Paul Fernandes held the door wide. Beckoning us in.

'If you're here to delete that email of yours, you'll have to kill me.'

Todd looked at Si with quizzical eyebrows. Si shook his head in dismissal.

Jean-Paul reclined in his leather office chair, one knee folded over the other, jiggling the Hush Puppy dangling from his toes.

'I understand the three of you represent T.H.S. Lustt?'

The three nodded.

'Am I ... speaking to her now?'

'Oh for God's sake, Jean-Paul. We don't have multiple personality disorder.'

'Some form of psychotic illness, though. You came here to commit a burglary in order to delete one email that required three brains to compose. Hardly the definition of mental stability.'

Todd hovered his whiskey under his nose then tossed it back. The glow spread down his arteries, warming his throat, his fingertips.

'Look.' Si pinched his nose. 'Let's cut to the chase. We need to compromise.'

'Do we, now? Because I have you dead to rights. Confessing in some sordid email; breaking into my office; attempting to burgle my computer.'

'That's not the literal definition of burgle—

'Macmillan Dictionary, 6th edition, 1973.'

'OXFORD ENGLISH. 2012. Burgle: verb, present simple: to enter a building illegally, usually using force, and *steal* from it.'

'Merriam-Webster doesn't—

'FUCK MERRIAM-WEBSTER. Can't you just, just not call security? Can't you just let us evacuate the building quietly?'

'Ernp. Correction. The building itself may be evacuated, but human beings cannot take on the active participle of the verb to— '

'We'll let you in the book,' Todd blurted. The men looked at him. 'We'll, I dunno, kill John Fernandes off or something. Is that what you want?'

'You'll retire the character. Send him to live in Bermuda as a Member of the British Empire.'

'And you'll stop publishing your mean stuff?'

'I take it you're referring to the sagas of Harriet Todd? Twould be a pity to reel her in. She has quite a following.'

'No more.' Si was standing now. 'That's what we're calling it. The book, I mean. *No More*. Final in the series. We'll, we'll... wind it all up, I guess.' Si made eye contact with everybody in the room, holding Jean-Paul's gaze the longest, until Harriet tugged on Si's sleeve and whispered something in his ear.

'She's asking if you'll give the book a good review. Since you're literary editor.'

'If I'll positively review the book from the series in which I had my—pardon my French—*salad tossed* by fireants? The series in which I met humiliation?'

Todd threw a cushion at Jean-Paul's face. 'Be grateful that shit's fiction. We'll do your stupid apology book. We cool or not?'

Jean-Paul's eyes scanned us all. The people who'd dared to outsell him, out-publish him. People who'd wriggled out from under his red pen and enacted terrible public revenge. Sent him a psychologically torturous email. Attempted to burgle his office. Described in detail fireants biting off slices of his rectal tissue and carrying the slices back to their nest. People who'd fought a literary feud with him were asking to meet in the middle. People who considered themselves worthy adversaries in a battle of brains, a war of words with the very integrity of literature at stake.

Jean-Paul rolled his eyes, reached out to shake his friends' hands.

'I believe we're cool.'

THIS GENERATION NEEDS A WAR

I'm standing around a rectangular hole in the ground and 40 rain-soaked Māori crying outside the marae and I totally have to get the fuck out of here.

Jeez, man. I drove six hours to stand here on the muddy grass with my so-called people. The deceased is Willie Wētere, a 120 kilogram professional bully who I'm reeeeally not sad to see dead. He was drunk and drove his farm bike into a wire fence and choked. Meanwhile here's me, about to graduate with honors from law school down in Wellington. I'm starting to think natural selection takes your life where it's meant to go.

I check my watch, sing a few bars of *Whakaaria Mai* to fit in, cast my long neck around. There are sheep less than ten metres away. This is hillbilly shit. Little Huria's rubbing peoples' hands and bending her spotty face in sympathy, 21 going on 55. I can't tell if she's enjoying herself or just playing the part.

We were head boy and head girl together, me and Huria. Duxes of the school, us two. They gave us special blazers with badges sewn into them. We always ended up eating lunch together when we weren't feeling like rugby or fist fights. Jerks tried to force our heads together at the school dance to make us pash. As if we were the same. As if our destiny was written.

Huria spies me and sashays through the black suits and hats and puddles. Anxious midget body, frizzy black hair pulled back into a tight hard arrogant bun, showing that big wide brainy forehead.

'Can't wait for our holiday, huh Tama,' she squeaks, all short and hunched and smily like a grandmother. Huria runs her hands up my suit jacket, making adjustments, smoothing crinkles, straightening my breast pocket handkerchief. She's a month older than me but tonnes shorter. I'm like a giraffe, looking down on her. Since we were born we've known each other inside-out. We've top-and-tailed in each other's beds, swum naked in the creek. I have this memory of Mum putting a bowl on Huria's hair and cutting around the edges. I buried her pet lamb when it died. She stitched my eyebrow shut after I fell off the quad bike. I'll never get inside her pussy, that'd be awkward and weird, we're too tight for that, but it's on the edge of my mind, woo-whee. I can't stop thinking about partying, lately.

'Europe's 25 days away and counting,' I say behind my hand, blocking out the song that's erupted as the coffin sinks into the earth. 'And I'm meeting you in Monaco, was it?'

Huria stands back. She's constantly finding reasons to be disappointed with me, this girl. Getting geography wrong is a war crime to her. 'It's MONTREUX, dude. The Chillon Castle's 800 years old! It's on an island in the lake! Didn't you get that itinerary I sent you?'

'Honest, Hu, I'm trying to be itinerary-free. I don't need paperwork, y'know—I need a blow-out. Need to get away from all this.'

The black mob moves, everyone squelches through the mud and gets in their cars and drives to the RSA. Ever the Girl Guide, Huria says goodbye to like twenty kuia and ten kaumatua, kissing each one and helping them bend into their cars. Me, I hit on a couple of cousins sitting in the front of a lowered Subaru, ask them if they're coming over to the pub. I was starting to get some panache during my time in Wellington, growing out of my teenage dork phase. I had a 50/50 success rate getting my dick wet, which was pretty good. In this inbred little hometown, though, I'm just some overachiever who's never killed a pig. No cred. The Subaru girls hide in their black hoodies, giggling. I move on.

The pub's so full of mourning Māoris the windows are white with fog. People's soaked shoulders steam. People have to suck their tummies in and squeeze each other with their handfuls of beer. I hit my head on the door frame as I enter. Head too high-up. My body hasn't caught up with my brain.

Grampop sloshes a handle of beer in front of me, grinning insanely. Grampop's been shrinking and his pants have soaked up mud from the tangi. He's dripping on the floor.

'Here's to your trip!'

I toast Grampop but Dad doesn't join in. Dad's been against my O.E. since I announced it. Dad's afraid of what's outside his super-boring small-town Māori life. Mum reckons Dad went wild in Singapore back in the 70s after he served in 'Nam but he clamped a lid on it for some reason and I've never seen Dad cut loose once.

Grampop rolls a smoke, even though you're not supposed to smoke in here.

'Sorry about him,' Dad says.

Grampop bumps his fist on the table. 'NEVER APOLOGIZE FOR NOTHIN'!'

Some of Willie Wetere's Neanderthal mates are filing past our table and they snigger at Grampop's outburst. I only see these guys when I come home for Christmas and funerals and their only progress is they've gotten fatter or been to jail or had another kid. Another rugby championship lost. Another pig stuffed. Another marlin mounted. Tennis courts with weeds growing out of them. People riding horses to the shop to buy bread. Nothing ever changes here.

Dad tilts his head at Philip Ropitini, whose wide arse has bumped our beer and his cup of tea. Philip Ropitini's great great great grandad fought heroically against Hongi Hika, so the legend goes. Ran into fire, ate the flesh of his enemies, if you believe the bullshit. Meanwhile jocks like the Ropitinis think my family are wusses 'cause dad's tupuna were kupapa and fought alongside the British. Soft, apparently, 'cause we do constructive stuff in the community, like Dad's a volunteer firefighter and he gives poor families food parcels. Families including the Ropitinis, actually.

We watch our wobbling beers slow down and still. The raffle wheel is spinning in the corner. Some old guy holds a meat pack triumphantly in the air. It's noisy as a waterfall in here.

'They're looking for trouble, I take it, those delinquents who bumped our table?' Dad goes. 'Remember, Tama: Queensberry rules if you plan on fisticuffs. And shake hands afterwards.'

'RUBBISH, NOW YOU LISTEN HERE, TAMA,' Grampop shouts over the noisy pub, squashing Dad out with his elbow. A medal swings off Grampop's chest and dips in his beer foam.

'This generation needs a war, y'unnerstand? Son, I had the best time of my entire life when I was stationed in fuckin' Europe after the war. Europeans looooove a Māori boy.' He raises his beer. 'We're good niggers to them.'

'Jesus, Grampop.'

'And son, tell you what: nobody knows how to party like them Europeans. If I had a shilling for every Fräulein I rooted in Düsseldorf, jeepers creepers... .' Grampop squeezes Dad's wrist. Dad shakes his hand free, looks away, adjusts his tie and cuffs.

'And a course I met the foxiest young lady in Sheffield and the rest was history. HISTORY! Traded her some pantyhose for a wedding ring, didn't I. Mattera fact you can claim yourself a passport through your British side, provided this Brexit malarkey doesn't go ahead. Betcha didn't know that.'

I look Dad in the eye to see if Grampop's bullshitting.

Dad plays with his teabag.

'Not factually incorrect, though I'd say your Kiwi passport's safer than the British.'

Grampop thumps his walking stick on the floorboards.

'Have two passports, why don'tcha!'

'Regardless,' Dad goes, 'You're going to take precautions while you're over there, yes?'

'Yeah pop. Totally. I'll probly just fly into London and hang out there a couple months.'

'You'll be needing a crateload of rubber Johnnies!' Grampop goes, laughing till he starts coughing into his elbow.

Dad's not even listening to Grampop. He's looking at me hard. I dip into the secret plans in my brain and pull out a report that will satisfy him.

Yes, Dad, I'll be looking for an internship in a good law firm as soon as my plane touches down, and I'll email you and Skype too.

Yes, I'll drink lots of water before I go to sleep each night, and eat a big kai, and I'll keep my hand over the top of my beer so kidney thieves don't whisk me to some dodgy warehouse in Serbia.

And yes, perfect squeaky little Huria can report back on me if she wants.

Honest, Dad, there's nothing to fret about. Just a quick O.E. then I promise I'll come home safe.

*

There's an African dude grinning down at me, tickling my armpits, saying something about playing, swings and slides, Come to de sandpit, mon. I can't understand his accent, at first. I've been sleeping for 30 hours. It finally turns out he's Jamaican and he's dragging the whole Commonwealth to this pub called Outback which is dripping with Australian-themed shit. There's a stuffed kangaroo at the door and a painting of Uluru and a lot of Fosters and Steinlager and VB Bitter on tap. A bunch of us huddle round tables sharing photos of Stonehenge and Iceland, making plans for predictable shit.

Outback Bar stops serving hot chips at 8 o'clock and ravers pour in as they cut the lights and the ceiling glitters and there's fingertips and pills and glowsticks and I'm talking to this chick from Perth in a Kombi van photo booth that's in a dark corner of the place with boomerangs glued on it and trying to make plans with her, it seems the polite thing to do, we'll go to a full moon beach party on Ko Samui, what's your email address, I'll write it down, but she laughs when I ask her name and tells me to quit my yapping and pulls her jeans down and braces against the wall, showing me her back, no kisses, no intimacy, and after a few minutes I'm pulling my pants up then bouncers chuck us out into Trafalgar Square and we're stumbling and the cold wet stone walls are pressing against us and JOEY'S BEEN ARRESTED! AUSSIE AUSSIE AUSSIE! OI OI OI! and we're playing rugby around Nelson's Column and I run smack into this huge Pakistani fella and his mates chuck a couple punches in and I get my arm twisted like a noodle by the cops and the sun's coming up and I'm puking a full English breakfast at the table then we're spending the morning in a pub playing darts and singing and they shake me awake miles away and we're watching Chelsea thrash Amsterdam and my phone is buzzing and it's my dad calling and Jacob takes the battery out of my phone while my dad's ringing and biffs it into the throng.

*

Oxford in summer is slow and hazy and quaint and warm and the trees drizzle petals and leaves. Squirrels sniffle and women push prams and the river is thick and green. Students in white shirts and wide brimmed hats are punting long wooden boats, falling in love. Their lives are safe and golden.

Huria sits across the café table from me wearing a straw hat that makes her look tinier than ever. She's smirking cause she's sipping lager and lime at 11 am. It's pretty much the naughtiest thing Huria's ever done.

I'm sighing and drumming my fingers on the table.

Huria has been doing kapa haka with this group called Nga Hau E Wha from the New Zealand embassy and her bus has arrived in Oxford and, lo and behold, I'm in Oxford too, at the Oxfordshire Folk Festival. It's actually not lo and behold whatsoever cause Huria's pretty much stalking me. She got epic-flustered when I was without a cellphone for a week. Fucking overachieving SuperMāori. I get enough of that cultural stuff back home. I've gone to the opposite side of the world to be European, to be hip, to be cool. Here, I'm something sleek and caramel and hip. The other day some honey at the train station mistook me for Italian. Another person thought I was from Malta. I am reinventing myself. I am a brown James Bond.

Huria slides a handwritten letter across the table for me and I take a peek. It's Dad's unmistakably square handwriting leading up to some whakatauki proverb at the end.

I slide the letter back, toss my drink into my throat and light a cigarette. 'Right: time to jet.'

'But you just got here?' Huria's saying, looking stung. 'And since when do you smoke?'

'I've got this thing. Up in Newcastle. I booked this Contiki party bus and I've just gotta go.'

'Newcastle? But we're meeting in Switzerland next week? Then you're looking for an internship, Ta-'

'WOULD YOU QUIT TELLING ME WHAT TO DO?'

I pull a wad of money from my jacket and chuck it down. I make sure the bank notes spill across the table and flutter onto the ground so Huria has to get down on her knees and scrabble after them.

I didn't want to do that to poor Huri—she's a homegirl, after all, she's like a sister, but it's not her I'm walking out on. It's me.

I get on my bus and head north for Newcastle with buds stuck into my ears. Six60 are jamming this fucking bongo-bongo dub tune that goes 'Don't forget your roots, my friend / don't forget your famileee.' It's so god damn saccharine I have to switch it off. I find some angry beats instead. *I am the Firestartah / twisted Firestartah / I'm the bitch you hated / filth infatuated/ I'm the self-inflicted mind detonator.* Yeah. That's my mood.

I watch the signs flick by on the motorway, watch the kilometres change, envisioning every shot of sambuca I'm gonna pound, every Marlboro I'm gonna suck down, the Jäger bombs, the vodkas and cokes and the so-called llello I find myself snorting from some Portuguese guy's credit card in the toilets while the black inferno shakes and rattles and I spill out sideways onto a dancefloor made of blue glass and I haven't eaten and my stomach bubbles and there are a hundred thousand people beneath me and this Norwegian chick's yelling into my ear and it takes ten repeats til I finally understand her accent over the bass, she's asking where I'm staying and I give her a comical Jim Carrey shrug, screwing up my rubber face.

I haven't a fucking clue, honestly. All I know is I have a backpack of underwear and books in a rental locker at the bus station.

She tells me I have to get on this overnight ferry from Newcastle to Oslo leaving at 10, arriving at breakfast, it's a once in a lifetime opportunity, the northern stars reflect on the black sea and you can see Ursa Major and Taurus and I'm sold, this is really happening, we're kissing for five, ten seconds at a time, and as we wobble down High Street leading to North Shields

Ferry Port (eh? Shield what? Where am I?) and stumble onto some gangplank and some boat I'm like Sweet, Iespardy, wuzzat, you won me to take little baggy in my sock, okay, Tama's a good boy, Tama takey baggy in de socky. I don't know which part of Newcastle Oslo is in, like some kind of a seaside suburb or something, but I enjoy the ferry ride, at least until I wake shivering on a slatted bench and we're bobbing on a dark indigo sea and there are some Germans bowing Thank You and scampering away, holding something triumphantly up under the moon and I wake with icy breath and diesel stench and rusty water dripping on me and the Customs cops are reaching inside my hip pockets, touching my nuts, just about, and I'm recoiling in the corner going Hey hey heyyyyy, who the fuck d'you think you're feeling up, boys?

Foghorns. Salt air. Seagulls screaming.

There is no little bag of crystal shards in my sock any more, just a smudge of lipstick where some gorgeous Norwegian chick has kissed my ankle. The last chain of tourists is filing off the ferry onto land, sneering over their shoulders at me.

The Customs cops don't put another hand on me, but they surround me so I can't run. I'm the last person on the ferry, the only one without a huge hi-vis jacket with reflective strips on it and it's obvious I'm in trouble. They politely invite me to follow them up the bridge and get in a brand new Prius so they can drive me to a holding cell and I'm like Sweet, bro, sweet. Free trip around—where'd you say this was again? Ostend? Onslow?

*

The holding cell has wide windows, double glazed. It's warm as a lounge in here. The view is of these narrow streets lined with birch trees filing down to the harbour. The buildings are all made of glistening granite or glass and steel. This city looks like Starfleet Academy. Best part of being locked up in Norway, though, is the fruit juice, because my body is miserable from being fed alcohol for days and my stomach is twisted and my breath is rotten. The juice comes on a tray with a salad and fruit and crumbed chicken. The Norwegian feds have put me in a detox spa, pretty much. Well, when I say ME, I mean US—I'm in here with these football hooligans called Gremlins, from Newcastle. They have the word tattooed on their necks. They're saying they're from Tyneside and I'm not sure I've been there then their leader with hurried, demanding eyes is saying to me 'Ow the fook d'ye get yer arse o'er here if it weren't froom Tyneside, like?' and after a few moments translating, I'm realizing Newcastle is where I've come from, and it's like on the port of the Tyne river.

Right. Gotcha.

'I think someone must've slipped me— '

'Loads of English here,' the hooligans' leader interrupts me from his bunk bed. 'We're due out tonight. Slap on the wrist, aw this. Four star 'otel, meart. Oi: ye want to squeeze in a little sparrin?'

I tell him no thanks then watch as the boys fill the day boxing, practicing ugly combinations of knees and elbows and headbutts. The toughest ginger twin, all hunched and acne'd, shakes the flowers out of the vase and he mimes cracking it over the head of his youngest droog. The secret to winning a fight is apparently to end it ASAP using whatever shortcuts or surprises you can get your hands on.

I roll away on my bunk, face the wall. I'm still yawning the party out of me. My brain needs to chill for a week. My liver needs to process whatever weird chemicals I've had.

A polite, cheery woman with red hair comes in once with hot chocolate on a tray and invites me to a private room, away from "these people." I know she's going to ask me about the girl who gave me the meth to smuggle in my sock. I'm about to leave the room when I feel the hooligan leader's eyes burn holes in my back. I can tell that if I tell her anything, I'm going to get my arse kicked. I take the hot chocolate and close the door on her.

She returns an hour later in a foul mood.

'We are needingk one description of your friend,' she goes. There is no warmth in her face.

'Just deport me,' I go, shrugging, 'I can't remember that night.'

After lunch and dinner, I'm signing a form promising not to return to the Kingdom of Norway without going through Customs then I'm driven to the docks and released. There are these big white iceberg-looking ships with glistening portholes. I try to scuttle up a bridge and board one but the albino guard-boy in his fluffy sweater makes a commotion and I back away and go roaming the streets, desperate for dinner. I've got my passport and my wallet and my new phone and the rest of my shit is in some locker somewhere. What status update are you supposed to put for a situation like this? I don't have tonnes of friends following me anyway. Fuck Facebook.

In a sinkhole just beyond the chainlink perimeter of the docks is a sailors' pub, anchors and lifejackets nailed to the exterior. I get an advance on some cash from the AmEx machine with a massive withdrawal fee that my dad would tell me off for agreeing to, then I'm shouldering open the door of the pub and walking into the centre. Anyone wants to jump me, jump me. I could use a week in a fancy hospital.

Someone puts their hand on me immediately and I flinch and seize the neck of the beer bottle I've ordered, ready to attempt to fight. Turns out the dude grabbing me with the long goatee and sideburns and shaved head is Gremlin, the hooligan from the cell with the impatient eyes. His chin beckons me into the booth and we hunker down low over the table top and get into a conspiracy with his boys. These dudes explain they sailed into Oslo cause they're waiting on a delivery from some Danish lads that's supposed to arrive. If I want to go ahead and speed things up and take two ferries down to Copenhagen to receive a delivery then fly back to the UK, they'll support me.

I'm trying not to blink, but it's a fuckload of information to take in.

'Ye got ye Kiwi passport 'n all, meart?'

I slap it on the tabletop.

'Fookin' five hundred thou for a good'un,' the guy explains to his boys. 'Oi: give us ye mobile, like.' I hand over my cellphone and he types some numbers into it for a quiet, tense minute. 'Nem's Poofin.'

'Like the bird,' I finally go, after decoding his accent for a few awkward seconds, and neck the rest of my beer, 'You're name's Puffin, you're saying... ?'

'Ah dorn't tend t'repeat mesel, pal. On ya bike. Ye've got yer orders. Good lud.'

Seems the right thing to do now is get up on unsteady legs and leave. It's 10 o'clock and the city's buried under glowing snow and I'm wandering black ice streets down to the docks and thank fuck, this Somali-looking woman with an unexpectedly bouncy accent is telling me the last ferry is at eleven. I fall asleep in a bundle of coats, keeping an eye on these dodgy-looking Egyptians wearing puffer jackets like armour. They begin texting as soon as they spot me. Fuck.

I find a safe booth and endure ranted conversation from this old Japanese witch who's climbed the highest peaks on four continents. She's been here exploring the fjords with nothing but a bumbag full of figs. Thanks, lady. Keep me company. Keep the hyenas from closing in.

When I wake up, it's summer morning in Denmark and I fall into a conversation with some crazy Swedish metalhead in an Opeth t-shirt who says I simply HAVE to go to Roskilde. It's one of the world's best heavy metal music shows.

We do it. It takes three days out of my life and I sleep in a tent with mud beneath us, getting all my calories from beer, but I do it.

Midway through the Rammstein set, I realize Puffin wasn't just putting his friends' contact details in my cellphone to be friendly.

He was memorizing my phone numbers.

I leave the concert and catch a taxi to the airport and get a flight to England before Gremlin kills my dad or tells him I smuggled drugs. I don't know which one's worse.

*

Heathrow breaks every backpacker except me. I watch two Kiwi dudes arguing with British Airways about their surfboards. I watch a pair of Canadian sisters crying in the corner cause they're out of money and have to wait two days to board a plane, sleeping on the carpet, living off coffee and crackers.

I score a ride on this insanely cheap Irish discount airline called Aer Grand, buying a ticket on my phone from this website where you play poker for discount airfares. My ticket costs just ten pounds, thank God. I'm lucky, that's it. I've been blessed. Nothing bad can truly happen to me.

The flight from London to Belfast is only ninety minutes and when I get off, the air tastes like smoke and seaweed. I'm in Northern Ireland, and there's a skinhead in a bomber jacket and kilt with his arms folded in front of the luggage carousel, except I can't remember where my luggage should be. Newcastle or Oxford or Oslo or—

'Ye'd be Tama then,' he says to me, yanking my bag out of my arms and marching efficiently away like a soldier. On the back of his shaved head is a wobbly green tattoo saying F.T.P.

His car is parked in a handicapped space and he's left the engine running.

'So oi understand yer not whoit, through and through,' the skinhead says as he starts the car. 'Listen: oi won't tell if ye won't tell.'

He plows through a gaggle of shocked tourists, honking the car horn.

I try to speak but I've lost my voice.

*

We take an elevator in silence up 20 floors, then 25, 30 then 33. The skinhead leads me to the apartment at the end of the hall and does three knocks, then two, then one, then waits. The door opens and fingers pull us inside.

We're ushered onto the couch and given a cup of tea each. Two pissed-off looking freckled guys in denim jackets are pacing the tiny flat, kicking children's toys out of the way.

I wish they would begin the conversation by asking me who the fuck I am and how the fuck I arrived here because I'm not sure myself. A friend of a friend... of a stranger...

'Guns cannae be bought or sold in Belfast,' they begin telling me. 'Only reliable place tae git yesel a gun in Europe is Switzerland, She's liberal as fook o'er on the continent,' they continue, lighting fresh smokes from a mountain of Benson & Hedges behind the couch.

After they've talked and talked about Uzis and Kalashnikovs and modifying trunnions and receivers, whatever the hell those are, the twins squat on the ground in front of me. I've finished my cup of tea and I'm busting to go to the toilet but afraid to ask.

'So how d'ye ken Parfin, eh?'

'Ye ken Parfin,' they say after I'm silent for too long, 'Tell us how.'

I realize they're asking how I know Puffin. *Ken* must mean *know* around here.

'Met him at f-football,' I stutter.

'Not much football where you're from,' the ginger twin on the left winks.

'There's nothing where I come from.' I'm surprised at my own words. First confident thing I've said in ages.

They take my wallet away and leave me to talk to the cat for an endless half hour. My FTP friend is asleep with his stinking black boots on my thighs. When they return, all the cards in my wallet are out of order and the photos of my dad and Grampop are where I usually keep my library card.

'Nice view,' I nervously say.

'Ye tryina be foony, meart? We're top o'the fookin council esteart.'

I nod at the Union Jack flag on the walls, the Fenians Must Die poster with a picture of Lord Kitchener, the WANTED and R.I.P. and BOBBY SANDS ROT IN HELL posters.

'So you guys are like enemies of the Irish....?'

'We ARE Irish, ya eejit. Did ye not cross the water when ye came here?'

The kinder of the denim ginger twins pulls me to a corner of the room while his brother smokes his glass pipe.

'Oi, this town, roit, she's fookin' starfed to the gill with Albanians, fookin' Pakis, fookin' Ukrainians, meart. We can't beat em so we're fookin' joinin em.'

'All that Brexit's shite's set tae majorly starf up our business loik, make it harder to get stoff off the continent and over to the UK,' the methhead brother adds.

'...which is how come we're garn with the away crew. Supporters, that's us.'

They wrap a Chelsea scarf around my neck and punch a blue and white chequered t-shirt into my chest and that's me, apparently. A football hooligan.

*

The Shipyard is the best club in Belfast and the twins pull me through the bouncers' wall of shoulders and push me into a corner and three bottles of vodka appear. Some guy who claims to be a friend of the twins keeps hassling me about the All Blacks.

'Yous Merries think you're the best in the feckin' wirld with your haka, trying to intimidate us, but we invented the feckin' game, meart,' and tries to convince me Ulster are the best rugby side in the world and I tell him 'Righto' and do my best to bury myself in the music, watching girls.

I'm sleepy and grumpy from smoking speed with these guys and I want to go home.

'Think you can intimidate me, pal?' he says out of nowhere. 'Try some of that haka shit right now, I'll fookin' drop ye.'

The guy makes fun of Chelsea. I reach out for support, grasp an ice bucket and hit him with it while my crew watches me, arms folded. I kneel on the guy I've hit and bash his skull till his hair sticks to a flap of bleeding skin hanging off his face like potato peel. The boys haul me up and push me into an elevator with a bored-looking Russian girl. She fucks me in her hotel room. I roll over, sleep for a year, wake up and gasp, stunned to find myself hundreds of metres above the ground in a sea of yellow plastic seats, looking down on a chorus of booming Chelsea supporters singing ONE MAN WENT TO MOW, WENT TO MOW A MEADOW.

There is a rectangle of grass in the centre of my giant bowl of seats and Chelsea fans. I scan the stadium walls. The Credit Suisse signs are in ...German? Holy shit. I think I'm in Zurich.

A whistle blows. The words Auf wiedersehen! materialize on the billboard. A wave of moaning collides with a current of cheers. Rolls of toilet paper arc through the air. A terrace seat lands on the grass. There's plasticky smoke coming from a fire somewhere. Bottles breaking. Another whistle. I hear English accents. Somebody shoves me in the back and I have to follow the tide out.

England supporters ooze onto the clean stone streets. We wash over everything. I see an old man get punched from behind, his scarf torn off and taken by some little kid. Guys are running at each other doing kung fu kicks. A paramedic is flattened with a paving stone. A police horse drops steaming shit as a bunch of guys pulls its bridle, ripping the rider off, punching the horse. The cops sprint to safety. We stampede after them, spilling into alleys, restaurants, pubs, a chocolate café. There's a Greenpeace thrift shop and the hooligans form a queue, sending out baskets of ammunition, shoes, bottles, dinnerware. People hurl plates and mugs at the police. The porcelain explodes in white puffs on their riot shields. The police retreat. England supporters file into a McDonald's. Men in yellow scarves are running out screaming and throwing trays and milkshakes and Wet Floor signs.

Clinging to a statue on a stone island with frightened tourists is Huria, looking miniscule under a thick woollen hat and a giant backpack, holding her mobile, stabbing it with a fingertip.

Something buzzes in my pocket. It's a text from Huria.

I HAVEN'T HEARD FROM U IM SCARED R U COMING 2 SWITZ?

I try to cling to the iron rails around a rubbish bin but I'm sucked downhill and I only stop when I slam into the arms of a grinning ginger twin who tells me he's been looking for me everywhere. Time to get back to work. This isn't a holiday, pal.

*

Armurerie de la Gare is right across the road from Lake Geneva. There are wet footprints leading up and down the stone. The doormat is moist.

Inside it's a palace, or it used to be. There's a chandelier, thick green carpet, shields and spears on the walls and a suit of armour. The staff are three blondes, 18 to 20-ish, standing at attention like hoteliers and wearing lederhosen and big leather boots and oversized name tags. They welcome me with big grins and flapping lashes. A guy carrying a stack of boxed rifles grunts as a grinning girl holds open the door for him.

The dude I'm following for the transaction is named Markus Thommen. I don't know if that's his whole name. It's just the name the ginger twins told me to expect as I waited on a park bench beside the lake, watching its jagged waves, wishing I could send pictures to a friend. Huria would love to sit with me and watch the wind shaving curls of water. She's emailed to say she's disappointed but she'll wait for me in Montreux on the 23rd then move onto Lausanne on the 25th, then I can get "back on track," as if I've derailed.

In a corner of Armurerie, amongst floor to ceiling racks of protein bars and silver canteens and fishing jackets, Markus Thommen bends his head down and gives me a hard look.

His accent is dictionary-perfect English like Hannibal Lecter. His hair is sheep-white. His accent is dark and hard.

'Don't fucking embarrass me. We get out of here, we get up the street, you get out of Switzerland.'

Markus Thommen pulls shades over his eyes. I don't understand why he's so jumpy. 'Kent Terrace in the city of Ka-waka, this is where you are coming from?' He grabs my collar and twists. Our noses press. 'I AM RECEIVINGK FIVE YEARS IN PRISON IF YOU ARE FUCKING THIS UP.'

I follow him as if we're in a three-legged race together. He moves metres away across the store then I let myself be elastic'd over towards him. The salesgirls don't seem to care. Markus Thommen asks for a trolley and they bring him this expensive wheeled table contraption made of stainless steel and wood with shiny golden fasteners. He fills the trolley with a few AR15s, then asks for a huge thing called an SG550 which sticks way out of the trolley like a giant folded music stand. He then wheels his trolley inside the elevator, moves up to the first floor, up on a deck by the chandelier, and stacks handguns into the trolley too, all Sig Sauers. By the time he's asking the milkmaids to put ammo in the trolley, he's having trouble moving it. There must be 80 kilos of metal in there. At least 30 guns. The trolley's wheels are getting stuck in the plush carpet.

Some baron-looking dude in an elaborate felt jacket with lions and fleurs de lis converses with Markus Thommen as the girls scan each gun at the counter. All I understand in the conversation is 'Lizenz under papierschein.'

Part of my job was to spill Coke on Markus's permit before we came into the store then dry the paper off, shaking it into the wind over the lake. I wanted to let go. I wanted to step into the water and disappear. But we got the fake permit and the fake licence looking used and authentic and now we're sliding it across the counter. This is me, now. Helping creepy strangers buy guns. Pointless to back out.

I leave the store first and wait on a park bench as they fill Markus Thommen's rental car with guns. He drives 500 metres up the street. I jog along the waterfront then arrive at his driver side window, panting. I've been smoking too many cigarettes.

Without leaving his seat, he unlocks the back of the car. He's transferred half of the guns into two suitcases so heavy they seem to be stuck to the ground.

'Here,' he says, handing me a raw, naked plastic-y feeling handgun with a label hanging off it, 'Your money is in de case. Two thousands. You are having fun in Knabenschiessen.'

'What?'

He snorts and rolls his eyes.

'You check into your hotel, you check out. If you are seeing the football supporter, you are not to approach. You put the suitcase on the bed, you check out of the hotel. Don't do a single other thing or I am cutting your fucking throat out, ja?' He reaches out from the steering wheel and slaps my cheek. I curl my fingers into a fist, ready to hit back.

'Ub ub ub!' He waggles a telling-off finger at me then takes out one of the duffel bags and dumps it at my feet. 'Your father, you are not wanting him to get punishment, no? We are having men in your country. Your father, his house, 371 Puriri the street, it is built of wood yes?'

'I—I guess so... ?'

He flicks his lit cigarette at me. 'Wood burns like a motherfucker.'

*

I'm linking arms with this Malaysian princess to get into Club Lange & Söhne in the medieval catacombs beneath Geneva, then I'm texting Dad cause I've forgotten his 60th birthday, then I'm holding the drunken walls of a passageway leading into Absolut Dungeon which is a medieval torture chamber with weapons and flaming torches on the walls and strippers and short thugs with wide elbows and big stomping boots then I'm boarding the 10.05 TGV Lyria to Paris which is apparently a high speed train doing 200 miles an hour which makes me feel sick and dizzy and I squeeze the arm rests and finger my phone, desperate to phone Grampop or Dad. Talk me out of this, you guys. Guilt me into stopping.

Under the Eurostar counter at Gare du Nord station in Paris, the ginger twins are waiting for me, dressed in their denim armour. Sewn on their blue jackets is a yellow flag with a red hand. They're behind a metal stand, peering past some cops' shoulders. I think they've been ordered to get back on their train to England, like there's some law that stops them from setting foot on the continent. They press against the barrier hard, though, and once their eyes lock on me, I'm captured.

'YOU'LL GIT ON THIS FOOKING TRAIN WITH OOS OR THERE'LL BE NO MORE WORK FOR YE, MEART!' one of them is bellowing at me across the station.

I disappear behind a pillar and catch my breath. Fuck. I don't wanna do the gun stuff with these guys any more. There was a documentary playing on the train about people bringing arms into Belfast. A seven year old kid got caught in the crossfire at a playground. He died with his face in a drinking fountain. Women are being sent death threats. Kids are in the gutters are addicted to smack.

'They make a lot of noise, your friends.'

The man in front of me has every inch of his face shaved except for his fluffy black eyebrows. He looks like a polished hazelnut in purple tracksuit suit. He must be Turkish or Greek or Azerbaijani or something. So are his bros, who detach themselves from their own pillars and bat their folded arms with newspaper and bottles of iced tea.

'You are lookingk for work?'

*

There is a tiny, shivering woman Mr. Eyebrows needs to get on the Eurostar from Paris into London. She cannot travel with her real people. They turn you away if you're in numbers. Luckily this woman comes from wealth back home. All she needs to get over the water into the UK is a pretend-boyfriend whose passport is from a neutral country. There is 20,000 Euro in it for me if I'm interested in helping. I'd like to find a backpacker hostel and think about it but the men nudge me into the tiled toilets and I'm surrounded and there's only one answer. They ask me to hand them my backpack. They finger my passports, my wallet, my letters from home, the medal Grampop gave me to keep me brave. They take me with them to a huge ugly Humvee and we drive into what looks like Morocco or Tunisia or something, except I know we're deep within Paris. Smoke and rugs and mezze and coffee and a market selling melons and cucumbers. I can just see a few skyscrapers leering over, but this is a ghetto. A foggy underworld.

They tell me to wait in a little woodshed. Three hours later it opens and she's standing there, the woman who's paying tens of thousands to get into the UK. I'm given a Manchester United flag to drape over us both, and ticket stubs from a match we supposedly attended. Proof of a quick jaunt to

Europe for a typical backpacker couple, now let us back into England, please.

I bury us in red and we return to the train station and I present my NZ passport and she presents an Australian one and we bite our fingernails till we've got our tickets to cross the Chunnel and we're tunnelling through the blackness, barely breathing till the train surfaces and she falls into the arms of her family.

*

They remind me of Huria, these women, the way they look anxiously at the world, expecting hurt. I bring them into England from Paris or Antwerp or Amsterdam. We practice our lines, our banter, our fake accents, we fill our phones with photos of football and fountains and Euro Disneyland then we smile through customs, make small talk about the Cup final with the guards then take our seat on the Eurostar, draping colored scarves and flags on our laps. Yobs and thugs and shirtless fat white men invite us to get up and dance and belt out Millwall or Arsenal songs. The women look at me with drowning eyes. They're really from Syria, Iraq, Eritrea and this is the only way they can connect with their family in England. Well, for most of them. Some of them are only crossing the water because men are pressing something back in their backs.

Two women I smuggle in have legitimate-looking families who they fall into, hugging and weeping and wailing. One other woman is picked up by a young Russian male who looks at me with wolf eyes. Another is led away by ten Bangladeshi guys. I limply follow, calling out my supposed girlfriend's name until we're out of the station and free in the city and we're in a grotty alley and one of them pulls two wheelie rubbish bins into the passage and blocks me off, looking at me hard.

Go home, son, he's saying.

*

Puffin finds me in a backpacker hostel in sleepy Norwich, even though I've changed my cellphone and my email address and I haven't told anyone where I am. Puffin's version of making up for the death threats is to take me out for a meal. We eat soggy nachos in a Wetherspoons pub.

Puffin promises that the "ragheads" I've been working for are out of the picture. They'll be getting a solid hiding next time Galatasaray crosses the ditch. Well, a hiding and a sit-down. No point in stuffing up business.

Puffin drives me all the way up the country to Leeds in his Fiat with the cracked windscreen to vouch for Markus Thommen and the ginger twins who are selling their guns to this seedy, stoned Indian student with an Isis flag on the wall of his dorm. The kid paces angrily in from of his bunk bed, ranting. He has the money though—shitloads of money, actually. He says it's his inheritance and he doesn't need it because he's destined for paradise. He hands over 30,000 Euro for five guns which we've smuggled into his apartment block in Christmas tree boxes. While my so-called friend tries to calm our excited roommate, I stare down at a nearby swampy farm. Pretty, down there. Hedgerows. Peaceful lambs nibbling buttercups. 30 minutes later, as we're about to get in the car and leave with two backpacks stuffed with Euros, I'm switching my phone on. Puffin is looking at me unimpressed.

'You really want to leave a trail ay fooking footprints, pal? Cellphones ping towers, that's you and me down the loo.'

'Ssh. I'm talking to my sister. Yo: Hu. It's me.'

'Tama...?'

I can hear her waking up and yawning. Her bed creaks. 'What time is it? Where are you?'

Puffin punches me in the stomach. I drop the phone. His knee breaks my skull open. My brains spill out into the wet gravel of the parking lot.

'*You're sitting in the back,*' he growls, kicking the side of his own car then swinging the backpacks of money into the trunk.

I scramble for my mobile. It's been swallowed by a pothole filled with milky coffee water. I roll back my sleeve and begin reaching in to retrieve my phone. Puffin charges his car at me, stops with a squirt of the wheels. His bonnet growls like a dog.

I get off my knees and stagger into the car. We race north. I beg Puffin to turn on the radio. I want to hear on the news if there's been a mass shooting at the University of Leeds. If it's not today it'll happen tomorrow, or maybe next week, oh God, what've we done, what've we DONE?

Puffin burns my hand with his cigarette, stomps on the accelerator and keeps driving north.

I'm woken hours later with a slap in the head.

Puffin drags me out of the car, plus my bag, and dumps me in front of X-Base Backpackers Edinburgh.

My job is to party with naïve drunken backpackers then rob them while they snore in the bunk beds. I slide their passports out of the arse pockets of their jeans like sliding cheese out of a mousetrap. I lock myself in the bathroom and take high resolution photos of each passport page. I sell these on a website I access with the slow, exhaustive wi-fi in the hostel. One guy I rob is a young music student who sleeps with his guitar in his arms. He has photos of his whanau in his wallet. The tokutoku written up his arms says he's from Ripiro Beach. Ngati Kuri. Half a world from home.

On top of the Gremlins and the fucking Ulstermen, the Albanians have been asking where I'm living. I haven't told them. But they know Dad's address.

I'm out of this. I quit. I can't get any more dirt on Dad.

It's breakfast when they invade. I'm at the buffet, filling up on eggs, and there is a tiny view of the street that gives me a five second warning I'm about to get fucked up. They're wearing black Kathmandu puffy jackets and gloves. I watch in a mirror as they walk behind the reception counter and demand to examine the computer to find out which room I'm in. I sneak out through the swinging door of the kitchen.

The Exit door tips me onto a pile of black bags filled with bottles. I sprint down Queensferry Road, then Ferry Road, avenues with lichen growing over the street signs. Spraypaint on an HIV billboard says *Welcome 2 Muirhouse*. The streets shine with broken glass and rain. There are weeds wrapped around ancient rubbish bins with mounds of bottles and cans. Concrete towers leer down at me.

I beg a woman walking a pramful of junk mail for help. I can see frightened eyes inside her burqa. She shakes her head. They're coming, the Albanians are, chasing me down red brick alleys, endlessly winding, no street signs, no numbers. Trash cans. A pitbull bellowing at me, straining its chain. I'm about to die.

I arrive in the middle of some nameless road, desperately lost, exhausted. Out of breath. Out of time.

An Uber squeals to a stop. Its door falls open.

'Tama, I take it?' calls the voice inside, 'Get in, meart. Your old man sent fae ye. Got you a plane ticket 'n all.'

GO HOME, STAY HOME

Daddy's in a lunchtime line at the bank waiting to get a letter with his bank account and address on it. The line is all folded arms and tapping toes and people frowning into their phones as they wait for a window to open.

Daddyyyy. It's taking foreeeever.

Daddy is nodding. We'll do some maths while we wait for this bureaucratic brachiosaurus to move, Daddy goes. How many seconds in eleven minutes, kiddliwinks? That's it. Do the tens first.

Daddy looks the security camera in the eye. One last chance, God. I'm asking you to your face. Make things easier on me.

A woman in a black and gold security uniform tells the line that Window 3 is now closed, unfortunately. The wait time increases to 18 minutes.

Tell the bank to stick their paperwork up their cloaca, Daddy announces, loud enough for everyone in the line to hear. Kids: you know what a cloaca is, surely? C'mon, basic feature of non-mammalian vertebrates. The intestinal, urinary and genital tracts combine into a common... I'm boring you.

The family walks out into the wind.

Look, we'll play Go Home, Stay Home when we get back, I promise.

What about your letter from the bank, daddy? You said you needed it real bad or we can't get your payment?

We need our dignity more than some letter, Cynth.

Daddy has been illegally parked for 50 minutes in a ten minute parking zone. He's pretty sure he can spot a fascist robot in a uniform bending over the bonnet of his tired Toyota. Daddy is receiving a ticket right now and the car is nearly too far away to stop the pressing of the buttons, the clicking of the pen, the issuing of the fine.

Hurry, kids, hurry!

They wheeeee as they drag Daddy down the street. Daddy is panting as he arrives in front of the fascist. She's an old-ish lady, hunkered over another car. She has left a ticket tucked under Daddy's windscreen wiper.

Hey, he begins. I was just at the bank. Need a bank statement so I can prove I'm eligible for a food grant, you know how it is. We're driving off now, is that copasetic?

The parking warden adjusts her cap over her bun. You should actually consider yourself lucky, mister—your tyre's touching the white line, which is a second breach of the by-law. However, considering I've given you an instant $400 fine because you're lacking a Warrant of Fitness, I can't add any extra infringements.

But I don't have any money? Daddy tugs the white cotton out from the pockets of his jeans. My wife's taken everything. I've got nothing. The bank's f-forcing a mortgage s-sale. They'll come for my kids next. PLEASE.

Good day, sir.

But the car's in perfect working order. I changed the brake pads personally, the fluids, the air filter. Even the transmission oil. C'mon, now. We don't need some government sticker to verify that.

Cynthia and Chad slip their fingers under his belt like tendrils. Can we goooo, Daddy?

Daddy grabs the disappearing shoulder of the warden, who is attempting to assess the next vehicle.

Hang on, sister—

YOU WILL REMOVE YOUR HANDS FROM ME RIGHT NOW.

Daddy does not want to go to court again. Daddy's been in court five times over the last two years, for refusing to give his name to police, for missing child support payments, for flying to the highlands of Papua New Guinea and immersing himself in a barter economy, for teaching Derrida when he should've been teaching chemistry, for the school suing him to recover their wages for breach of contract, for renouncing capitalism till the bank sent some people round and said they were taking the house back unless he caught up on payments.

The parking warden is fingering her earpiece. She's reporting Daddy to the cops.

C'mon, kids, Daddy goes, tugging the kiddliwinks back up the street. Legally it's your mother's car and I was supposed to surrender it. In summary, we can't deal with the authorities right now.

Is it summer, dad? Daddy? Daaa-deee.

Daddy herds the children into an alleyway. They hit the bricks at the end and leap the wall and land in a bathtub full of cabbage, laughing. They skulk from parking lot to fence to tree to shadow, pretending they're cats, backs against the buildings, forefingers and thumbs curled over their eyes to make binoculars. They get to the park and the brook and the boardwalk and slow down and Daddy checks every direction to make sure they've lost their tail, exhales and spreads his fingers on his knees. They're safe by the bush.

Whew—close one. His face melts into a smile. Right, kiddliwinks, attention: genus and species of each tree, if you please. Quercus rubra is known in English as what? The northern red oak, correctamundo, well done, Cynth. And this, my diminutive disciples, is the swamp oak AKA titoki, Latin name Alectryon WHAT, please Chad? C'mon, you excel at this one, get it? Not *electron excelsus*, son, a-*lec-try*-on. Attaboy.

They take a seat on the lower steps of the boardwalk where tourists launch yellow pedalboats and lick ice creams.

Daddy—where's mama?

On a yacht with Rajiv, sipping mimosas, I believe. Sorry-*DOC*tor Rajiv.

What's mimosas?

Opium of the masses. She took the blue pill. Look, your mother has forced a mortgagee sale because I won't take half of the house. Compromise kills, kids. We're not losing our home. Cause when the landlord say your rent is late, and he may have to lit-i-gate... finish it for me, guys.

Don't worry, be happy?

Bobby McFerrin, what year, please?

Ummmm.... 1988, I fink?

Chad earns a kiss on the top of his forehead.

There's hope yet.

*

Daddy finds his best crowbar and uses it to force the padlock from the back door. He's impressed the so-called authorities have stuck a *Foreclosed: Do Not Enter* notice all the way back here. They've utilized their so-called brains and predicted Daddy's patterns of movement. Points to them.

Daddy ushers the kids inside, drags the kitchen table to barricade the door. He sits on the cold lino to read a faded 1997 *Scientific American* magazine from the stack. After they've found something to play with—a box of old Duplo and blocks in the basement—the kids are summoned to Daddy for another quick lesson, sitting on upturned pots on the kitchen floor. Over the past months, Daddy's spent days coloring and drawing for hours, face-down on his belly with the kiddliwinks.

Some days they've luxuriated in the downtown library until closing time. Some days they've waited til dusk then snuck onto the playfort at the kids' school. It has a swing bridge, a flying fox, a roundabout, and a two storey slide. It's the best-est playfort in the world, and even Daddy can fit through the plastic tunnels. Some days it's all gardening in the soil behind the garage, harvesting brassica and cucurbita. The Truancy Services people keep leaving their card in the door saying to give them a call cause Daddy's not supposed to be homeschooling without approval, but Daddy knows what he's doing. Daddy fights the phonies.

Recap from today, guys. Myco-rrhizal, like we practiced. Spell it for me. Tax-o-nomic ge-nus. Lin-nae-us. Chad: looking over here.

The sun is almost out of energy. Dad's getting purple rings around his eyes.

Please can we get a Happy Meal, dad. Pleeeease?

You want to subscribe to the lunacy of the corporate fast food model, you tell me what the proportion of water in the human body is. You haven't been to school in five weeks. The least you can do is learn.

You were loony, Daddy. Mummy said you were in the loony bin.

It would have been loony to have *stayed* there. Big differ-ence. Just because the government compels you to go into an institution under the Mental Health Act 1977 section 4, doesn't mean you can't leave. I escaped, didn't I? A puerile place, 'twas. Puerile means disgusting, Chad. A woman hanged herself with her knickers from a coat hook while I was there. Does that sound like effective healthcare to you? Hmmmm? Kids, d'you know humans are the only species that commits suicide be-cause of lack of happiness? Returning to my thesis, then: it is hyper-capitalism and runaway economics that causes ennui. And we're not going to subscribe to that, are we.

Daddy, what's—

Ennui is letting so-called authorities get inside your home, Chad. It's borrowed from the Old French *enuier*, meaning annoyance, case in point the *ANNOYANCE* of letters from the bank declaring it trespass to enter *MY* property which *YOUR FORMER MOTHER* should have sided with me on. Anyway, kids, I've got more of a weltschmerz than ennui. It's German. It means the world hurts. My point is we're not letting the government inside this home. Or the bank. The bank'll come first, technically, but those Quislings will ask the government for backup, the police, who are technically not an arm of government, in fact our whole system is supPOSED to be built around separating the legislative, judicial and executive... Cover your mouth when you yawn, Chad. Fair enough, I've exceeded your attention span. Thank you for your concentration today.

Daddy rolls onto the floor, puts his hands under his ear like a pillow.

You said we could play Go Home, Stay Home. Daddy? You promised.

In the morning, Cynthia. In the morning.

Promise?

Promise.

*

Cynth is tugging Daddy's eyelids.

They're here. Outside. You said to wake you.

The family drops to their knees, crawls across the floor, climbs out the laundry window and pours into the head-high grass. They weave through the stalks til they arrive at a mountain of potting mix. From up the summit, they can pull the cornstalks and sunflowers aside and see the Gestapo peering in the windows.

Kiddioes: crab walk.

Shuffling on all fours with their butts in the air, they crawl over Potting Mix Mountain til they reach the ladder behind the garage. Soon as they're positioned on their bellies on the creaking garage roof, Daddy instructs the kids to slow their breathing. Get your heart rate down so the infra-red can't find you. Their hearts ebb. They watch a gleaming glassy invader settling on the driveway's gravel. Slamming car doors. Glazed metal.

That's them. They wanna take you away, Daddy whispers. They're jealous. The Government wants to put you in a cage. Kids! *Do not engage.*

Tēna koe, brother, I'm Ricardo, we just wanted to introduce ourselves in good faith, a man in a collared shirt is calling through his megaphone hands. He spins 360 degrees, unsure where to direct his voice. Just a quick powwow 'bout how the kids are getting on. There are fines, I have to let you know up front. If they're not being brought to school. Ricardo looks at his partner and whistles. Maximum fine is, what, 150 thousand I believe, Trudy? And me and Trudy here don't want you to have to face prison time.

The peel of a siren. The crunch of boots on concrete. Fists banging the weatherboards.

PLEASE TALK TO US, SIR. WE KNOW YOU'RE IN THERE.

As the snoops start trying to force windows open, Daddy and the kids retreat. They've trained for this for months, practiced in chilly grey rain, rehearsed under a punishing sun.

'Kids: GO HOME STAY HOME.'

They hurl themselves off the roof, crash into the potting mix, leap the fence, hit the bulrushes and willow trees and tall grass, slosh through concrete sewer tunnels, paint themselves in mud. Half a click up the river, they each have a suitcase stashed in the bushes beside the filtration plant, a suitcase with military rations, water purifying tablets, changes of clothes, a compass, a pocket knife, a first aid kit, an encyclopaedia each and one toy.

It's not for long, you guys, Daddy pants. I'll find us a place. That's a promise.

*

Fruit trees are easy to raid. All you do is sidle up along someone's fence, test the hinges on the gate, ease on in. Chad carries a leafy branch in front of his head. The human eye is trained to recognize faces, so he won't be spotted as quickly if he pretends to be a bush.

They wash their bums in the river then play Hide & Seek and Marco Polo and their favourite, Go Home, Stay Home. The kids try to make it from the wildnerness back to their home base safely without a brute leaping out of its hidey-hole and terrorising them with tickles.

Cynthia is on bread duty. There's a cabinet beside the boat pond where the supermarket donates stale bread to feed the ducks. It takes two days to work out the delivery boy's timing—9.15, every morning—and Cynthia brings back loaves and rolls and bagels.

Daddy returns with dumpster pizza every night, and Chad wakes up to his favorite for breakfast. It's too unsafe to light a fire—the concrete castle of the water plant looks directly down on them, and the workers would surely call the cops—so they eat every pizza cold.

They live in an old maintenance shed sinking into the boggy river banks. The floor is on a slant and Cynthia's water bottle keeps rolling away. The only thing to read is Playboy magazines from 1968. In the back, Gore Vidal interviews Norman Mailer for 10 pages.

When Chad screams and pulls leeches off his inner thigh and cries as Daddy pops them and he is splotched with his own blood, Daddy tells Chad in every life you have some trouble / but when you worry / you make it double.

Guys, c'mon, where's my chorus, huh? Is this about the McDonald's thing again? You're a fool if you think a Happy Meal will literally make you happy, kiddo.

Chad's eyeballs ripple. He bursts into tears hard as hail.

Cynthia punches Daddy on the arm. Her face is an angry snarl.

Having said that, I'm... open to debate?

*

McDonald's is a new experience for Daddy. He strokes the colorful walls, the glittery hardfoam of his booth, reads every word of the paper placemat on his tray, runs his finger over the health and safety warnings on the plastic play fort. Utterly, utterly fascinating, all of it. An anthropologist's dream.

Daddy is warned not to tear open the chemical sachets to heat his MRE army meals on McDonald's property, but Daddy informs the manager that the manager is attempting to assert something he legally has no right to assert. They try to impose far too many unjust laws for a so-called restaurant which doesn't exactly have the moral high ground, considering its investment in blood diamonds. Even just walking through the McDonald's drive-thru they get told off. Daddy points out he's not even holding up the line. There is no conceivable reason why he can't order some milkshakes for his kids from the drive thru window. Finally Daddy is caught boiling noodles in the bathroom and they are escorted out.

School holidays begin tomorrow, anyway, kiddliwinks. This place would become flooded with parents and teachers likely to recognize Daddy and report him. Best keep moving like the Gimi people of the Maimafu highlands. They're hunter-gatherers, Chad. Go on. Guess the definition for me. Attaboy.

They drift across overpasses and along cycle lanes, dragging suitcases stinking of mandarins and avocado. They have to buy a pack of gum to be allowed to use the toilets behind Mobil. They scrub between their legs and under their arms with liquid soap from the dispenser.

The smell of chicken soup coming from the Baptist church is so strong Chad can almost see little bits of onion and meat in the air. Daddy knows the principal of the kids' school will surely be in the congregation, though. He's a real do-gooder.

We'll be spotted, kids, hate to say it, Daddy explains. Can't have the cops called. They'll lock Daddy in a cage. We have to keep moving. Your school's not far. We'll settle in the playground, yeah? Recalibrate.

Over the motorway bridge, crouching behind the substation so the police prowler doesn't spot them, between the big barn retailers, and sprinting to the traffic island and beyond. They hit the edge of the grass and the kids dump their suitcases and run towards the fort.

The school is empty for the holidays so Daddy breaks into a shed and comes jogging back with a can of creamed rice, a box of UHT milk and three packets of Oreos. Daddy won't let the kids play Hide and Seek until they've eaten, but the kids say they won't eat unless Daddy agrees to play Hide and Seek, and as soon as Daddy can peel his eyes off the cop car crawling along the horizon, he will.

Cynthia, who hasn't eaten since yesterday, begins sprinting towards the bushes. She looks like a tawny brown wig atop two broomsticks. When Daddy catches Chad, the boy is also way down in weight. Melting, disintegrating. Some wasting disease Daddy promises to diagnose.

With some slurps from a punctured can of sweetened condensed milk, the kids catch up on calories. You'll need it, Daddy explains, crouching, squeezing the kids' shoulders, taking a sample of each. I'm gonna make you hide for a looooong time. But trust me: I'll be seeing ya.

Okay, kids. Now we can play. You go hide—go, now! Run, Chad, get outta here! I'll come find you! 100 second countdown, y'hear? Hide real good. Hide *well*, I should say.

The police car veers off the road and onto the grass. They call Daddy's name. It has to be 90 metres away. So are the kids.

I'M COUNTING TO THREE HUNDRED, Daddy calls across the field, FOUR HUNDRED! SEVEN! JUST HIDE, ALRIGHT?! AND DON'T COME OUT UNLESS IT'S ME.

Chad cuts through the scrapey bushes and the spindly saplings and the raised gardens where the kids from his class are growing string beans and doubles back around the swimming pool until he shrieks with surprise as he collides with his big sister. They're out of breath. Their eyes weep with excitement.

Cynthia rattles the handles of the gym shed, the caretaker shed and the garbage shed til the last shed opens up. Inside are towers of plastic chairs, stacked 20-high. The kids slide the doors of the shed shut and wriggle between the legs of stacked chairs. Nervous, giddy, desperate to pee, they keep their eyes covered until they've counted to one hundred, then Chad points out Daddy said something about three hundred, and if Cynthia's heard the words on the wind right, it's actually seven hundred. They count and count until they lose their place and have to start again. Now it's more exciting than ever. Silly Daddy. He might not see them for years.

LEAP

Tonight my inbox is nothing but rejection. There have been 51 submissions to fiction publishers over the past five months. Each failure I've charted on a spreadsheet. The last submission cost 20 euros and maxed out my credit card.

Heavy wet drumming on the roof. My flat is uninsulated; condensation dribbles down the windows. The weather is never going to get better, nor are my hopes of making a living from literature. Cluttering my desk are letters from Visa saying I'm shifting funds between credit cards too much. It's hard to earn a living when you've pledged to only work for ethical companies.

I tiptoe past the baby's crib to bed, put my head on the pillowy cream folds of my wife's belly. She rubs healing oil into my stressed scalp while I turn my latest novel in my hands. The book cost $9 for each copy; I ordered a thousand. The *North & South* adverts for the book cost eight grand. It sold 22 copies at its launch. 800 books sit in unopened boxes under my bed. A poet was supposed to perform at the launch but he had a nervous breakdown. A student TV channel interviewed me then lost the footage. I got in trouble for taking time off work to chase the exhilaration.

My wife rubs my oily skin, pauses, swallows. I can hear her summoning some difficult words into her mouth. After the massage is complete, she explains that to get a decent job, I'll need to chop the literary achievements out of my CV. I came runner-up in my library's short story competition, sure, nobody can take that away from me—but that stuff's just not essential on a résumé. Start over, honey. Emphasize the floors you swept when you were 21, babe. The summer gig delivering furniture back when you bounced through your days, splurging on shoes and caps and beer and bongs. Tossing my surfboard into the sunset after a day of sticky summer work.

I trudge back to my computer and prepare to quit. I have a few grams of energy left to give my email a final check and confirm there's no miraculous publishing contract waiting in my inbox. Sleep is pulling me into a black well. Do this before it gets worse, dude. You're costing your family.

I prepare an email to my university, my fourteen fans, my hermit publisher, telling everyone this whole famous writer thing is an expensive joke and I'm quitting. Doesn't matter if I have an agent in London telling me my next manuscript might break through and she'll fly me over to tour bookshops. Nope. Not worth the hours of risk. Can't be away from the babies. Too big a leap. Could get killed.

I hit the Send button, tell the world I give up.

*

Within a month I'm bending and hammering and sweeping every day. Construction work begins at minimum wage but the pay goes up pretty quick once I've got my SiteSafety ticket. My hunched spine straightens out. Food and water and coffee tastes better gulped on a sweaty smoko break when every minute counts. I stop taking my Prozac. There are no monsters lurking, no upsetting emails. Everything's reliable. Do the hours, get a paper pay stub. No more waiting for drip-fed dollars from Kindle. No more shifting money from Visa to Mastercard and back.

The days pass quickly. The boys are impressed by the way I bring big words into my jokes. I roll onto the advanced course in framing and truss. It gets me ahead of the others. I begin doing seven hour shifts, dawn til two, then having a shower, changing into a button-up shirt and studying at night. The boss starts asking me for input on plans. I show him where on the designs he can make the structure smarter, save on materials, labour, consent costs. It's strange, feeling essential, getting thanked. Writing always seemed to be about cutting the world with criticism till I could sew myself inside the wound.

One day my publisher phones while we're doing a concrete pour—well, *former* publisher. My books've been selling three a month, he reminds me, and if I write a good essay for *Landfall* we can surely hit the ten mark.

I hang up while he's shouting in my ear. Shoulda killed that whole risk-taking author thing yonks ago. Shoulda strangled the impulse.

*

Because I have years of experience handling stakeholder conflicts in my writing, contracts and tenders are a breeze. I write convincing proposals about how my firm can realize this tunnel or that foundation with the best suppliers for the best price. I back my words up with market trends, charts, price points. After a year it makes sense to start my own firm, get a couple boys under me. Residentially Engineered homes are prefabricated for the future. They're built more quickly with fewer fuck-ups and with a higher chance of building inspector approval, saving clients $40K per house. My outfit gets $25,000 of that saving. Half of it's profit. Multiply that by 1000 RE homes a year, the numbers are satisfying. Understanding markets is everything. Stupid that I wasted a decade standing outside the literature market complaining about it.

Four years after getting into the construction game, my wife can't keep up with the numbers so we get an accounts lady, then two, plus a fella to handle HR and a girl on front desk. I can't remember all my builders' names. I can barely keep up with my kids, either.

The wife has this drunk little smile on her lips all the time now, a blissed-out smirk, amused how our lives are going, like she's in dreamy disbelief. Laughing at our old selves. She likes landscaping so much we jet to Bali so she can select statues and birdbaths to import. After Bali we head over to Hong Kong to see Cantonese theatre, that's a must, then it's a 14 day tour of China including Beijing's Forbidden City. While I'm there, it makes sense to get talks going with John Holland Group in Shanghai. They control all Chinese supply to Australia. We put figures on some charts. I have to get my numbers a lot more lean if I'm going to scale up and do business with them. Get my pre-frames designed in Guang-zhou, nailed in Manila then freighted to Tauranga. Get those import and rebrand costs competitive enough and over the next half decade I'm looking at ten figures a year revenue, with plenty of profit.

In the office, people treat me like a king on a throne. Spose I do look a little like Henry VIII on my chair, worried mouth stretching my jowls down, chest starting to droop. I don't have time to walk places and I eat most of my meals at my desk. They bring me coffee, fried chicken, birthday cake. They reckon 65 hours a week is too much work. I tell 'em the company doesn't run itself. My kids've got motocross lessons, piano, ballet to be paid for, plus the company's sponsoring my boy's school's rugby shirts. The bills add up.

Weekends I used to agonize over pages of text, sweating and typing and worrying what critics think; now weekends are all about the boat. The *Family Free*, she's called. She's a brand new Maritimo M51. 45 feet, 670 horsepower Volvos on her; burns 300 dollars of diesel just getting out of the harbour. I've got new rods, too, obviously, and you can't cook snapper on a dirty barbecue so I've had a six burner installed. The fellas in my fishing club, they're hardskinned business boys. You can say anything to these people and they won't run off crying and publish a blog about it.

We see each other at conferences most months—Melbourne, Auckland, Vegas. Our favorites are the ones in Rarotonga. We wear white shirts with short sleeves. Our neckties trickle over our bellies. We ogle the waitresses, stroke their flowers, our drunken eyes softened. After the agenda's done for the day, us business boys file off into our shacks one by one. We all get a woman. Gotta feel alive, don'tcha.

*

My son's Wednesday night prizegiving begins with a haka up on stage, then waiata songs, bagpipes then some motivational speaker jackass. Buried in the black audience with my phone secreted under my shirt, peering down my chest, I manage to clear 22 emails before the wife slaps my wrist and tells me to concentrate. Here eyes are glued on Motivation Boy. She must have a wide-on for the prick. She's not happy about the sneaky roots I've been having. She's been sleeping in her own bed, wants to separate. I'd better behave. Be a good boy. Kill my risky impulses.

The motivational speaker is some young pup in a suit jacket and skinny jeans. He keeps pausing on the lip of the stage, using his fingers to enunciate. Some bigshot wet-behind-the-ears author with a slideshow. I yawn, eat potato chips off my belly, look around the walls. God, I went to this school. I have memories of locking myself in a disabled toilet at lunch cause I couldn't take my eyes off *The Catcher in the Rye*. Everything else in my world turned grey while Holden Caulfield throbbed, radioactive. The book burned the veneer off the phony world.

The young fool in front of the projector screen is concluding his speech, ordering everyone to go off and follow their dreams. He finishes with an arrogant bow. Applause popping and cracking like fireworks. I use the distraction to peer at the screen stashed under my vest and send a firm message to the fuckers in Wellington trying to suck the nutrients out of our deal: *100 orders or no. Please confirm and I'll courier contract Monday. Regards.*

People are standing and clapping and whistling for some reason. I excuse myself, stumbling over kneecaps towards the toilet, regretting the bourbon I've drunk to get numb enough to sit through two hours of this.

The bourbons come out into the urinal in a golden stream. I have the toilet to myself, for thirty seconds.

The door swings open. Applause leaks in. Someone enters. In the mirror I see the jacketed young man—that writer prick—rinse his hands and push wet fingers through his hair. I sneak up behind as he dips into the basin. My thick forearms make a knot around his neck. I haul the young man's body backward, tipping to maximize gravity as I choke him. He kicks. We fall across the bathroom, bang into a toilet stall. The soles of his shoes scrape the walls. He is about to walk on the ceiling then, with a twist, he struggles free, hops onto the iron radiator, pushes a casement window open. Cold night pours in. He glances behind at the force that wants to kill him, looks down, sees it's a risk, and takes the leap anyway.

ABOUT THE AUTHOR

Michael Botur, born 1984, is a writer originally from Christchurch, New Zealand, who now lives in Whangarei with his two kids.

Botur's heritage includes English, Irish (County Longford), Scottish (Clan Macintosh), Polish and some obscure ancestors from Rawalpindi, Pakistan.

Botur is author of four acclaimed indie short story collections and one collection which hardly anybody read. He published the new adult sci-fi novel *Moneyland* in 2017 which has had thousands of reads on Wattpad, published the sequel *Moneyland: Payback* on Wattpad in 2019 and published literary fiction novel *Crimechurch* on YouTube in 2019.

Botur holds a Master's Degree in Creative Writing from AUT University and a Graduate Diploma in Journalism Studies from Massey University, as well as degrees in arts and literacy. Botur makes a living from communications, content and copywriting.

Botur has published creative writing in most NZ literary journals and has won various prizes for short stories and poems since beginning writing in 2005. He has been making money from creative writing since the age of 21 and in 2017/18 was included in collections put together by University of Otago (*Manifesto 101*) and University of Canterbury (*Bonsai: Small Fictions*).

Botur has published journalism in most major NZ newspapers and magazines and news websites including *New Zealand Herald*, *Herald on Sunday*, *Sunday Star-Times*, *The Spinoff*, *Noted*, *Mana* and *North & South*. In 2017 Botur launched the only online 'gallery' for NZ short story writers, http://www.NZShortStories.com, where he makes all of his short fiction free to read and download, including #100NZStories100days.

ABOUT THE PUBLISHER

The Sager Group was founded in 1984. In 2012 it was chartered as a multimedia artists' and writers' consortium, with the intent of empowering those who create art—an umbrella beneath which makers can pursue, and profit from, their craft directly, without gatekeepers. TSG publishes books; ministers to artists and provides modest grants; and produces documentary, feature, and commercial films. By harnessing the means of production, The Sager Group helps artists help themselves.

ALSO BY MICHAEL BOTUR

Crimechurch -2020
Loudmouth (poetry) 2019
True? - 2019
Moneyland - 2017
LowLife - 2017
Spitshine - 2015
Mean - 2013
Hot Bible! -2012

ALSO FROM THE SAGER GROUP

Vetville: True Stories of the U.S. Marines
Straight Fish
The Lonely Hedonist
Stoned Again
The Devil and John Holmes
High Tolerance, A Novel
The Someone You're Not
Revenge of the Donut Boys
Lifeboat No. 8
The Living and the Dead
Three Days in Gettysburg

More Books From The Sager Group: TheSagerGroup.net

THE SAGER GROUP
Artifex Te Adiuva

www.ingramcontent.com/pod-product-compliance
Lightning Source LLC
Chambersburg PA
CBHW051653180726
48284CB00006B/1977